American Meltdown

Book Two of The Economic Collapse Chronicles

Mark Goodwin

ISBN: 1494961954
ISBN-13: 978-1494961954

ACKNOWLEDGMENTS

I would like to thank Jesus Christ, the Messiah. "For in Him we live and move and have our being." Acts 17:28

Thanks to David Kobler for the extensive tactical knowledge provided on his SouthernPrepper1 YouTube channel used in the research for this book.

Thanks to John Jacob Schmidt and everyone at RadioFreeRedoubt.com and Amrron.com for the radio and digital communications information used in the technical research for this book.

Thanks to my wife and family for their prayers and support in the good times and the bad.

Thanks to Janice Matthews for much more than editing. Her comments and suggestions made a better book and a better writer.

Forward

American Meltdown is a work of fiction, but the threats that materialize in the book are real. Many of the numbers stated in the book are forward projections made by the author and based on real numbers. American Meltdown looks at the current political and financial problems our country is facing and simply does the math. Plan accordingly.

Technical information in the book is included for educational purposes and to convey realism. The author shall not have liability nor responsibility to any person or entity with respect to any loss or damage caused, or allegedly caused, directly or indirectly by the information contained in this book.

For more information on preparing for a financial meltdown or other natural or man-made disasters, visit the author's website at www.PrepperRecon.com

Except for a few people and one cat whose real names were used with permission, all of the characters, places and incidents are products of the author's imagination or are used fictitiously. Any resemblance to actual people, places or events are entirely coincidental.

PROLOGUE

The American Economic Collapse

Matt Bair and his wife, Karen, moved from South Florida to Kentucky shortly after the EBT card riots the previous fall. The handwriting was on the wall. The country had entered into the throes of death and it was time to get out of the cities.

Bailouts to prop up US deficit spending from the International Monetary Fund came only with the conditions of deep austerity cuts. All government employees, military programs and entitlement programs had been slashed by 15%. Despite the Federal Government's best efforts, they could not make ends meet.

Municipal bankruptcies were spreading all over the country. Police and other municipal service workers were laid-off or had large pay cuts that made it not worth working any longer. Many police departments had simply locked the doors and the officers walked away. In those cities, the gangs and criminals were now in charge. The collapse had begun and the debilitating effects were spreading like wild fire.

The abandonment of the dollar by foreign nations made it impossible for companies like Walmart, who depended on a strong dollar and weak Chinese yuan, to stay in business. Despite China's determination to suppress the yuan and America's attempt to prop up the dollar, markets proved to be stronger than the central bankers who tried to manipulate the currency trades.

Inflation was now in double digits, even by government standards which constantly changed the metrics to make the reported inflation numbers appear smaller than they actually were. This manipulation instilled a false sense of confidence in the heart of the American consumer. If folks knew how bad things really were, the economy would have fallen apart years ago.

In the last few months, OPEC had canceled oil trade settlement using US dollars and had moved to gold settlement. Many other nations had abandoned dollar-based settlement for international trade. The BRICS nations- Brazil, Russia, India, China and South Africa- had instituted their own trade settlement bank and trading currency. The new currency, called the Bric, was made up of a basket of the member nations' currencies. BRICS member nations used the Bric for trade settlement between other member nations but, unlike the Euro, retained their own currencies for use among their respective citizens. This massive move by the rest of the world meant the value of the dollar was in free fall. The trillions of dollars printed through various quantitative easing programs rushed for safe-haven assets. This caused gold, silver and other commodities to skyrocket against the dollar. Average American families were unable to keep pace with the rising costs. Homes were foreclosed, cars were repossessed and credit cards were canceled. The domino effect sent shock waves through the economy like an atomic bomb. Businesses closed, federal tax revenues plummeted and people could have really used some assistance from government programs. Sadly, now that it was a real need, the money simply was not there.

America had spent decades building an entire class of people who were made comfortable in poverty. They were taught that the government would always take care of them through welfare programs. They learned from previous generations to milk the system and attain a standard of living that surpassed most of the rest of the world. Their only required task to sustain that standard of living was to show up to the polls every few years and vote for the gravy train candidates.

The financial burden of maintaining the dependent class had hit critical mass years ago. Combined with military spending that surpassed the military budgets of all the other countries on Earth, entitlement spending had taken America's debt into the abyss. The warnings had been ignored and now the day of reckoning was here.

CHAPTER 1

"He trains my hands for battle; my arms can bend a bow of bronze. You give me your shield of victory, and your right hand sustains me; you stoop down to make me great."

-Psalms 18:34-35

Matt Bair dreamed someone was knocking at the door. The sound came again but harder. It wasn't a dream. Matt was getting in the habit of waking up at sunrise, but this still felt early. He looked at the clock. It was 4:30 in the morning. Then he remembered, it was the first day of militia training. He groggily stumbled to the door and opened it. His cousin, Adam, was standing there, fully awake.

"Rise and shine, city boy," Adam said cheerfully.

Adam Bair was Matt's cousin who lived in Eastern Kentucky since he returned from active duty in the Marines.

Matt got dressed and made a strong pot of coffee. "I'm just going to make a quick breakfast. Would you like some cheese eggs and toast?" He asked.

"No thanks," Adam replied, "but I'll have a cup of coffee. We have a little time. Eat a big breakfast. It'll be two days before you'll be back in your warm house with the comforts of a kitchen. A big meal now means the food in your ALICE pack will last that much longer."

The All-purpose Lightweight Individual Carrying Equipment or (ALICE pack) was used by the US Army for years. When it was finally retired and replaced by the Modular Lightweight Load-carrying Equipment or (MOLLE pack) ALICE packs became dirt cheap on the military surplus market. The rugged construction of the ALICE pack made it a low-cost favorite of preppers and militia members.

Matt's pack was heavy. It had the essentials he needed for the next two days of training. It held a two man tent and a full-size sleeping bag. These items were heavy, but he wouldn't last long without proper shelter. It was January 2nd and the mountains of Kentucky were ice cold. The high for today was supposed to be 30 degrees and the low for the next two nights would be around 14 degrees.

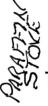

Matt packed several homemade paraffin stoves, (similar to Sternos,) for boiling water and making hot coffee. They were really just cardboard coiled around inside of an old tuna can and filled with candle wax. They didn't burn as clean nor as hot as a real Sterno, but in hard times you use what you have.

"What do you have in that big old bag?" Adam asked.

Matt said, "Since there is little risk of spoilage with the low temperatures, instead of bringing canned or dried food, I packed mostly regular food that was already cooked. The bigger threat to the food is to keep it from freezing. I packed the food in the middle of the pack in hopes that my body heat will radiate through just enough to keep it from freezing. I have a huge chunk of meatloaf, some cornbread pancakes and a two cans of vegetable soup. I also have two entire batches of Nana's No-Bake-Cookies."

The cookies were closer to fudge than cookies, but that's what they were called. The sweet treats were made in a large sauce pan on top of the stove rather than in the oven, thus the name "No-Bake-Cookies."

Adam said, "I love those things! They're the perfect trail food. (The oatmeal provides fiber and complex carbohydrates)(The cocoa gives you some caffeine, antioxidants and that general good feeling you get from eating chocolate. The peanut butter provides good fats and protein and of course the sugar is a reliable source of quick energy.")

Matt said, "Nana's no-bake-cookies are always a big hit any time I take them anywhere, so I made a batch to eat and another batch to share."

"Do you have a good medical kit in there?" Adam asked.

Matt said "I have a small hygiene kit and a good-sized medical kit. The medical kit has aspirin, a small bottle of Betadine, a small bottle of alcohol, antibiotic gel, Band-Aid Tough-Strips, a medical instrument kit, sutures, antibiotics, Tylenol 3 with Codeine that was left over from dental surgery Karen had a few years back and an Israeli Battle Dressing."

The Israeli Battle Dressing or (IBD) was a sterile, self-contained, six-inch compression bandage for severe wounds. Israeli soldiers had started carrying them many years ago. The design had caught on and now soldiers around the world carried them into combat.

Adam asked, "What type of antibiotics do you have?"

Matt answered, "Amoxicillin. The brand is Fish Mox which was manufactured for fish tanks, but I would rather take drugs for fish than risk getting gangrene. We also have a good supply of Fish Flox, which is Ciprofloxacin. Cipro is much harder on the stomach, but if an infection has already set in, it is a more sure method of killing it. Cipro is also one of the few antibiotics that's effective against Anthrax."

Adam asked, "How are you set for tools and equipment?"

Matt said, "My pack has the usual suspects in the tool and equipment arena. I have a small hand saw, a folding shovel, a fixed blade field knife, a coffee pot and an old steel French military mess kit. My Leatherman Wave multitool stays on my belt."

Matt grabbed his pack and threw it in the back of Adam's truck. He went back in and geared up. He had never bought a hydration pack for his ALICE pack, so he carried a traditional canteen on his

FIRST AID

belt.

Matt had found a tactical vest at the flea market back in November. It had to go under his heavy winter coat which wasn't ideal for combat training, but the coat could be shed if need be. He wore a thick hooded sweatshirt under the vest which would keep him warm for a while. The tactical vest had a cross draw holster for his .45 caliber Glock 21 and pouches for his pistol and rifle magazines. It had a pouch on the shoulder for a walkie talkie and a side pouch where he kept a spare IBD.

"Where's your brother?" Matt quizzed as he got in the truck.

"Still getting ready," Adam said. "We have to swing back by and pick him up. He ain't worth no more than a city boy."

Matt smiled as he took the ribbing. At least he wasn't the only slacker in the bunch.

They drove back to Adam's to pick up Wesley. When they pulled up, Adam honked the horn. Adam said, "I told Wes to be waiting outside! He's having a hard time getting away from his new wife; that's why he wasn't ready when I left to pick you up."

Wesley appeared through the door, wife in tow. Matt and Adam watched as he gave Shelly one last kiss and closed the front door. Wes quickly sat his rifle and gear in the back of the truck and jumped in the cab.

"Hey," Wes said when he got settled. "Cut me some slack! I've only been married a week."

Matt asked, "So where are we going to be training?"

Adam answered, "This weekend, the training will be at Lieutenant Joe's. Joe Rollins is a retired U.S. Army Lieutenant who served in Vietnam. He maintains a traditional flat-top haircut and folks around here always address him as Lt. Joe. Joe has a little over 300 acres above Wood Creek Lake near London, Kentucky. His place is pretty central for most of the Eastern Kentucky Liberty Militia members, so he offered to have the training on his property. The large amount of outdoor space ensures we'll have plenty of room to train without bothering the neighbors."

When they arrived, Matt could not believe the amount of men there.

Wesley said, "The militia commander, Franklin Johnson, told me he expected about 300 new men in addition to the 85 we had before the meltdown. But it looks like there are already over 400 men here, and more are still trickling in."

Adam added, "Franklin and a few other members of the militia came out to Lt. Joe's last night to coordinate parking, draw up maps for camp sites and decide where to dig latrines.

"We'll have a few drills teaching basic troop movement, but this meeting will be focusing on information. We'll be doing a basic gear check and establishing a communication relay system."

When everyone had checked in, the total was more than 500 men.

Matt said, "It seems that President-Elect Anthony Howe's promise to ban all semi-automatic firearms by executive order has motivated quite a few men to sign up. Howe pledged during his campaign that he would sign the order on inauguration day. That's less than three weeks away."

Adam, Wesley and Matt checked in and got their campsite assignment.

"Good morning, Sergeant Bair," the man at the check-in station said to Adam. Adam had trained with the original 85 militia members several times in recent years. Wesley had also, but not quite as often as Adam. Adam had seen his share of combat in Afghanistan and Iraq, and had been put in charge of some of the militia training in the past couple of years.

Adam was given a photocopied map of the area when they arrived.

He looked at the map and said, "The campsite is divided into quadrants. Each of us is assigned to a quadrant depending on where we live. The campsite is over in that lightly wooded area. There is really nowhere on Joe's property with enough open space to accommodate all of us. It was probably hard enough to pick a spot that was relatively level and had access to the creek. The water is frozen, but I saw some men cutting blocks of ice out with chainsaws. They have a boiling pot going over by that fire. I guess that is to melt the ice and ensure there's plenty of water for everyone.

"Looking at the map, it appears that each quadrant represents the direction the men are from in relation to the lake. All the guys from the around the Mt. Vernon area, which is northwest from the lake, are in Quadrant I. The men from around McKee, which is northeast, are in Quadrant II. We all live southeast from the lake, so we're in Quadrant III. Somerset is southwest of the lake and men from around there are going to Quadrant IV. Quadrant III is more crowded than the other quadrants, but I guess Commander Franklin Johnson is more concerned with keeping all of us together with our neighbors than having the numbers evenly distributed.

"The guys from Manchester are also in Quadrant III with all of us from the London area. That probably puts the total number of militia men in Quadrant III at nearly 200, roughly double the size of the other quadrants. I'll talk to Franklin about breaking the militia into five separate companies. Each quadrant can be its own company except Quadrant III. We should break Quadrant III into two companies. We could split it up according to whether we lived closer to London or Manchester. That will be consistent with the Commander's philosophy. Commander Franklin believes the camaraderie of neighbors who know each other will form a stronger militia and greater morale."

After Matt, Adam and Wesley pitched their tents, Adam went to find the commander. Franklin Johnson approved Adam's recommendations and elected him Captain of his company. Johnson elected a captain for each company that would report directly to him. Each captain was to elect three lieutenants to lead three platoons. The platoons were broken down into two or three squads and staff Sergeants were assigned over each squad. Everyone was arranged to be in squads with the militia men who lived in the closest proximity to one another. The platoons were arranged likewise. This made for an efficient information relay system in case they had to rely on walkie-talkies or person-to-person communications. It would also allow them to rendezvous with their squads and platoons using the least amount of movement to be detected by the enemy.

The companies were named after the closest town. Adam Bair's company was called London Company. The men set up their camps in their assigned spaces and spent a while meeting the other men in their companies.

At 11:00 a.m., everyone gathered around Franklin Johnson as he explained the methods of training that he had in mind for the individual companies. He had to almost yell in order for everyone to hear him, but he got it done without a PA system.

Wesley explained to Matt, "Several of the new members are having trouble with the fact that Johnson has no military experience, especially those who served in the military. Those of us who have been in the militia with Franklin for a while know better. Franklin never joined the military because he didn't trust the government's decisions. (He has no problem fighting or dying for his country,) but he feels the military ambitions of the past few administrations, from both sides of the political aisle, had little to do with defending American soil. Franklin paid money out of his own pocket to get advanced weapons training. He studied military strategy and tactics and he worked his way up the ladder in the US Postal Service. That gives him a good understanding of logistics. He was promoted to upper level management with the Post Office and has good people skills."

Franklin began speaking. "I would like to thank everyone for coming out today. I know it's cold and you left your warm homes to be here. We don't know when or if we will have to stand up to the tyrant, but we will do what is required to be ready if that day is thrust upon us. We must be ready to meet him in the snow or rain or blazing sun."

Wesley nudged Adam and whispered, "You can tell he worked for the post office."

"Shut up," Adam said as he fought to keep from laughing.

Franklin continued, "None of you men need a lesson in the Constitution nor in the Bill of Rights. You are well aware of your rights granted by your Creator and the supreme law of this land. That is why you're here. Today we'll be working on information relay procedures, gear checks and some general combat techniques. After today, you'll only be training with either your individual companies or, in most cases, your platoons.

"I felt it was necessary for us to all come together this one time to see each other and be encouraged by knowing the number of men committed to this effort. In general, however, gatherings of this size will draw unnecessary attention. You're all aware of the need for discretion. Even here in Eastern Kentucky, there are some among us that are loyal to the tyrants who have hijacked our nation. Those of us who have been in the militia for some time now affectionately refer to the loyalist as Tories. The moniker comes from the Revolutionary War. Tories were those loyal to the crown."

Johnson continued speaking for about an hour explaining the protocol for reporting intelligence, measuring progress, and receiving orders. He spoke briefly about the minimum requirements for weapons and provisions for packs. He went on to give some advice about keeping a low profile.

Johnson said, ("Try utilizing a bivouac whenever possible as most of the tents I see around the camp range in color from bright orange to sky blue. They aren't the most tactically advantageous forms of shelter.) When you are moving discretely through the country and have to shelter overnight, you can use the overhang of a cliff or build a shelter out of branches and leaves laid over a fallen tree to maintain a low profile."

After the meeting the men broke for lunch. Wes, Adam and Matt worked together to get a fire going before they ate. Matt shared a bit of his meatloaf with Wes and Adam.

"Is this from that deer I shot?" Wes asked.

"It's mixed," Matt said.

"With what?" Wes inquired.

"It's mostly that deer you shot," Matt said.

"And what else?" Adam could tell Matt was trying to be evasive and that caused him to wonder as well.

"Possum," Matt said.

Adam's eyes opened wide. He had just taken a rather large mouthful of the delectable meat loaf.

Wesley looked at the meal in front of him for a minute, then decided to give it a try. "Not bad," he said.

After the initial shock wore off, Adam said, "Actually, it's really good. But why did you put possum in it?"

"The deer meat is a little too lean for meatloaf. Possum is a good source of fat. I put a good amount of Worcestershire sauce in it to bring all the flavors together," Matt said with a wink.

CHAPTER 2

"Discipline is the soul of an army. It makes small numbers formidable; procures success to the weak, and esteem to all."

-George Washington

Matt woke up just before dawn. He was freezing. He had done all he could to stay warm, but he was still shivering. He hated the thought of getting out of the sleeping bag. The night before, he had used hot rocks to get his tent warm. He had put several larger rocks in the camp fire to get them red hot. He built a small platform of rocks inside his tent to act as a hearth. He used large sticks like oversized chop sticks to transfer the rocks from the fire pit to the hearth in his tent. The hearth kept the hot rocks from melting the bottom of the tent which was made of plastic. The hot rocks worked well for a while. When he had first gotten into the tent it was toasty and warm. As the rocks cooled, the tent became frigid again.

Matt said to himself, "There is no use fighting it. I better get up and start moving to get some body heat going."

Matt did thirty pushups in the tent to get his internal temperature up. He put his boots and coat on, got out of the tent and started a fire. He placed a pot of water over the fire for coffee and got back in the tent to do another set of pushups. Outside there was not much of a breeze, but it still felt warmer in the tent. By the time the coffee was ready, he could see the first sliver of dawn in the eastern sky over the adjacent mountain. While it would be a while before the sun would warm the air, it was a sign that the coldest part of the night was over. There had not been much snow this year. Matt was thankful that he didn't have to contend with the added discomfort of the moisture from the snow.

Adam and Wes shared a tent and Matt figured their combined body heat kept them a bit warmer through the night than he had been. Adam and Wes woke just as first light was breaking from behind the mountain.

They all shared the things they brought for breakfast. Adam brought a thick piece of country ham to have for breakfast with eggs. Matt brought biscuits that were already cooked.

Matt commented on the biscuits "Just one day after I made the biscuits, they're already hard."

Adam said, "A quick remedy for stale biscuits is to make us some red-eye gravy."

This was done by pouring coffee over the country ham after it was finished cooking, but while it was still in the pan. This rinsed off the excess grease and salt and made a sort of country au jus.

Wesley said, "What would breakfast be without red-eye gravy."

The Bairs had all grown up with red-eye gravy. It was something of a family favorite.

The day's training started with building shelters and camouflage. Adam taught a class to all five companies on constructing a ghillie suit and basic camouflage.

He began the class with a short description of the suit. "A ghillie suit is camouflage made from long strips of fabric that are sewn onto an over-sized outer garment like a jacket and trousers or a one-piece jump suit. Traditionally, the strips are made from burlap, but use whatever you can find. Any fabric in earth tones will work. Greens, tans, dark greys and browns are the colors that you want to use for the underlying garment as well as the fabric strips.

"In the case of snow, you can use a simple white sheet as a type of poncho for camouflage. Your weapons can easily be concealed under the sheet and brought up to a firing position with little obstruction. We will also use face paint to break up the shape of the human face and match the colors of the seasons for the surrounding terrain."

After a lunch break, they reconvened for more training. Afternoon classes explained basic troop movement. Matt and the others learned wedge, diamond and file formations. Matt learned the difference between traveling, traveling over watch and bounding over watch.

Dave, the instructor, explained, "Traveling is simply moving in formation when there is little threat of enemy contact. When enemy contact is more likely, squads will put more distance in between the individual fire teams, this is called traveling over watch. Bounding over watch is used when contact with the enemy is expected. This method has the two fire teams of each squad leap frog forward, one at a time so one fire team is covering the other fire team as they move. For those of you who may not know, a fire team is simply a team of four or five guys. There would typically be two fire teams in a squad, so the squad size will ultimately define the size of the fire teams rather than some preset number."

When the troop movement lecture was over, all five companies broke up into platoons and practiced their troop movement. Double time file movement, low crawls and high crawl movements quickly revealed that many of the men in Matt's platoon were in poor shape. The men practiced by marching for about ten miles total that afternoon and finished well after sundown.

Adam gave a short pep talk to his platoon after the training. "I don't want to sound harsh, but I hope this will serve as a wake-up call for many of you who realized that you're more vulnerable because of your weight or poor cardiovascular conditions. As your platoon leader, I am going to make it my personal responsibility to get this platoon in shape by meeting more often than the required two days per week for training."

As Matt, Wes and Adam were returning to their campsite, Matt said, "The temperature is dropping fast and my clothes are wet with sweat. I'm going to make a pot of warm water and take a quick cat bath with a wash rag inside his tent. I'll get into some dry clothes, then meet you guys for dinner."

Afterwards, he felt cleaner, but not really clean. He put on dry clothes and met the guys at the fireside.

Wes said, "I'm done with this. I'm so ready to get home to a shower and a warm bed."

"Me too," Matt said.

Adam smiled and shook his head.

"What's up, brother?" Wes asked.

"Y'all better enjoy this little boy scout jamboree, because we start training for real next week," Adam said.

"What do you have planned for us, Cousin?" Matt inquired.

"You'll see," Adam said with a mischievous grin. "I don't want to torture you guys, but you both are way too soft for combat. It's unlikely that I will be able to simulate the 'festivities' of Paris Island, but I'll do my best to prepare you for a fight."

Matt wondered exactly what Adam had in mind. They stayed one more night in the freezing cold. They were dismissed the next morning at first light. The extra night was not meant as punishment, it was just conditioning so they would be better prepared to operate in the elements.

CHAPTER 3

"You said in your heart, 'I will ascend to heaven; I will raise my throne above the stars of God; I will sit enthroned on the mount of assembly, on the utmost heights of the sacred mountain. I will ascend above the tops of the clouds; I will make myself like the Most High.' "

-Isaiah 14:13-14

Inauguration Day

Anthony Howe sat in the back of the limousine as it drove up Pennsylvania Avenue. He had waited for this day for what seemed like forever. He felt just like a little kid on Christmas morning. He had asked Santa for the world and now it was sitting there, under the tree for the taking. The country was descending into economic chaos. Impossible choices lay ahead, but Howe was in it for the rush of power. He really had very little concern for the masses, who were suffering. This was his moment in the sun and no amount of trouble amongst the 'peasants' could take that away from him. This was the moment when the whole world would look at him as the most powerful man on the planet.

The lead Secret Service agent said to Anthony Howe "Due to the political turmoil in the recent election, we're advising you not get out of the limousine to walk the traditional last length of the presidential parade up Pennsylvania Avenue to the inaugural proceedings."

Howe thought back to all the turmoil he went through to get here. The election had been a three-way race and none of the candidates had received the required 270 electoral vote to be elected through the Electoral College. The vote fell to the House of Representatives. The independent candidate, Texas Senator Paul Randall had received the most electoral votes and had won the popular vote, but in the end, The House chose Democratic New York Governor Anthony Howe.

The agent continued, "We've picked up chatter on the internet that suggests many of Randall's supporters are ready to fight against the government."

Howe countered, "I know you boys have your work cut out. Randall has convinced his followers that I have launched an all-out assault against the Constitution, but you can handle it. I appreciate your concern, but we'll stop the limousine three blocks from the podium where I'm to be sworn in. These people have come out in the cold today to see their new president and I intend to fulfill their wish."

Howe and his wife, Jenna, exited the car and began to wave to the crowds lining both sides of the avenue. These people were among his most loyal followers who bought every empty promise he made in the campaign. The crowd was enamored with Howe. The president preceding Howe, Mustafa Al Mohammad, had cultivated a personality cult among the liberals and Howe knew he was inheriting that hero worship.

Howe's smile grew larger as he drank in the cheers and the applause. He thought, *This is the attention and respect that I deserve.* He absorbed the praise and basked in the knowledge that all this pomp and ceremony was just for him.

At the podium, Howe met Chief Justice Rosa Espinosa. Howe repeated after The Chief Justice, "I will faithfully execute the Office of President of the United States." The section about defending the Constitution had been removed from the oath as well as the bit about solemnly swearing. Howe also dropped the tradition of being sworn in with his hand on a Bible citing that the Book had been a source of division and contention for too many years in America.

Howe had pre-arranged to have the oath altered from the oath required by the Constitution which reads in Article II, Section I, Clause VIII "I do solemnly swear or affirm that I will faithfully execute the Office of President of the United States, and will to the best of my ability, preserve, protect and defend the Constitution of the United States."

The Chief Justice had deliberated with several other Supreme Court Justices and they determined that the document was written in a different era and that the present age called for more flexibility in the interpretations.

Great amounts of liberty had been taken in the interpretation of the Constitution for many years now. The very people who had derived their authority from the Constitution were the ones who had relieved it of a vast portion of its substance. In fact, the portion of the Constitution that granted their power was the only part they held sacred.

The crowd went wild as the band played and ceremonial canons fired in the background. Howe was announced as President of the United States and he stepped to the podium to make his inaugural address.

"My fellow citizens, I am humbled by the outpouring of support I have received from you today. Our nation has been cast into a turbulent period both by unfortunate economic circumstances and political division.

"A member of our own government has called for Americans to stop paying taxes and join him in his financial terrorism against this country. We will show Senator Randall that America is stronger than he anticipated. We will show him that this great country will not fall apart simply because he is a sore loser.

"But I will not lie to you. Many weak-minded people in this

country have succumbed to his blasphemous rhetoric and followed his septic advice. His so-called 'American Exit Strategy' has convinced millions to quit participating in economic activity and start illegal black-market barter networks which have abandoned the use of US currency."

Howe knew he was only eight days from a major fiscal short fall in the federal budget. He needed to start damage control right away. It was true that millions of people had dropped out of the current system and followed Paul Randall's advice to establish barter networks, but millions more had lost their jobs due to the recent financial turmoil.

Anthony Howe continued his inaugural address, "I will seek out and find Paul Randall and his co-conspirators. Once they have been dealt with, I will bring our lost sheep back into the fold and restore our economy.

"Paul Randall has also called for an armed resistance. I will not stand for this. I have left much room for the right to bear arms in my plan to remove weapons of war from our streets. As I promised in my campaign, I will be signing an executive order to ban all semi-automatic weapons later today. I have sought to maintain the rights of hunters and collectors to register and keep revolvers, single-shot and pump-action shotguns as well as bolt-action rifles that hold less than seven rounds of ammunition and do not have detachable magazines. These allowances will be suspended for any states, cities or territories where resistance to the ban is supported by state or local governments or law enforcement agencies. To ensure seamless compliance to the new law, DHS agents will be assisting state and local law enforcement in the collection of the banned weapons. We will join the rest of the civilized world that has for so long viewed Americans as savages in the Wild West.

"I expect resistance in the less refined areas of the country and will make examples of those who openly defy this edict. We have brought home hundreds of thousands of our military men and women from foreign bases. They have been tested in the fire of battle and are well trained to deal with insurrection. The criminals who have predetermined not to comply with the new regulation will soon find that they have bitten off more than they can chew. A fist full of farmers and rabble-rousers will not long contend with the most powerful military force in the world."

Anthony Howe put a stern, self-righteous expression on his face. He raised his voice to a low shout as he continued. "No more will this country be the laughing-stock of the world. No more will this country be mocked as our schools, streets, malls and theaters are painted red with the blood of gun violence victims."

The crowd cheered their new warrior of peace.

CHAPTER 4

"The beauty of the Second Amendment is that it will not be needed until they try to take it."

-Thomas Jefferson

Adam clicked off the television in disgust. "This guy is the real deal. He's the devil incarnate. He just blamed the collapse on Paul Randall and established himself as their savior. He said he intends to use the US Military to march on American cities! He'll use that insubordination clause for most every state to completely ban all firearms. I've got news for him, there's an awful lot of Marines that will not comply with the order to disarm the American people."

"Lock and load," Wesley said.

Matt said, "He has stood in absolute defiance to the Constitution. He has absolutely no legitimate authority. I hope leaders at the state level will stand up to this criminal. They should arrest him but it looks like he has enough support to get away with it, at least in D.C."

Matt was in the habit of being at Adam's any time there was a significant announcement to be made on television. Matt signed up for internet and satellite TV, but the companies laid off so many people, that service had never been hooked up since he moved. The increasing number of people dropping service because they could no

19

longer afford it was putting a severe strain on communication companies across the country. Most were operating on a skeleton crew that just did the minimum to maintain service to paying customers. Matt could still get two local channels. Two others had closed their doors for lack of sponsorship. It was hard to say how much longer these two stations would be around. The Lexington channel came in with a weak signal, but it was the one most likely to make it financially.

"Does this mean we're going to fight?" Shelly asked. Shelly was Wesley's new wife. Everyone knew that war meant people would die. No young wife wanted to lose her new husband to battle.

Adam said, "We hope that won't be necessary, but we'll talk about it later." Adam nodded to Mandy and Carissa, his two daughters.

He whispered to Shelly, "We never keep things from them, but there's no use worrying them ahead of time."

Shelly whispered to Adam, "Sorry. I would never want to scare the girls. I just spoke without thinking."

Janice, Adam's wife, patted Shelly on the shoulder. "It'll be fine."

Wesley lived with his brother before the beginning of the collapse. He had decided to marry Shelly right after the first signs of the breakdown. Now, he and Shelly lived in Adam's farmhouse together with Janice and the girls.

Karen, Matt's wife, squeezed Matt's arm tight when Shelly mentioned fighting. Matt knew she didn't want to lose him, but he tried to make her understand that he was not willing to live under the oppression of a criminal government.

Janice went into the kitchen and Karen followed her. Janice was simmering a pot of homemade venison chili.

"I don't know if I can handle the guys getting into armed conflict," Karen said.

"Well, you'll learn to pray," Janice said. "I hope I don't have to go through it again. At least he'll be here this time, instead of some far off desert. He'll also be fighting for something he believes in. I think that's what made it so hard for him over there. Adam went in thinking he was fighting for America, but he soon realized it was about controlling resources and global influence."

"How did you stand it?" Karen asked.

Janice stirred the pot of chili. "I prayed, then I cried, then I prayed some more. After that, I usually cried. When he got home, he was so messed up and drugged out, I cried and prayed until I couldn't take it anymore."

"Well, God heard your prayers and rescued Adam from all of that. He is an amazing, godly man today," Karen said.

"Yes, he is," Janice said. "Nothing could be as hard as all of that was. Not even losing him."

Everyone sat down to eat and dug into the delicious chili.

Adam asked Mandy, "Why aren't you eating?"

His 12 year old daughter was just stirring the bowl and not eating.

"I'm not too hungry," She said.

Matt figured that she sensed trouble was in the air. Carissa was only 8 and didn't seem to have caught on to the somber mood since the inaugural address.

"You better be glad Matt didn't make that chili and just eat it," Wesley said to Mandy.

She cracked a little smile as she asked, "Why?"

"Ain't no tellin' what he might put in it. That's why," Wesley said cryptically.

Now Carissa was curious as well. "Why, what does he put in

chili?"

"I told you there ain't no tellin' what he puts in chili. But I can sure tell you what he puts in his meatloaf," Wesley baited.

"What?" Mandy asked intently.

Matt shook his head. He knew from the beginning where this was going.

"Possum," Wesley said.

Mandy curled her nose as she said, "Eww."

Carissa screeched, "Eeeek!"

"No, he doesn't!" Mandy demanded of her Uncle Wes.

"He does and I ate it," Wes countered.

Matt could tell that Karen was begging to get suspicious. He tried to avoid her glance before she figured out that this was not all just for the amusement of the children. She didn't have to say a word. The way he was avoiding her was as good as a confession. She had just eaten that meatloaf a couple of weeks ago. She slugged Matt's arm as hard as she could.

He drew back and winced with a muffled, "Ouch!"

After the excitement died down, Mandy began to eat her chili. Wesley's distraction technique had worked; everyone's mind was off the trouble at hand and they talked and laughed for the rest of the meal.

CHAPTER 5

"Every citizen should be a soldier. This was the case with the Greeks and Romans, and must be that of every free state."

-Thomas Jefferson

Pastor John Robinson and his wife were unboxing the few items they brought from the house. Like many of the congregants of Liberty Chapel, they had relocated to Young Field. It was a combination of two farms the church now owned. Young Field was several miles north of Boise, Idaho where the church property was located.

Pastor John said, "I didn't expect so many people to come out. We began constructing permanent buildings, but there's no way they'll be adequate to house all of the people who're coming to Young Field. We might have to stay in this little camper trailer longer than we planned."

His wife replied, "We'll get by. We're all in this together. There's quite a mix of campers, trailers and fifth wheels among the rest of the congregation."

Pastor John said, "After the election results, I knew a show down was coming between the rogue government and what was left of the true Americans. I think we made the right decision to make our stand here."

Pastor John continued, "I considered making our stand at the church. After thinking it over, I thought it would be best to get out of the city. That'll make it easier to spot troop movement. I'm humbled by the amount of congregants that followed us out here."

There was a rap at the trailer door. It was Albert Rust, the church range master. Liberty Chapel was committed to the Second Amendment and even had an indoor range at the Boise property. Church attendees could shoot and take concealed carry classes there. Albert also served as the commander of the 12th Battalion of the Free Idaho Militia. The 12th Battalion agreed to make their stand with Pastor John along with three other battalions from the northern part of the state. "Battalion" had been a bit of a stretch prior to the buildup, but with all of the new recruits, the 12th had swelled to nearly 450 men. The other battalions saw similar growth.

"Hey, Pastor," Albert said. "These are the two men I was telling you about from the Appleseed Project. This is Trey and Bill. They are both trainers. Bill typically gives the history presentation and Trey heads up the marksmanship training."

"It's so very nice to meet you gentlemen. I really appreciate you coming down to do the class," Pastor John said.

Trey Dayton replied, "We're with the 29th Battalion of the Free Idaho Militia out of Coeur d'Alene. We'll be making our stand here with you in Young Field, so it's in our best interest to help get these good folks as prepared as possible. More than that, this is what we feel God has called us to do."

Mrs. Robertson said, "Remind me again what Appleseed is."

Albert said, "Appleseed is a project that's been around for several years. It seeks to provide an in depth look at the history of The American Revolution, giving particular attention to the events surrounding Lexington and Concord. The history segment of the program looks deep into the hearts of the men who made a stand against the most powerful military force on the planet in their day.

"The marksmanship part of the course teaches the basics of shooting a rifle with aperture sights in standing, sitting and prone positions. The course is also designed to familiarize shooters with quick magazine changes. Participants shoot at small targets at short distances which trains them to hit larger targets at longer distance. Several hundred rounds are usually shot by each participant over the length of the two day course, so .22 long rifle is the recommended ammunition. Even with recent ammunition shortages, .22 long rifle is still the most affordable round for heavy training. The Ruger 10/22 is the most popular gun used at the training clinics, but Marlin manufactured a .22 rifle called the Marlin Liberty Training Rifle. It's perfect for the marksmanship class. It comes with a sling, adjustable aperture sights and two detachable magazines which, like the 10/22, is now illegal under the executive order that Howe signed two days ago.

"Trey and Bill will be giving the class to all of the people at Young Field who're interested. Most of the folks probably have a .22 to train with, but Trey and Bill brought about 30 Liberty Training Rifles that were donated to the Appleseed Project. For those taking the class, the next two days will be completely dedicated to the heritage of the men who made their stand against tyranny two centuries ago and to becoming proficient with a rifle. You should take the course Mrs. Robertson."

Mrs. Robertson said, "If I won't be in the way, I think I will. Thank you Albert."

CHAPTER 6

"The liberties of our country, the freedom of our civil constitution, are worth defending against all hazards: And it is our duty to defend them against all attacks."

-Samuel Adams

In his office at the National Guard Armory, Texas Senator Paul Randall stood up to greet his friend. He was glad to see General Alan Jefferson.

Jefferson said, "I see you're still keeping a low profile Randall. You've been in hiding since Al Mohammad sent DHS agents to arrest you for inciting an insurrection. I would imagine Kimberly is getting tired of living in a military installation."

Since the election, Randall's supporters were being very vocal about their opposition to Howe and very defiant about his plans for the country. Former US President Al Mohammad had tried to detain Paul Randall under the 2012 NDAA which contained a clause that allowed indefinite detention of American citizens without having to charge them with a crime. It was a very convenient law to have on the books in this particular instance.

Texas Governor Larry Jacobs tipped Paul off to the movement of the DHS agents before they arrived at his ranch and the Randall's had bugged out. They hid out at a family friend's cabin for a while, but their location was discovered by insect-sized micro-drones that operated robotically without a human operator. The micro-drones used facial recognition software and swarm programming to cover large areas. After the Randalls were located, a kill team was sent to the cabin. A firefight ensued and one of Randall's twin sons, Robert, was killed in the standoff. Governor Jacobs had body guards positioned at and around the cabin. The Randalls and the guards took out the kill team. The surviving Randall family members were relocated to the Texas National Guard Armory to hideout.

"How are the reassignments coming along?" Randall asked Jefferson.

"I had absolutely no problem until Inauguration Day," Jefferson answered. "Our plan to get sympathetic military brass reassigned to key bases was moving right along. I think we covered most of the bases in the states that are likely to side with the patriot movement."

General Allen Jefferson was the Commanding General, US Army Forces Command or CGFORSCOM for short.

The general said, "Prior to Howe taking office, if I couldn't get a reassignment, I knew enough people in Washington to make it happen. There are people in the military from top to bottom, and even in the Pentagon that don't support the turn our country has taken. Of course Howe has no shortage of lap dogs either. Sometimes it's a bit of a challenge to know who is who.

"Strategic bases in Texas have been fully staffed with officers who are dedicated to their oath to defend the constitution. Fort Hood will be a clean sweep when the announcement is made to choose your sides. The officers in charge at Fort Hood are making sure all accommodations are made for representatives from Oath Keepers. Those representatives will present Oath Keeper values and try to get commitments from new soldiers and those who are just waking up to what was going on inside the White House."

Oath Keepers was an organization that sprouted up years before, when the first signs of the police state became apparent. (Oath Keepers consisted of military and law enforcement that reaffirmed their oath to protect the Constitution as well as specifically enumerated unconstitutional orders which they pledged to refuse.)

Jefferson continued, "A few of the orders Oath Keepers have pledged to disobey are orders to disarm American citizens, blockade cities, impose martial law, hold American citizens as enemy combatants, invade states that assert their sovereignty or hold citizens in detention camps. All of which are on Howe's agenda.

"Have you talked to Larry Jacobs?"

Randall replied, "Governor Jacobs has been in contact with several other state governors who are willing to stand up to Howe."

General Jefferson said, "And you have the American people, who voted to elect you president, behind us."

The wheels had been set in motion for a Coup d'état.

CHAPTER 7

"All the perplexities, confusion and distress in America arise, not from defects in their Constitution or Confederation, not from want of honor or virtue, so much as from the downright ignorance of the nature of coin, credit and circulation."

-John Adams

US Treasury Secretary Melinda Chang answered her phone. "Hello."

Commodity Futures Trading Commission Chairperson Nora Brooks was on the line. "Secretary Chang, this morning's bond auction appears to be creating some anomalies in the secondary markets."

"Nora, the Fed is buying all of the bonds from this morning's auction. Why would the auction have any effect on markets?" Chang shot back. She knew the CFTC Chairperson had earned a bit of a reputation as being a worry wart. Brooks had been preaching a message of the "end is nigh" that nobody wanted to hear. The Fed and Treasury were working with the major Wall Street banks and the rest of the Plunge Protection team to keep kicking the can down the road for nearly a decade. It had worked this long. Sure, things weren't good, but they had been able to manage the decline and avoid freefall.

Brooks said, "Yes, ma'am, but it's the secondary markets. There are a lot of sellers and no buyers. There's also a lot of 30 day and 60 day Treasuries maturing today. The Fed bought the new issues, but I just spoke with Ivan who is overseeing the transaction process and he said they were under the impression that the market would buy the rollover debt. They're not authorized to buy any of the short term rollover debt."

Chang noticed a tone of panic in her voice that was more pronounced than usual.

"Nora, relax. We'll figure it out. We always do. This is really not your problem in the first place. You need to let us handle it," Chang said in a condescending voice.

"I don't mean to argue Madam Secretary," Nora replied politely, "but it is my problem. Interest rates on 10-year notes are up 280 basis points today. This is catastrophic. The interest rate swaps are not sufficiently structured to withstand that much of a spike in such a short time."

While still wildly unregulated, interest rate swaps were derivatives that fell under the jurisdiction of the CFTC.

Nora Brooks continued her explanation, "These derivatives are based on risk formulas which assume this type of one-day increase could never happen. This is the equivalent of a car insurance company that insures every car in the world. All of a sudden, every car in the world just had a wreck. No insurance company could cover that. What's worse, because no one would listen to my testimony before congress, there is no regulation on who can buy those insurance policies. Back to the car insurance analogy, every car in the world just had a wreck and every one of these cars are insured by 20,000 other people against loss. It's really much worse than that, but it's the only analogy I can come up with at the moment to try to get you to understand what is happening right now."

"Okay, and what is the total value of derivatives based on interest rate swaps?" Chang was starting to understand that this was a bigger problem than she realized.

"$700 trillion," Brooks said somberly.

"I am sorry," Chang needed clarification. "Did I hear you correctly? Did you say billion?"

"No, Madam Secretary," Brooks answered, "I said trillion."

Chang sat her phone down. She felt weak in the knees and light-headed. The voice on the phone, it couldn't be real. Deep inside, though, she knew it was true. She felt sick all of a sudden. She sank to the floor, paralyzed by fear.

Nora Brooks could tell Secretary Chang wasn't going to be much help, so she called the Chairperson of the Federal Reserve, Jane Bleecher. She explained the activities within the derivatives market.

"So the 10-year is now 18.35%?" Bleecher asked.

"Yes, Ma'am, up 280 basis points since this morning's bond auction. That represents an 18% increase in the 10-year rate, in a matter of hours. There are no buyers for the existing US debt." Brooks explained.

"How could the banks have so poorly mispriced the risk in the derivatives?" Bleecher asked.

"The risk models are all based on historic statistical data," Brooks explained. "There has never been a one-day rate increase like what we saw today. We have never seen more than a 100 basis point jump in a single day. These derivatives are priced using the same risk formulas that have always been used. The pricing models aren't that much different than what insurance companies use. This is an extreme outlier event, probably in the neighborhood of 9 standard deviations from the mean."

"Thank you, Nora," Bleecher said, "I have to call the President right away."

Howe answered the phone. "Jane, they are telling me this is important. I hope it is, because you are interrupting a very important meeting."

Jane explained the situation. Anthony Howe had come from a Wall Street family. His father was the co-founder of the Wall Street mega firm Howe Clancy. He understood the implications right away.

"Jane, I want you to hang up with me and call the SEC. Have them close all the markets in 30 minutes. Call Brooks back and have her halt all commodities and derivatives trading. Also get the FDIC and tell them to shut down the banks in 30 minutes. I want everything to close down simultaneously in 30 minutes. Do you understand me?"

"Yes Mr. President. I'll get straight to work on all of that." She hung up.

Howe got straight to work as well.

He called his financial planner inside Howe Clancy and told him, "Sell everything and get as much physical cash out of the system as you can. Wire the rest to Zurich. After that, go to as many coin shops as you can and clean them out by any means necessary; cash, check or credit card. Move fast, buy any silver or gold the shops have available."

Soon the rumor of Howe's move had spread throughout the building at Howe Clancy and everyone knew this was the big one. Most did not have time to react before the banks and markets were closed down.

CHAPTER 8

"Paper money has had the effect in your state that it will ever have, to ruin commerce, oppress the honest, and open the door to every species of fraud and injustice."

-George Washington

Matt was bringing some wood up to the house on the dolly. Adam Bair pulled into Matt's drive and got out of the truck. Matt called out from across the yard, "Hey, Cousin!"

"Why don't you drive your truck down there and bring up a rick or two at a time?" Adam asked.

"It's my exercise," Matt explained. "I can only stay in the house for so long. This gets me out and keeps me warm while I'm doing it. Plus, it saves gas."

"Well, they just shut down the banks and the markets," Adam said.

"What happened?" Matt asked.

"An interest rate spike triggered some type of derivatives Armageddon according to CNBC," Adam answered.

"Do you still have anything in the bank?" Matt asked.

"A few hundred that I kept to pay bills with," Adam responded.

"You should probably try to spend that with your debit card," Matt suggested.

"I tried," Adam responded. "All the credit cards are shut down. There are zero banking services operating in the US. I can't even sign in to my online banking account."

"Do you mind if we shoot over to your house and check out a few news sites so I can try to get a feel for what's going on?" Matt requested.

"Let's do it," Adam said.

"Karen will probably want to go also. I'll get her." Matt went in to get Karen, but she was busy making some cookies.

"You go ahead, I'll walk over when I'm finished," Karen said.

"Drive the truck over. I don't want you walking around by yourself," Matt said.

"Is a bunny going to eat me?" Karen joked.

Matt had not gotten past his overprotective paranoia from living in South Florida. Crime was so bad when they left, he was constantly worried about Karen when she was out by herself. Now, they were in the middle of the woods and he had to remind himself that she was finally safe.

"Okay, walk but bring your pistol," Matt negotiated.

"I don't leave home without it," She said.

Matt and Adam jumped in the truck and headed to Adam's house.

When the guys walked in, the rest of the family was gathered around the television. The story had moved past the financial channels and had permeated all of the news stations.

Matt watched for a few minutes then went to the computer to check out Zero Hedge. He knew he would get the most accurate version of what happening from Zero Hedge. Matt read what they had posted and checked a couple more sites before returning to the living room.

"It looks like all of the big banks are bankrupt," he announced to the rest of the room.

"What does that mean?" Janice asked.

"It means they owe a lot more than they have, and the holders of the interest rate swaps want their money now," Matt said.

"Won't the government bail them out?" Shelly asked.

"They owe about $700 trillion this time, Shelly. I don't think anybody can bail them out," Matt said. "Even with the out-of-control money creation by most every central bank in the world, the global M2 money supply is still less than $50 trillion dollars. The banks owe 14 times more than all the money in the world. If they're going to get a bailout, it's going to have to come from another planet."

"But depositors will still be covered. Right?" Janice inquired.

"The 2005 bankruptcy reform act, pushed through by our good friends at Howe Clancy, Goldman Sachs and JP Morgan Chase, made sure that derivatives holders would have super priority in case of a bankruptcy. Depositors are now considered unsecured creditors," Matt explained.

"But that's the depositor's money!" Shelly protested.

"Not according to US bankruptcy law," Matt said.

"The FDIC will still make good on insured amounts, though," Wesley said. "I bet they knew this was coming. Maybe that's why they dropped the FDIC insured amount to $75,000."

"I don't know. This event would have been hard to pinpoint when it would happen. The interest-rate market is built purely on confidence," Matt said.

"Unless someone planned this event," Adam added.

"It's possible, but folks on our level will never know if that's what happened," Matt said. "As far as the FDIC reimbursing depositors, they only have about $30 billion in the fund insuring over $10 trillion in deposits. So yeah, the first one third of a percent of depositors should theoretically have no problem getting their money. The other 99.7% are on their own."

"But the Fed can just print the money to reimburse them," Wes stated.

"And nearly double the money supply in doing so," Matt said. "Either way, the paper money won't be worth having by the time this is all over with."

"So should we run out and try to buy stuff with the little bit of cash we have left?" Adam asked.

"If there are staples you need and think you can get, yes," Matt said. "There will probably be a run on anything like food and personal supplies. We'll probably see worse rioting than we saw in the last EBT riots. If there are no banks, credit cards and EBT cards won't work at all this time. In addition to the dependent welfare class rioting, everyone who put their faith in credit cards will also be joining the show. If you're just looking to get rid of the rest of your dollars, I would wait. In the short run, we'll probably see a major liquidity crisis where people who haven't prepared are looking to sell everything of value for a few bucks. We might see jewelry, ammo, tools, farm animals or even farms being sold for pennies on the dollar to try to get cash. If the grid stays up for a while, Craigslist may be a gold mine in the next few days. Once the smoke clears though, dollars won't be good for anything except lighting fires."

"Well," Adam said, "I guess we're pretty well set on staples. Ladies, why don't y'all write a list of everything you would like to buy if this was the last day grocery stores were going to be open. Me and the guys will go to Kroger and pick up what we can find."

"Sounds like a good plan," Matt said, "But, I think we should try the Piggly Wiggly. It's a little more out of the way. Piggly Wiggly is less likely to have trouble and more likely to have the stuff we're looking for."

"Good call," Adam said.

"Karen is coming over in a while; tell her I'll be right back," Matt said to Janice.

"You better get something for her," Janice said.

"Oh, I know what she'll want," Matt said.

"What's that?" Janice inquired.

"Cheese, mostly extra sharp Cheddar. Maybe a little Swiss; Brie if I can find it. That's not likely at Piggly Wiggly, though," Matt said.

The guys loaded into Adam's truck and headed out.

CHAPTER 9

"The rich rule over the poor, and the borrower is servant to the lender."

-Proverbs 22:7

Anthony Howe sat in the oval office with Treasury Secretary Melinda Chang, Fed Chair Jane Bleecher, his new Press Secretary Jared Campbell and his new Chief of Staff Alec Renzi. It was hard to say how long Jared and Alec would last. In the high stress environment of the financial meltdown, those two positions were likely to have a higher-than-average turnover rate.

"People, this is not pretty. Everyone needs to understand that the next few weeks are going to be tough. The press is going to be attacking us and the people are going to be blaming us for this mess we walked into. Get over it and do your job. When we send soldiers into war, everyone knows there are going to be casualties. People accept that with no problem. They are going to have to accept the fact that there are going to be some losses in this crisis.

"We all knew a crunch was coming, I just wasn't expecting it today. But it's here so let's just roll with the punches. I'm open to any ideas you have about holding the country together. A lot of it is going to be damage control. Jared, you are my man for that. Spin this to be

Paul Randall's fault. Say whatever you have to say. I'll sign off on anything you come up with as long as you make us look like we're doing everything we can. Just let the public know we're up against impossible circumstances. I don't even need to see what you're going to put out. You know what they need to hear to make them feel better, so write it up and roll it out.

"Alec, get the military, FEMA and DHS together and come up with a plan to keep order. I want it finalized and ready to go into effect by sundown. I am declaring martial law and suspending the Posse Comitatus Act. I want troublemakers detained at the first signs of civil unrest. Anyone who breaks dusk-til-dawn curfew is to be detained. Anyone who resists detainment is to be shot on sight. We are not playing around with rioters for the next month like Al Mohammad did last year in the EBT riots. If people went nuts over that, you can bet they'll go stark raving mad over this. People are going to get upset when we start shooting Americans, but they'll get the message that we won't tolerate chaos.

"Melinda, if you're not up for this, I need to know now. You had a little meltdown earlier. If you need to tap out, tell me now. I can promote New York Fed President Sydney Roth to Treasury Secretary. Nobody will think any less of you."

Chang had adjusted herself with a couple of stiff drinks prior to the meeting. "I think I'll be okay, Mr. President. It was just the initial shock."

"Jared," Howe said, "I am leaving you in control of the fort. People need to see you in the White House Press Briefing Room to feel like things are normal. You'll be staying in the White House subterranean bunker. Marines and Secret Service will be with you. The bunker is designed to withstand a bomb, you'll be perfectly safe there from a few protestors. You can bring your wife and kids, but absolutely no one else can know about it.

"The rest of us are relocating to Mount Weather in Virginia. It's not far, and it'll be a much better place to work. Same thing goes for the rest of you. Bring your spouse and children and nobody, and I mean nobody else knows where you are. I am not threatening you with your job. If it leaks out and causes me more trouble, you will be prosecuted."

The intercom phone buzzed."Mr. President, Stanley Klauser from the IMF is on the line."

"Didn't I say I was not to be disturbed?" Howe shot back.

"Yes, Mr. President, but he said if you don't take the call, not to bother calling back," The voice said.

"Put him through," Howe growled.

"Mr. Director," Howe said.

"Mr. President," Klauser said over the speaker phone. "Are you free to speak or do you need to take me off speaker?"

"I am here with my staff, but they need to hear our conversation. They'll be involved with the decision process of our crisis," Howe said.

"Very well then," Klauser said in his thick German-Swiss accent. "We seem to have something of a conundrum. As we discussed previously, the IMF was depending on a percentage of the deposits in your banks to secure additional relief monies for your fiscal shortfall coming up at the end of the month.

"It is my understanding that much of those deposits are now evaporated by today's action in the derivatives market. Most of the money in the banks has already been carted off by the derivatives investors to other countries. I also understand that if there were more money, that the derivatives investors who were not able to cash out would be first in line to receive it under your current bankruptcy laws.

"I am very much unable to secure additional financing for the US unless you can come up with another way to produce good faith capital. The other member nations have been very patient with your country in taking the recommendations from our last agreement."

"Mr. Director," Howe said, "we have made the 15% across the board cuts to all of our military, government and entitlement programs. This deep cutting austerity has been in the face of very high inflation which has caused the strain to be much more for our citizens and government employees to bear than the nominal 15% cuts."

"Mr. President," Klauser countered, "The International Monetary Fund put those requirements in the last deal as mandatory austerity measures. It was our expectation and the expectation of the other member countries that America would continue to find other areas to reduce spending. You still have more entitlement spending and more military spending than any other country in the world. America asking for more is the equivalent of the CEO of a company going around and begging for change from the people in the mailroom. The mailroom clerks are none too happy about lending money to the man they see ride around in a limousine while they are struggling to put bread on the table. I am sure you see my position."

The mailroom analogy sent a shot of anger to Howe's brain. His face was glowing red, but he knew he had to endure the abuse. He knew Klauser was loving every minute of it.

"Does the Director have any recommendations?" Howe said like a dog with his tail tucked.

"Of course, I would have to run it by the board of directors and have any agreement ratified by the member countries but I may have a thought or two," Klauser said.

Howe knew he was toying with him. Klauser had the board and the new Council of Member States that ratified agreements eating out of his hand.

In the past few years, the IMF and the UN had grown closer and closer. The Council of Member States had been formed as a permanent committee to function in the role that the Troika had filled in the previous European crisis. The Troika was made up of representatives from the European Central Bank, the IMF and the European Union. Financial woes were spreading around the world and an international board was needed to help govern the bailouts and bail-ins in a way that made all member countries feel included in the process. New international law continued to change the procedure used to grant loans and reduce the sovereignty of nations. Now, accepting loans from the IMF was tantamount to selling your soul to the devil. Klauser already had a list and Howe knew it. Klauser would have never initiated the call unless he knew the terms he was going to dictate to Howe.

"First, you must cut your spending across the board by 50%. Your economy has collapsed and you will soon have no tax revenue whatsoever," Klauser said.

"So another 35% on top of the 15% cuts made last year?" Howe asked.

"No!" Klauser shot back somewhat annoyed. "50% from current levels."

The audacity of the IMF Director infuriated Howe. "There is no way I can cut military spending, social security, government payrolls, health care, and government assistance programs by 50% in one swipe, Stanley!"

There was silence on Klauser's end. Howe had just yelled at the only person who could help him and in front of his staff to boot.

"Then descend into chaos, Mr. Howe and let the vultures lick up the scraps! Good day!" Klauser yelled as he hung up the phone.

No one in the Oval Office said a word. Melinda Chang helped herself to a glass of brandy from the decanter on the shelf. No one noticed. Not even Howe, who would have usually sent a staff member home for drinking his brandy without it being offered to them.

Howe yelled at his staff, "Don't you people have something to do?"

The room cleared in less than 15 seconds without anyone saying a word.

CHAPTER 10

"The fate of unborn millions will now depend, under God, on the courage and conduct of this army. Our cruel and unrelenting enemy leaves us only the choice of brave resistance, or the most abject submission. We have, therefore, to resolve to conquer or die."

-George Washington

Paul Randall called Texas Governor Larry Jacobs. "Larry, are you issuing a statement about martial law?"

"I Informed the National Guard that federal troops or agencies were not to be allowed to take any action in the state," Larry said. "I drafted a letter to the White House telling them that Texas will not surrender semi-automatic firearms. I also informed them that federal troops or agencies taking action to disarm Texan citizens would be arrested. If they resist arrest, they'll be fired upon. The National Guard is coordinating with militia to set up perimeters on border roads leading in and out of Texas. I am placing a couple of Guardsmen with each militia group to relay my orders regarding the borders and action against federal troops. That will free up the Guardsmen to help secure civil unrest inside the state. I don't want militia getting involved in policing right now. Protecting our borders will keep them busy enough. I'm sure we'll see quite a mess by evening.

"This is going to be a battle on two fronts. We'll have massive rioting and looting in our cities by sundown and we will be fighting to keep the US military from marching on our streets and enforcing this unconstitutional gun ban. I won't have our citizens disarmed at the time they need their weapons the most."

"Have you floated this by any other governors around the country to see if anyone else is with you?" Randall asked.

Governor Jacobs said, "South Carolina Governor Hayden Nicholas is sending an almost identical letter to D.C. Idaho, Montana and Wyoming are coordinating their own styling, but the three of them will be sending one letter that represents the intention of all three. It is being termed the Northwest Coalition. They have invited North and South Dakota to join. eastern Washington and eastern Oregon have filed for an emergency partition vote to separate from the western halves of their two states. They are threatening violence if the partition is not granted. The liberals on the west coast have fought the partition for years, but they may be willing to grant it now. The irreconcilable differences are a bit more obvious now. If they get the partition, eastern Washington and eastern Oregon will also join the Northwest Coalition."

Governor Jacobs paused a moment. "Did you speak with General Jefferson?"

"I did." Paul Randall said, "The brass at Fort Hood are holding a meeting right now explaining the intentions of the leadership on the base. They will offer any soldiers or officers who remain loyal to D.C. the opportunity to leave provided they are off the base by 8:00 a.m. tomorrow morning. Anyone who stays will be treated as a deserter if they leave or suddenly decide to renounce their allegiance to Texas.

"Fort Bliss, Fort Sam Houston, all the Air Force Bases and Naval Bases in Texas seem to be coordinated to give the same opportunity. The good General offered to get some Bradleys, Cougars and Humvees out of Red River if you think you would have any use for them. Maybe a couple of those would be a good show of strength at the border roads; if the militia won't mind that is."

"That would be much appreciated, Paul," Jacobs said. "I am sure Jefferson is aware of the Northwest Coalition. There aren't many bases up there, but the ones that are, would be worth locking down. There are some heavy hitters up that way. Specifically, Malmstrom Air Force Base in Montana and Warren Air Force Base in Wyoming. They're two of the three that "officially" control Minutemen ICBM Missiles."

Paul replied, "I know he positioned leadership up there in hopes that Montana and Wyoming would side with the patriots. Jefferson is also hoping the partitions go through, specifically for Washington. Fairchild Air Force Base is right outside Spokane. The official story is that all of their nuclear silos were decommissioned, but General Jefferson seems to think that may not be entirely true. Same story with Vandenberg Air Force Base located in the People's Republic of California. Not much hope for getting control of that one.

"The only other active silo site "officially" is in Minot. We would have all of the official nuclear missile silos if North Dakota sided with us. Of course ICBMs are only one point of the nuclear triad. Weapons storage, B-52s, B-2s and nuclear subs armed with Tridents are sprinkled all over the country. If we're talking quantity, there are over 2,000 warheads still waiting to be dismantled at Pantex, right here in Texas. Well, mutually assured destruction has kept us all alive this long. Have you thought about what you'll do with the federal agencies inside Texas borders?"

"I'll wait until the military bases get settled and then issue eviction notices as soon as I know we have the support from the bases," Jacobs said.

"What about controlling the riots?" Paul asked.

Jacobs replied, "I'll issue a statement that everyone needs to stay home. I'll make a point of reminding everyone of the Castle Doctrine and extend it to include their right to use deadly force in defense of their neighborhoods, but we don't have the manpower to keep every street safe. Even if we had every soldier from every military base in America, we couldn't stop this. The banking system just collapsed and no one can get a nickel out of their bank, write a check or use a credit card. I hope people took the opportunity to get prepared after that shot across the bow last November with the EBT riots.

"I also hope all the good folks of Texas have guns and are ready to defend themselves. The bad element will have a heyday with this one. Not only has the government taught people that they will take care of them financially through welfare, they've taught them that the police are responsible for their safety. That's a bigger lie than the welfare system. In the best of times, all a police officer can do is come file a report after the crime has already been committed. Sometimes they can catch the guy who did it, but even if they do, the damage is already done. I hope folks have figured out that they're responsible for their own security. Tonight would be a bad time to come to that realization."

Randall stated, "I'm going to let you go. I'm going to get in as many phone calls as I can this evening. I want to get as much support as I can. We have a lot of work to do."

As soon as Randall had hung up with Larry Jacobs, General Allen Jefferson called. "Paul, Lejeune and Bragg are all set, the leadership is just waiting for the Governor of North Carolina to make a commitment. Do you think you could call him and try to get a definitive answer? We put a lot of good officers there hoping that we can work with the state."

"Sure, General," Paul said. "Governor Taylor supported me in the campaign. I hope we can get him onboard with the effort."

"Tell him it's time to man up!" Jefferson said, "We fight now or live as slaves for the rest of our lives."

Paul Randall said, "Good-bye" and put in the call to North Carolina Governor Ronald Taylor. Randall quickly explained the support the movement had in Texas, the Northwest Coalition and South Carolina.

"This is a tough call, Paul. I hope this will all blow over and things will get back to normal," Taylor said. He was obviously torn on what to do.

Randall replied, "Howe is going to be disarming the American people whether the financial crisis blows over or not. He couldn't be more straightforward about his intentions to confiscate weapons. This fight was already coming. The banking system collapse just pushed it up on the calendar."

Ron Taylor said, "You're right. We have been discussing that in the North Carolina State Senate. We just haven't made a final decision on how to handle it."

Randall continued to explain, "General Jefferson put a lot of faith in you to do the right thing by positioning key leadership in Camp Lejeune and Fort Bragg. It's all patriot brass running those bases thanks to Jefferson's planning. He won't be able to move them around again. If you don't commit to this effort, we may not be able keep America alive. I'm not being melodramatic, Ron. The freedom of this nation may very well depend on your faithfulness to the Constitution."

Taylor reluctantly committed to the effort. "Knowing how much I would be letting you and Allen Jefferson down, I'll call an emergency meeting with the General Assembly. I'll try to get this through tonight,"

"You're doing the right thing, Ron," Paul assured him.

"You and Jefferson are going to have to hold my hand through this, Paul," Taylor replied. "I don't have much experience with coups."

Continuing his plan to solicit support, Paul Randall called the Governor of Kentucky. With the dollar going away, it would be good to have the gold reserves being held in Fort Knox. There was no chance of getting at the gold reserves in the New York Federal Reserve. Randall was unsure of the amount still being held in Kentucky, but Fort Campbell was also there and it was a large military base. Since Kentucky had voted for Randall in the presidential election, he knew he had the support of the people. Governor Simmons talked with Paul for a long time, but in the end was unwilling to make a personal commitment.

"Governor, are you willing to let the Federal Government march on your state and disarm your citizens?" Randall asked.

"I will put it to a vote with the state legislature, Paul. This is not my call," Simmons said.

"Those people elected you to make crucial decisions for them, Governor," Paul said. "They overwhelmingly voted for me in the presidential election. You know where they stand. I am just asking you to hold an emergency session and to personally support it. You carry a lot of weight in the Kentucky General Assembly. I know a lot of those votes are going to go in the direction you recommend."

Governor Simmons was silent for a moment as he contemplated Paul's words. "You are very convincing, Paul, but I can't give you an answer right away. I'll think it over and get back to you on it. I owe it to the people of Kentucky to examine all the angles on this one. The repercussions are tremendous. I can tell you that we'll likely support you, but I don't make decisions this big in the blink of an eye."

"I can respect that Governor," Paul said.

He contacted the remaining state governors in quick succession. Several of them were on the fence including Nebraska, Louisiana, Mississippi, Tennessee and Alabama. Northern Colorado also demanded an emergency partition vote to separate it from the rest of the state. If it went through, Northern Colorado would become part of the Northwest Coalition. The economic problems, the political discord between parties, and the friction between states and the Federal Government had been building up to a flashpoint for years. No one could have ever imagined it would all erupt on the same day.

CHAPTER 11

"Our contest is not only whether we ourselves shall be free, but whether there shall be left to mankind an asylum on earth for civil and religious liberty."

-Samuel Adams

When Matt, Wesley and Adam returned from Piggly Wiggly, the girls were all gathered around the television watching the news coverage and eating the cookies Karen had brought over.

"What's happening?" Matt asked.

"People are freaking out," Shelly answered. "This is going to be way worse than the EBT riots. L.A. already looks like a war zone and it isn't even dark yet."

"How was Piggly Wiggly?" Karen asked.

"There was a lot of tension," Adam said. "Several people are trying to pay with credit cards and they're very upset that they can't."

"How could people forget so quickly?" Janice asked. "We just went through this with the EBT riots. You would think that people would've been a little more prepared and have some cash around."

Matt said, "The news and the government told them it was a mistake and that it would never happen again. People always believe their lies. That's why they keep putting these people back in office and keep watching the same old news channels."

Wes asked, "What's happening in L.A.?"

Shelly answered, "People are walking out of the grocery store with full carts and not paying."

"Why are the managers letting them get away with it?" Wes asked.

"Everybody is doing it," Shelly replied. "They can't stop everyone, so they're just letting them walk out. The police are trying to lock down individual grocery stores, but they can't be everywhere at once. Store owners in Koreatown closed up their shops. They're all posted up with their families around their neighborhood with shotguns and pistols tucked in their pants."

"At least some people have a good memory," Wesley said. "The police aren't confiscating weapons?"

"Not yet," Shelly stated. "The amnesty period lasts until March first."

Wesley countered, "Yes, but police are authorized to start confiscating any firearms on the ban list if they come into contact with them in the normal course of duty."

Shelly responded, "I guess they figure Koreatown is one area they don't have to secure if the residents are policing it themselves."

Matt turned his attention to the television.

CNC News correspondent Patrick James was reporting in a Chicago suburb. "We're getting reports of looting and food riots from all over the city of Chicago. While this area we're in now is safer than some, the situation around us has been deteriorating as dusk approaches. We'll continue to bring you live coverage as long as possible.

"Right across the street from us is a Target that was closed earlier today by management due to looting. Looters were seen running down the street with a wide assortment of goods. Some people had clothing and tennis shoes, others were carting off big screen televisions. I suppose if this situation proves to be the end of our civilization, one would like to witness it in HD."

Despite the flippant comment, Patrick James had a look of disgust on his face.

He continued reporting, "High inflation already caused most Walmarts to close. People in the neighborhood turned to this Target store when the Walmart down the street closed. Now that Target stores have been raising their prices to keep pace with inflation, sales have dropped to a critical level. Corporate losses are quickly eating away at company cash. The new round of riots may be the straw that breaks the camel's back. This store across from us may never open again after today.

"Two blocks from here is a Kroger grocery store that closed their doors only to have looters break through the front glass and clear out the shelves. We saw people running out with cases of beer and others wheeling away grocery carts overflowing with food items. As the shelves emptied, looters were fighting each other over the last few items on the shelves.

"Other retail stores are also closing as the sense of civil unrest is rising throughout the city. Police departments here in Chicago have been stripped to unsafe levels by budget cuts just as they have in the rest of the country. The Chicago Police Department was already ineffective against the level of criminal activity taking place prior to the rioting and looting. This renders the city completely helpless. President Howe has pledged to send military support to help maintain order in major metropolitan areas. But if they don't get here soon, there will be nothing left to defend.

"As many of you may remember, I was in Detroit last fall reporting on the EBT riots. We witnessed violent clashes between police and protestors. Several people were killed right in front of our cameras. The city never recovered from those riots. What little resemblance Detroit still held to the civilized world was lost during those riots. Now, standing here in the Southside of Chicago, it feels eerily like the early evening on the night that the EBT riots destroyed Detroit.

"President Howe has enacted a curfew beginning at sundown tonight. Here at CNC, we are encouraging all of our viewers to stay indoors until the curfew is lifted tomorrow morning at dawn. If the riots last fall were any indication of what we are facing, this is going to be a rough night. We are going back to the CNC studios where Ed Nolan is bringing you some breaking news."

The television screen cut to the studio where Ed Nolan sat behind the desk.

Nolan said, "Thank you Patrick. Be safe.

"We have just received word from a confidential source inside the White House that Texas has issued a statement telling President Howe that federal troops will not be allowed to enter the state to enforce martial law. The letter is said to have come from Governor Larry Jacobs who was an avid supporter of Senator Paul Randall in last year's presidential campaign. We will be monitoring the situation closely and we will let you know what the response from the White House is, as soon as we have more information.

"Earlier, President Howe issued a statement to the press stating that he would be using all of the resources available to him, including US military troops to maintain an environment of order and to enforce his dusk-til-dawn curfew.

"Several conservative lawmakers have said the move to employ the military in a domestic peacekeeping effort is a precursor to an invasion of areas around the country that are known to be vehemently opposed to President Howe's semi-automatic gun ban. These lawmakers have long claimed the gun ban to be unconstitutional and say they will encourage their constituents to disregard the ban. None have said if they intend to defy the ban to the point of violence against the Federal Government.

"We have seen states assert their rights in defiance of federal laws in the past, but if the report about Texas turns out to be true, it will be the most defiant act by a state towards the Federal Government since the Civil War."

Matt looked over at Wesley and Adam. The three men exchanged nods and smiles. Karen caught the look between them. It was obvious what they were thinking.

Matt recognized the look on Karen's face and he quickly lost his smile. He felt for his wife. He didn't want war either. That had not been why he was smiling. Matt was smiling because he saw hope. He knew it only took one kid in the playground to stand up to the bully. After that, others would be encouraged to take a stand as well. Soon, the bully and his cronies would be outnumbered and he would be put in his place.

While Paul Randall continued to give speeches of encouragement over the internet, no other leaders had publicly taken a stand against Howe.

Matt said, "If this is true, if Texas Governor Jacobs is really standing up to the President, this is a game changer."

CHAPTER 12

"Whenever a man has cast a longing eye on offices, a rottenness begins in his conduct."

-Thomas Jefferson

Howe was still scowling. He had a drink in his hand and his tie was draped across the chair. The White House Chief of Staff Alec Renzi let himself into the Oval Office.

"Mr. President, you need to read this." Renzi handed the letter from Texas to the President.

Howe quickly scanned the paper. His scowl deepened. "Get General Jefferson on the line. Have him send a platoon from Fort Hood to detain Texas Governor Laurence Jacobs under the 2012 NDAA Indefinite Detention Clause. Send Jacobs straight to a CIA black site before anyone gets a chance to talk to him. This is getting out of hand. I can't have another Paul Randall running around sowing discord. Cut this off before it gets started."

"Yes, sir," Renzi answered.

One thing Howe had learned from Al Mohammad, there was no negotiating with these people. Individuals like Paul Randall and Larry Jacobs were stuck in the past and still clinging to the antiquated notion that they could govern the same way people did 200 years ago. Times had changed. Governing had to be done with a strong hand. That is what people needed.(Unfortunately, the founding fathers had not understood how dangerous it was to let men speak their minds.) Jacobs had to be silenced before he started another brush fire like the one Paul Randall ignited. With Paul Randall hiding out, it was easy enough to label him as a kook, but if state governors started dissenting, it could incite rebellion that might cause Howe serious problems.

"General Jefferson is on the line, sir." Renzi handed Howe the receiver.

"General," Howe said.

"How can I assist you, Mr. President?" Jefferson asked.

"I need you to have Texas Governor Jacobs arrested," Howe said.

"What is the infraction?" Jefferson quizzed.

"Insurrection!" Howe's voice was harsh.

Jefferson began laughing out loud. "Mr. President, an insurrection would be the act of a group or an army against a government or power. Are you sure that is the charge?"

"Don't quibble with me, Jefferson, and don't you dare mock me. I'll have you busted down to sergeant," Howe barked. "Have him detained. I don't need a charge. Send a platoon from Fort Hood to bring him in. Take him straight to a CIA black site."

"You won't have to bust me down, Anthony, I resign. I have a new position as Secretary of Defense." Jefferson spoke with a light-hearted tone that infuriated Howe even more.

"Are you delusional? Scott Hale is the Secretary of Defense," Howe said.

"Not of the Sovereign State of Texas," Jefferson said.

Howe was further angered by the tone of satisfaction in Jefferson's voice. Howe slammed the phone down. This situation was getting away from him. It had to be contained right away. Howe called Secretary of Defense Scott Hale into his office.

"Hale," He growled, "you have to reassign Jefferson's position right away. He is in Texas and conspiring to overthrow the government with Paul Randall and Larry Jacobs. You also have to send troops from Fort Hood to Austin to lock down the Governor's mansion and all of their state government offices. I want Jacobs and Jefferson detained before they disappear into the night like Paul Randall. They are trying to stage some kind of ...." Howe was at a loss for the word.

"Insurrection, sir?" Hale said.

"Yes, Hale, an insurrection," Howe screamed.

Secretary Hale struck a sore spot when he said "insurrection".

Hale rang the commanding officer at Fort Hood to relay the President's orders.

"We are no longer accepting orders from the White House," the officer informed Hale. "Our orders come from the Sovereign State of Texas."

Hale and his staff started calling all of the military bases in Texas. He soon realized this was a coordinated event that had been in the works for some time.

Hale informed the President of the situation. Howe was unresponsive.

Jane Bleecher let herself in and said, "Mr. President, I am afraid you are going to have to come to some type of reconciliation with the IMF."

"I know, Jane," The President said somberly. "Why don't you call Klauser and tell him we would like to start over."

"I hardly think that would be appropriate Mr. President," Bleecher said.

"Just do it, Jane," Howe said calmly, but in a way that let her know not to argue.

Scott Hale took the opportunity to escape while Jane Bleecher was speaking with Howe.

As soon as her business with The President was finished, Jane made a quick exit as well.

Not more than a minute passed before Alec Renzi was back in the room. Renzi said, "I'm sorry to have to bring you more bad news, Mr. President, but we just got another letter from South Carolina. It is almost an exact replica of the one we got from Texas. They must have planned this together."

The lead agent of the Secret Service knocked, even though the door to the Oval Office was open.

"Come in," said Howe.

"Mr. President, we feel it is time to move you and your family to Mount Weather. The streets are getting very bad. Protesters are all around the front fence on Pennsylvania Avenue and Ellipse Road. Marine One is 15 minutes out," The agent said.

"Has anyone told Jenna?" Howe asked.

"Yes, sir, the First Lady is packing as we speak," the agent said.

"Alec," The President said. "Get everyone in here. I am going to need all of my core staff to get on Marine One with me in about 20 minutes. Secret Service will send vehicles to pick up everyone's immediate family later to bring them to Mount Weather. As soon as we get there, we need to put together a plan. Have Scott get the Joint Chiefs together and start coming up with a military response to Texas and South Carolina."

Alec Renzi's phone rang. Howe knew it had to be more bad news. The call was brief.

"Mr. President," Alec began, "Idaho, Wyoming, and Montana have delivered a joint document stating similar objectives to the letters from Texas and South Carolina. They are referring to themselves as the Northwest Coalition. In addition to those three states, Eastern Washington, Eastern Oregon and Northern Colorado are seeking to partition themselves from the other parts of those states to join the Northwest Coalition. North Carolina has also adopted the letter from South Carolina."

Howe threw his brandy glass across the room. It hit the wall near the door and shattered. He had been willing to deal with an economic meltdown, but not a civil war.

"Make sure the Joint Chiefs know all the details. This has to be stopped right away!" Howe snarled as he walked out of the room to prepare to evacuate.

CHAPTER 13

"Everyone must submit himself to the governing authorities, for there is no authority except that which God has established."

- Romans 13:1a

Pastor John Robinson held the Wednesday service just after lunch because everyone could meet together in the barn. There was no other meeting area at Young field. The barn held four wood stoves which helped quite a bit, but it was still drafty and cool. The temperatures had been mild. The highs had been near 40 degrees which was not bad for Idaho in late January.

Pastor John began with prayer then went straight to the announcement of the states and territories that had decided to secede from the authority of Washington, D.C.

"Church, we have known for some time that a season of testing was coming for our nation. We know that the enemies of freedom have taken root in our nation's capitol. We were able to reasonably predict that the economic disaster, which has now fallen on us, would come. No one knew the day, nor could we guess the severity of the collapse, but simple fourth grade math told us that this day would inevitably come. Now, it is upon us. We have done the best we knew to prepare, and we'll trust God to take it from here. As I have said many times, 'do your best and trust God with the rest.'

"With that being said, I can't tell you how thrilled I am that those who have been elected to lead us have submitted to the governing authority. Here in America, the governing authority is the Constitution. The first line of the Constitution plainly spells out who is in charge of seeing that the governing authority is followed. The framers, who established that authority with God's help, wanted to make it abundantly clear who were to be the ultimate overseers of that authority. To accomplish this, they wrote those words larger than any other words on the document. Can anyone tell me what those words are?"

Four or five people near the front row yelled out at roughly the same time, "We the people."

"We the people," Pastor John echoed. "When we read Romans 13, we must keep that in mind. It is the guidestone to correctly interpreting this area of scripture which I will be speaking on today. Romans 13:1 reads 'Everyone must submit himself to the governing authorities, for there is no authority except that which God has established. The authorities that exist have been established by God.'

"So we have determined that the Constitution and the Bill of Rights are the governing authorities that were established by our founders. Verse one also states that they were established by God and, in fact, there is no authority except that which has been established by God. The entirety of our legal system and our government system has its foundation on that governing authority. If any of our leaders are to derive authority, it must come from that ultimate authority that was originally established by God.

"Romans 13:2 reads 'Consequently, he who rebels against the authority is rebelling against what God has instituted, and those who do so will bring judgment on themselves.'

"Our present administration has risen up in rebellion against that authority. The Bible says that the present administration is rebelling against what God has instituted. They have rebelled against the authority established by God by going against the Bill of Rights. They have rebelled against the First Amendment by suppressing freedom of religion for the very men and women who have fought to keep this nation free. Our military are no longer free to speak of their religion if they are Christian. They can be punished for belonging to a Christian church or even donating money to a Christian church. They are not allowed to pray in the name of Jesus.

"The press is no longer free. Any member of the press that crosses certain lines can expect to be arrested or harassed by the DOJ or the IRS.

"I don't think I have to mention the infringements against the Second Amendment which reads 'A well-regulated Militia, being necessary to the security of a free State, the right of the people to keep and bear Arms, shall not be infringed.' I won't insult your intelligence today by enumerating the infractions by this administration in violation of the Second Amendment.

"The constant snooping by the NSA and the increasing warrantless searches of homes, personal effects and automobiles are gross injustices against the Fourth Amendment.

"The Fifth Amendment states that no one shall be deprived of life, liberty or property without due process of law, yet even Senator Paul Randall is hiding out from a criminal government that sought to assassinate him in the middle of the night.

"The Sixth Amendment guarantees a speedy trial, yet the 2012 NDAA Indefinite Detention Clause allows our government to indefinitely hold citizens without charging them. This unjust law also violates the principles in the Eighth Amendment which prohibits excessive bail. I would say indefinite detention would have a more egregious effect than excessive bail.

"And finally, the Tenth Amendment is grossly violated. It states 'The powers not delegated to the United States by the Constitution, nor prohibited by it to the States, are reserved to the States respectively, or to the people.'

"The Federal Government has taken over education, welfare,

healthcare, agriculture and many other areas that no government, state or federal, has authority over. Laws about what drugs are allowable for medicinal purposes ought to be the decisions of a state. If a person feels the laws in one state are excessive or too relaxed, they ought to be able to move to a state where they are more agreeable. States ought to be in charge of their own food regulations. If Idaho wants to drink raw milk and folks from Utah don't because of the health risk, so be it. All the minor rules of day-to-day governing are supposed to be set by the states. The Federal Government has a very, very small role to do in defending our borders, maintaining a post office, writing bankruptcy laws and coining money. Notice the government was allowed by the constitution to coin money, not print it.

"Romans 13:3 and 4 says, 'For rulers hold no terror for those who do right, but for those who do wrong. Do you want to be free from fear of the one in authority? Then do what is right and he will commend you. For he is God's servant to do you good. But if you do wrong, be afraid, for he does not bear the sword for nothing. He is God's servant, an agent of wrath to bring punishment on the wrongdoer.'

"For this verse we need to know who the rulers are. Does anyone remember who the Constitution puts in the top position of authority?"

This time, most of the congregation yelled out almost in unison, "We the people."

"You guys are catching on!" Pastor John complimented playfully.

The congregation laughed.

"Okay, this one is a little bit harder, but I'll give you a hint." Pastor John continued to teach the heavy subject with a light heart. "We just went over it. Who is granted the authority of bearing the sword by the constitution? Who is the one that Romans 13:4 calls the agent of wrath to bring punishment on the wrongdoer?"

The same group in the front that had answered the first time answered somewhat together, "The militia."

"Everyone up here in this front section gets an extra piece of cake at dinner tonight." Pastor John kidded. The room laughed for a bit then quieted down to hear more of what the pastor had to say.

"The militia is the only group specifically tasked by the ultimate authority established by God, the Constitution, with the security of a free state." Pastor John continued, "Now I want everyone to get extra cake at dinner, so you folks put your thinking caps on because this one is tricky. Who is the militia?"

The crowd cried out in perfect unison, "We the people."

Pastor John smiled as he said, "I think you've got it!"

He continued, "Romans 13:5 and 6 says, 'Therefore, it is necessary to submit to the authorities, not only because of possible punishment but also because of conscience. This is also why you pay taxes, for the authorities are God's servants, who give their full time to governing.'

"So that is why we pay taxes. We are to support those who have given their time and energy to following the ultimate authority established by God which we have identified as the Constitution. We are not commanded by God's word to pay taxes to support those who are in rebellion to authority which is the Constitution. Remember, we are God's agents of wrath to punish the wrongdoer, not reward them for their bad behavior.

"We are not commanded by God's word to pay taxes to support the sluggard. Quite the contrary, II Thessalonians 3:10 tells us, 'If a man will not work, he shall not eat.' Not only are we not to pay taxes to support the sluggard, we are not to pay taxes to support the poor and needy either. I am not saying that we should just let them all starve, but the Bible instructs the Church to fulfill that mission, not the government. James 1:27 says 'Religion that God our Father accepts as pure and faultless is this: to look after orphans and widows in their distress.' If the government does this with our money by the barrel of a gun, they deprive us of the opportunity to do it out of obedience to God. And if you don't think it is by the barrel of a gun, try not paying your taxes or don't show up for court after not paying your taxes. When the IRS agent shows up at your house, tell him you won't let him in and you aren't going with him. I bet if you look real close, you'll be able to see down the barrel well enough to tell if that is a hollow point or full metal jacket bullet pointed at your head.

"We're not commanded to pay taxes to support endless wars across the globe. Paul tells us in I Thessalonians 4:11 'Make it your ambition to lead a quiet life, to mind your own business' and in Romans 12:18 he says 'If it is possible, as far as it depends on you, live at peace with everyone.'

"Let us be grateful that we have leaders that are willing to stand up to those who are in rebellion against the authority that has been established by God. Let us ask God for strength as we fulfill our duty as his servants, as agents of wrath to bring punishment on the wrongdoer."

After the service, everyone came together for a late lunch. There was an established custom where the congregation ate lunch together and everyone ate the rest of their meals with their individual families.

CHAPTER 14

"They sow the wind and reap the whirlwind"

-Hosea 8:7a

Howe's Chief of Staff Alec Renzi brought him the phone. "It is former President Al Mohammad, sir."

"I'll take that in private." Howe waved his hand dismissing Renzi.

Al Mohammad had some video evidence of personal indiscretions committed by Anthony Howe back when Howe was governor. Al Mohammad let Howe know that he would be acting in an "advisory capacity" throughout his administration. He also let Howe know that he wouldn't take "No" for an answer.

"Anthony, how are you?" Mustafa Al Mohammad asked in a tone that let Howe know he really didn't care.

"Just peachy, Mr. President," Howe replied. He was sickened every time he had to talk to this man.

"You may call me Mustafa now, Anthony. I believe you have earned that right," Al Mohammad said.

"Thank you, Mustafa," Howe replied. Being granted "permission" irked him even more than referring to him as "Mr. President."

"Stanley Klauser just spoke with me," Al Mohammad began. "He is very concerned that if things aren't resolved with the American financial system, it will have a domino effect around the world. He said that communications broke down between the IMF and the White House."

"Jane called him last night to try to work things out and he wouldn't accept her call," Howe said. "We're trying to work this out ourselves."

"And how is that coming along?" Al Mohammad asked sarcastically. "You're President of the United States. You don't have your staff call the Director of the IMF when you are in an economic crisis. Certainly not when it's a systemic failure of this magnitude."

"You know how he is, he wants to dictate to me..." Howe started to respond, but Al Mohammad cut him off.

"Stop it!" Mustafa scolded. "You offended the only person in the world that can help you keep the country together. States are seceding. You're hiding out in a bunker. The banks are closed. The stock market is closed. Credit card machines are not taking payments. People can't get benefits, they can't go to the ATM's. People are looting grocery stores, hardware stores, department stores and convenience stores. Fast food restaurants are being robbed not for money, but for food. People are starving. People are rioting and burning down cities. Do you not understand what is happening? This is not about your pride. This is about whether or not America is still a country tomorrow. And it may be about whether or not you still have a head tomorrow. Mount Weather is quite a fortification, but so was Versailles in its day. Never underestimate a starving crowd."

"Fine!" Howe conceded. "I'll call Klauser."

Al Mohammad continued, "Make sure you start out with a very sincere apology. I'll let you get to work."

"OK," Howe said.

"A simple thank you would be in order, Mr. President," Al Mohammad said.

"Thank you, Mr. Al Mohammad," Howe said. He bit his tongue to keep his anger in check. Howe was seething. He knew Al Mohammad was probably right about apologizing to Klauser, but the way he held it over him, the way he had just scolded him like a child, the way he was blackmailing him to keep a noose around his neck, he could not tolerate. It was time to start shopping around for someone who could find a permanent solution to this problem with Mustafa.

Howe poured himself a stiff drink as he came to terms with what he had to do. He had to lay his pride down for just a moment and make the call. This is something he never had to do, until Mustafa came along. Howe had grown up as a child of absolute privilege. His father's financial firm was among the largest in the world. All through school, college and all through life, everyone respected Howe. Even his teachers and professors were careful about the way they spoke to Anthony Howe. When he had done things against the law as a youth, the police and judges knew better than to prosecute him.

Howe refreshed his drink and made the call. "Mr. Director, I just want to start by saying how sorry I am for the way things were said yesterday."

"The way things were said, is not the problem, Mr. Howe. Your defiant, aggressive tone that you spoke to me with, that is the problem. Would you like to apologize for that?" Klauser was making him grovel.

"Yes sir, I apologize," Howe responded.

"For what, Mr. President?" Klauser asked.

"I apologize for the aggressive and defiant tone with which I spoke to you yesterday, Mr. Director," Howe choked out.

"I do not accept your apology, Mr. Howe," Klauser began, "but in the interest of the global economy, we'll do what we can. I am not negotiating with you, Mr. Howe. I am going to lay out the terms by which the IMF will agree to aid the United States.

"First I will clarify the terms where we left off yesterday. The US will cut spending by 50% from current levels. When I say spending, I am referring to necessary government activities such as military and programs that your citizens have paid into such as Medicare and Social Security. I am not referring to wealth transfer payments to your citizens who have not paid anything into the system. Those programs are to be cut by 75%. I would recommend starting some type of a triage operation to find out who the truly disabled and needy are as this money will not go far; particularly in the hyperinflationary environment that is about to overtake your country.

"Our previous arrangement which we had discussed loosely was that the IMF would seize 90% of all deposits over $50,000 dollars from US banks. This is no longer possible as the entirety of all US banks have lost their liquidity in this present derivatives debacle. Fortunately, the FDIC limits were not reduced from $75,000 to $50,000. We will have the FDIC payout the insured amount to the depositor's accounts. From there, the IMF will assess a bail-in tax of 90% of the deposits over $5,000. All depositors with $5,000 or less in the bank will not be affected by the bail-in tax. I think that represents the majority of your citizens as your government has never encouraged them to save, so this should not be as politically dire as you may think. Those with more than $5,000 will keep the first $5,000 and 10% of the amount over $5,000. I doubt most of the ones with more than $5,000 in the bank were your constituency anyway."

Howe thought this must be Klauser's way of being gracious. It probably made Stanley Klauser feel magnanimous, but it rubbed Howe the wrong way. Howe sat and listened as he poured himself yet another drink.

Klauser continued, "China has agreed to purchase your excess military equipment for 25 cents on the dollar, which I think is very generous. What is more, they have agreed to pay in gold."

"Mr. Director," Howe interrupted, "I humbly apologize for interrupting, but it will be difficult for me to get the congress to agree to give up military equipment which has top secret technology to the Chinese."

"You'll find a way, Howe. America's days of being a superpower are over. Your country is going to have to come to terms with reality. The reality is, if you want this assistance to stabilize your currency and prevent the death of most of your citizens, you will have to agree to all of these terms exactly as they have been presented.

"The remaining gold reserves in the US will be held by the IMF as collateral until all loans made in SDRs are repaid in SDRs with interest at the prevailing rate. Currently, that rate is 19%."

SDR stood for Special Drawing Rights. SDRs were the currency of the IMF. It was a completely fiat currency just as all the other currencies on the globe. The value of each SDR was determined by a basket of currencies of all the member countries, in proportion to their economies. The IMF loaned money in SDRs as opposed to the currency of the debtor country to keep them from devaluing the loan by printing excessive funds.

"The IMF will lend the money to keep the US Government operating at the spending level we discussed for six months. Payments will be made each month to your treasury after a monthly approval process by the Council of Member States. You must be found to be in compliance with the terms of the agreement each month or the monthly payment will not be credited to your treasury's account. If your country descends into a civil war or fragments into more than one state claiming authority, the IMF will be unable to help you until the domestic issues are solved. We will overlook those issues until the end of April, but on the first of May, you must have these issues with seceding states resolved. The IMF retains the right to alter this agreement as it sees fit and when necessary to protect the vested interest of member countries.

"You may announce this agreement to your citizens tomorrow morning." Klauser hung up the phone without so much as a "goodbye" or "have a nice day."

Immediately after the call, Alec Renzi walked timidly into the room. It was obvious that Howe was livid.

"Sir," Renzi began, "the mob has breached the fence on the White House lawn. Secret Service recommends that you evacuate the remainder of the staff."

Howe stood up. He still had authority over this situation, and he intended to use it. "Tell Secret Service to have the Marines to fire on anyone who breaches the fence. All of the remaining staff are in the subterranean bunker. They are safer there than anywhere else."

Renzi responded, "Yes, sir, but they could be trapped there for days."

Howe yelled, "I said leave them there!"

CHAPTER 15

"Remember that it is the actions, and not the commission, that make the officer, and that there is more expected from him, than the title."

-George Washington

It was cold outside. After the animals were tended to and the firewood was cut and stored, Matt Bair had little else to do in the way of chores on his new homestead. He and Karen generally went over to Adam's house after lunch. It was only a couple of miles away if they walked through the woods rather than taking the road, so they usually walked to get the exercise. Karen and Matt typically tried to get back home before dark. This got them home before the frigid night air made walking outside unbearable. It also served to ensure they would not wear out their welcome at Adam's. Miss Mae, the cat, tended to get a bit destructive when left home alone for too long as well. Tearing paper or scratching up the couch was her way of protesting when she felt ignored.

When they arrived at Adam's, everyone was right where they left them the evening before. They were watching the crisis unfold on television. Matt and Karen found a seat together on the couch and turned their attention to the drama du jour.

Patrick James of CNC was reporting from the White House fence.

"People are climbing the fence onto the White House lawn. We have not received official word, but we're sure the President is not there. Marine One was seen leaving yesterday, and we assume the President and most of his staff were on board.

Press Secretary Jared Campbell gave the press briefing last night that did little more than stonewall the press on the crisis. That briefing was done in the White House Press Room last night. It was after we saw Marine One lift off, so we assume that Campbell is still in the White House."

POP....POP, POP...POP. Gunfire rang out from the White House lawn. Patrick James dropped down on his stomach. James had climbed the ranks at CNC by never thinking twice about accepting risky assignments. He had been in harm's way on a regular basis throughout his media career. This had boosted his status with the network and taught him to always be aware of the situation. The cameraman and the others stationed with Patrick James followed his lead and got down behind the CNC van. Patrick crawled over to the cameraman and continued reporting.

"Gunfire has broken out on the White House lawn. We don't know who is firing, but we'll try to move to a safe location and keep filming as long as possible," James reported.

James and the cameraman low crawled to the back of the van where they could see the White House Lawn. Several civilians were lying motionless on the lawn. The Marines guarding the White House were yelling indiscernibly between themselves. Four of the Marines were stripping off their Battle Dress Uniform shirts and walking away from the White House. Several others were yelling at them and two of the Marines were leveling their M-4 rifles at the Marines who were walking away.

Patrick James began to comment on what he was seeing. "It appears the Marines fired on the protestors who breeched the fence. I can't say at this time whether any of those protestors were armed or not.

Four Marines appear to be abandoning their post after the shootout. They have taken off their jackets bearing the Marines insignia. They seem to be checking on the victims of the firefight. They may be checking for weapons, but it looks like they are assisting the victims or checking for a pulse. The Marines still at their posts have rifles trained on the four that are walking away, but are not firing."

Matt and the others watched intently as the four Marines moved from body to body.

Patrick James continued, "They are now approaching the fence."

Matt squeezed Karen's hand as he continued to watch the live action scene on the television.

The Marines jumped the White House lawn fence, faced the crowd and held up their right hands with only their three center fingers extended and their thumb and pinky fingers crossed over their palms. They yelled, "Oath Keepers," as they held up their hands. The crowd of protestors cheered for the four men.

Matt looked at Adam. "Is that the Boy Scout pledge sign they just made?"

Wesley interjected before Adam had a chance to answer. "It's also the sign people made in the Hunger Games movies to show solidarity."

Adam answered, "It may stem from either or both of those things, but it has been adopted by the Three Percenters. The first American Revolution was started by only three percent of the population at the time. The three fingers represent The Three Percent. They are a different group from Oath Keepers, but I suppose these four guys are identifying with both groups (The philosophy of the two groups are not that far apart.")

Shelly asked, "I saw some bumper stickers at church with the roman numeral three followed by the percent sign. Is that the insignia of the Three Percenters?"

"That's them," Adam replied. "From what I hear, Oath Keepers across America are ready to go absent without leave. They are just waiting to see which of the states will secede so they know if they will be leaving or not. They also need to know which states will back the movement so they know where to go. These four guys may have just pulled the trigger on that plan. I think they are calling it Operation AWOL."

"AWOL is short for absent without leave?" Janice asked.

"You got it," Adam said.

CHAPTER 16

"If Congress can employ money indefinitely to the general welfare, and are the sole and supreme judges of the general welfare, they may take the care of religion into their own hands; they may appoint teachers in every State, county and parish and pay them out of their public treasury; they may take into their own hands the education of children, establishing in like manner schools throughout the Union; they may assume the provision of the poor; they may undertake the regulation of all roads other than post-roads; in short, everything, from the highest object of state legislation down to the most minute object of police, would be thrown under the power of Congress.... Were the power of Congress to be established in the latitude contended for, it would subvert the very foundations, and transmute the very nature of the limited Government established by the people of America."

- James Madison

Anthony Howe paced around in circles while he tried to get the video room at Mount Weather to look less like a bunker.

"This isn't going to work," Howe chided. "Can't you people set up a green screen in here and just cut and paste me in front of the fireplace of the Oval Office?"

Howe was furious. He regretted not having Jared Campbell here. This was his job. He should be the one telling these idiots what to do.

The woman who was handling the filming of the President's speech made a suggestion. "Mr. President, may I recommend that we drop a maroon crushed velvet drape over this wall and flank you with the flag of The United States and the Flag with your official seal? We have a nice wood desk where you can be seated. While it won't be the Oval Office, it will certainly look presidential."

"Okay," Howe grunted. "But get this mocked up to look like the White House by tomorrow. Bring furniture from there or whatever you have to do. It's only 40 miles away. It shouldn't take an act of Congress to get some authentic furnishings in here."

Howe went into the boardroom to meet with Bleecher and Chang. He started speaking as he sat down. "Ladies, I am going to tell the American people that the banks will be open on Monday. Will the two of you be able to make sure that goes smoothly?"

Jane Bleecher spoke first. "Mr. President, the Fed can produce the funds, but I expect the people to withdraw every dime they can get. I would recommend restricting withdraws to $500 per week. That will likely deplete most of the physical bills in the vaults in a couple of weeks."

"We can do that, but I am giving them enough bad news today. I'll let them figure out the weekly limitation on Monday when they get to the bank." Howe turned his attention to Chang. "Can we reopen the markets on Monday?"

"I don't think you should, Mr. President," Melinda Chang said. "I think it would be a blood bath of selling."

"Then when do we reopen them?" Howe asked.

Chang scribbled nervously in her note book on the table before she replied. "I would wait until we can come up with a plan to restore confidence."

"How do you propose we do that?" Howe asked.

Bleecher answered, "We need a new stimulus program that will inject funds directly to the people to spend."

Howe shot down the idea. "Hyperinflation has already set in. Pumping money into the system at this point will just make the currency completely worthless. We are getting reports that people aren't accepting dollars in individually-owned grocery stores as it is. Paul Randall's barter system idea is already creeping into grocers and gas stations."

Chang recommended, "Maybe we need to let the smoke clear and come up with a revalued currency. Perhaps we could back it with a basket of commodities. Then it would have a fixed value, based on the aggregate value of the commodities."

"That would be admitting Paul Randall was right," Howe rebutted. "We would lose all control to that maniac. I'll watch this country burn to the ground before I admit he was right about backing the dollar with silver and gold."

Bleecher proposed an alternative idea. "What if we began paying government employees and government benefits in ration tickets? The government could easily commandeer needed commodities such as food and fuel under the National Defense Resources Preparedness Executive Order 13603. This would turn the ration tickets into a de facto commodity-backed currency without naming it as such."

Howe perked up. "That's right. Mustafa signed Executive Order 13603 in his first term. It was the National Defense Resources Preparedness Act. It allows the government to seize resources in times of emergency. Jane, I think you are on to something."

Melinda Chang jumped right on the bandwagon. It was obvious to Howe that she was trying to prove her value to him. She said, "The ration ticket would likely start to trade as a currency for other goods and services. We would maintain some control over these transactions as we would be issuing the de facto currency. At least it would keep the consumer market attached to the government. That's more influence than we have in the barter networks Paul Randall is advocating."

Howe was actually smiling. "Good work ladies. Get this all ironed out and come up with a proposed timeline. Consider the full power of the US military at your disposal for implementing this plan."

As they left, Howe realized he was going to be in absolute control now. That is what he really wanted. The people would have to accept it. They could fall in line or starve to death.

Anthony Howe walked the short distance down to the video room from where he was to give his address to the American people. He was walking a bit lighter than just an hour before.

Howe complemented the woman who was coordinating the filming of the presidential address. "Well, the desk and backdrop look very nice."

"Why, thank you, Mr. President." She looked surprised by the sudden change in his demeanor.

Howe sat down at the wood desk and the camera focused in as he began his address to the nation. "America, the acts of economic terrorism committed by Paul Randall and other co-conspirators within our own government have collapsed our economy. As several state governments are now vowing to rebel against the United States Government, markets panicked. The anticipated loss of revenue from those states sparked a deterioration of confidence in the bond market as investors questioned how our nation could pay its obligations with a divided nation.

"Despite this attempt to completely derail our country, I have successfully negotiated an agreement with the IMF to restore our economy until these bands of traitors can be dealt with. We will be able to fund entitlement programs and reopen the banks on Monday morning. Unfortunately, the IMF did ask for a temporary security deposit in order to secure the needed assistance for these rescue measures. All deposits lost in the derivatives meltdown will be reimbursed by the FDIC up to the insured amounts. Those accounts will then be made available to the depositors for the first $5,000. Amounts above $5000 will be allocated to the depositors in full. The first 10% will be immediately available and the remaining 90% will be on deposit with the IMF as security for the loan. As the loan is paid off, the remaining 90% of the deposits up to $75,000 will become available incrementally.

"Those of you who receive benefits from the government will begin to see portions of your transfer payments as early as Monday. We are asking for patience while we work on getting your benefits restored to their full amounts as soon as possible. As funding is limited for these programs, we will not be funding benefit programs in states that are in open rebellion. I understand that many of you in those states are not in agreement with your state governments, but cuts have to be made. I would encourage you to contact your governors and state representatives and demand that those governments step down and turn over power to the Federal Government. For those of you who live in those states, this is the best way for you to have your benefits restored. If they will not listen, take to the streets, protest at the governors' residences and the military bases and demand that they comply.

"For those of you in states that still want to see our country prosper, you have nothing to worry about. Life will be getting back to normal very soon. So please, obey the curfews, relax and take it easy this weekend. The banks will open on Monday and we'll get back to (making this country great again.)

"Take care of each other."

Howe forced a smile until the cameraman signaled he was off air. He got up and went to his office alone. He poured himself a stiff drink and looked in the mirror. "Salute," he said to his reflection as he lifted his glass.

CHAPTER 17

"I believe that banking institutions are more dangerous to our liberties than standing armies. Already they have raised up a monied aristocracy that has set the government at defiance. The issuing power (of money) should be taken away from the banks and restored to the people to whom it properly belongs."

-Thomas Jefferson

Larry Jacobs' ranch was a fortified position. It was a large 400-acre ranch near Gatesville, Texas. It had a main house, guest quarters and staff housing. The ranch had good infrastructure to support a fair amount of people, so he set up the Texas command center there. It was staffed with Special Forces dressed in typical ranch hand attire to avoid unnecessary attention. Several Bradley fighting vehicles and Mine Resistant Ambush Protected or MRAP vehicles were parked inside the barns.

Paul Randall and his wife stayed in the main house with Larry and his family. Sonny Foster, Paul Randall's right-hand man also stayed in the main house with them. Sonny had been Paul's campaign manager during the presidential campaign last year. Paul had hoped to make him his Chief of Staff if he had won but even now, Sonny was indispensable.

General Allen Jefferson had been invited to stay at the ranch with them, but the general insisted on staying at nearby Fort Hood. It was close enough that he could drive up most weekdays to discuss the developments.

Paul, Larry and Sonny sat out on the porch with their coffee early Friday morning while they waited for breakfast to be ready.

Sonny broke the silence. "Can you believe American bank depositors lost everything they had in the bank? This is just like the 1930's. The FDIC was set up to guard them against a loss of their deposits."

Paul Randall nodded. "The FDIC has proved to be a false sense of security. Now it seems the FDIC served only to make people neglect to consider the destructive practices by the banks. Had there been no FDIC, folks would have paid more attention to what the banks were doing.

"The public thought the FDIC would bail them out, so why should they worry if the banks were using their money like poker chips in the casino? Had there been no FDIC, things would be different. If depositors knew their deposits were at risk, and bank A had deposits tied up in highly leveraged derivatives and bank B stayed with safe investments, where do you think the public would have put their money?

"The banks stole everything in the interest rate derivatives collapse. Howe is letting the IMF step in and take the FDIC insurance money that was supposed to cover depositors for the loss."

Larry set his coffee cup down. "The fox isn't just watching the hen house, he is making the rules and managing it. There seems to be more foxes than you can shake a stick at and they are all fighting over the hens."

Sonny agreed, "It's a bad day to be a hen."

Larry looked over at Paul. "Well, you've been warning folks to get out of the banking system for a few years now. We all know how corrupt it's become. Folks that listened to you shouldn't have lost too much."

Paul said, "They've lost more through the stealth tax of new money creation by the Fed over the past several years than they did in the derivatives collapse or the IMF bail-in. They just see the numbers disappearing from their bank accounts this time. The Fed has been stealing the value of their dollars while leaving the same nominal amount in their accounts for over 100 years."

One of the staff stepped out onto the porch to alert the men that breakfast was being served.

"Let's go eat!" Jacobs exclaimed.

General Jefferson came in as everyone was sitting down for breakfast. His wife, Candace, was accompanying him this morning.

Paul Randall's wife, Kimberly, greeted them both warmly. "Candace, I am so glad to see you. General, it is good to see you as always, but you don't bring your beautiful wife around here much. It's such a pleasant surprise."

Alice Jacobs chimed right in. "Do come in. We have places right here for you at the table."

The Jeffersons joined the others for breakfast.

Larry passed the biscuits. "General, I am used to seeing you in your battle dress uniform, but not Candace. I am assuming you two were trying to blend in when you left."

"There was quite a gathering at the front gate of the base this morning," Allen replied. "It seems Howe has convinced government benefit recipients that they can break us by protesting at the gates of the base."

Paul Randall said, "So, they have weaponized the welfare class."

"I think that about sums it up," Jefferson said. "I saw several chartered buses dropping people off at the front gate with professionally printed protest signs. Howe has people inside Texas organizing this. I would never impose for myself, but I may take you up on the offer to stay here for a few days, for Candace's sake, Larry. That is, if it wouldn't be too much trouble for you, Mrs. Jacobs."

Alice was quick to reassure the couple. "It is no trouble at all. Kimberly and I will love having another lady around."

"Thank you very much." Candace smiled at Alice and Kimberly. "I told Allen that I would be fine at the base, but he thinks there could be trouble."

Allen explained, "I wouldn't put it past Howe to send in some serious rabble-rousers to instigate violence. If he can get us to fire on civilians, it will be heavy political capital in this war for public opinion. I have instructed the men to set up a deadline ten feet in front of the gate using barricades. If it's breached, they are instructed to fire tear gas. If the protesters approach the gate, they are to use rubber slugs in their shotguns. And if the gate is breached, they are to shoot to kill."

"Rubber slugs won't kill them?" Alice asked.

"It is a projectile fired from a shotgun," Allen answered. "It can kill a person, but they are not designed to. The term is 'less lethal' but the possibility exists. Tear gas canisters can kill a person if they hit them in the head when fired. All weapons carry the potential for lethal force. That's why we try to avoid it all together."

Sonny Foster paused from eating. He looked serious. "This is going to get ugly. Millions of people were just cut off from the government program they have been trained to be dependent on for decades. The ones who got them addicted to the handouts, then cut them off, are blaming this on us. Not to mention, Howe blamed the derivatives panic on the secession movement. All of the letters from the states came after the Wall Street meltdown. The so-called 'secession' letters specifically named military intervention within those states for crowd control as being the line in the sand. Declaring martial law was Howe's response to the riots erupting from the market crisis. I can't believe anyone is buying his lies."

Paul Randall replied, "They've been buying his lies ever since he first announced that he would run for president. I call it political denial. It's like an abused wife that won't admit she is getting beat up. She looks in the mirror, sees the bruises and thinks he still loves her."

Larry said, "I'm glad Howe is managing to live up to his predecessor. He had some mighty big shoes to fill. Al Mohammad could just about beat the devil in a lying contest."

Sonny said, "Ladies, I am so sorry to talk business over breakfast, but I did receive some very good news this morning. Kentucky and Tennessee have joined the Carolinas to form what they are now calling the Southern Coalition. Mark Shea, Montana's Governor, has suggested to the other governors in the North West Coalition and the Southern Coalition that Paul serve as Commander in Chief of what is being called the American Coalition. All of the governors of those states, as well as Larry, support the motion to make Paul Commander in Chief."

"What do you say, Paul?" Larry asked.

Paul knew the governors had in mind to appoint him to a leadership role. "I am honored. Of course I'll serve."

Kimberly was speechless. She hugged her husband as tears streamed down her face. She had witnessed the disappointment when the presidency was taken from him even after he had won the popular vote. Finally she said, "I'm so proud of you, and so happy to see your opportunity to lead America back to a good path."

They finished their breakfast and the men retired to Jacob's study to talk strategies.

CHAPTER 18

"These are the times that try men's souls. The summer soldier and the sunshine patriot will, in this crisis, shrink from the service of their country; but he that stands it now, deserves the love and thanks of man and woman. Tyranny, like hell, is not easily conquered; yet we have this consolation with us, that the harder the conflict, the more glorious the triumph. What we obtain too cheap, we esteem too lightly: it is dearness only that gives everything its value. Heaven knows how to put a proper price upon its goods; and it would be strange indeed if so celestial an article as freedom should not be highly rated."

-Thomas Paine

By late Friday evening, the riots in Texas and the other Coalition states were getting completely out of hand. Matt and Karen stayed home and watched the evening news on their television which only picked up two channels. It had snowed the night before and they had no desire to get out in it. Miss Mae was curled up in Karen's lap. She was happy to have them home all day for a change.

Matt's phone rang. It was Jack, Matt and Karen's next door neighbor from when they lived in South Florida.

Matt answered, "Jack, What a nice surprise. How are you and

Tina?"

"Not good," Jack replied. "Elvis and Blaine were shot to death last week. A bunch of guys who looked like gang members drove up to the checkpoint at the top of the street and opened fire on them. The gang had AK-47s. Elvis and Blaine never stood a chance with their pistols and shotguns. Dan and I were at the other end of the street. We wanted to get up there and help them out, but we were pretty much pinned down by constant gunfire. I can't explain it. There were probably ten guys shooting up Elvis and Blaine. It seemed like thousands of bullets were flying. I don't know how long it lasted. It felt like an hour, but it was probably less than two minutes. I feel terrible. I wish I could have stopped it.

"Trevor is dead too. Some thugs pulled a home invasion on him in the middle of the night. There have been several other home invasions around here. They always kill the people in the house when they rob them.

"We quit the block watch. There aren't enough guys left to hold it down. Everyone left or got killed. We just stay up all night, then try to catch a couple hours sleep in the daytime, with one eye open. This is an unimaginable hell. Everything is falling apart around here. It's like we are living in a third world country. I know you said it was going to get rough around here, but I don't even think you could have imagined ...."

The signal went dead. "Jack?" Matt said, "Hello?"

Karen asked, "What happened?"

"I don't know," Matt answered. "It was Jack. The call just dropped. Sounds like things are really bad there. He said Blaine, Elvis and Trevor are all dead."

Karen covered her mouth with her hand in shock. "How?"

"They were all shot to death." Matt was sad to hear of his former neighbors' deaths.

The phone rang again. It was Jack's number.

"Hey, Buddy," Jack said. "I only have one bar on my phone. Cell service is really bad these days. I only get one bar. I don't really know why. It could be some of the towers were sabotaged back when we could actually call police. Maybe it's because of the power irregularities from the fires. The internet is completely out. Cable too. I think Comcast just gave up. Not that they were worth a bucket of horse manure when times were good. If the call drops, I'll call you right back."

Matt tried to lighten the mood. "Oh yeah, I remember good old Comtrash. It was an enigma to me how they were able to stay in business with the horrible service and lousy customer care even before the collapse. So you guys still have electricity?"

Jack chuckled. "Comtrash, that's a new one. I always called them Comcrash. We have power most nights. There have been a lot of fires. There are blackouts in areas where they had to cut power because of downed lines from the fires. Those areas are zombie apocalypse territory. Anyway, I suppose they also lost some reducing stations in the fires and can't keep the power up 24/7. Most days, we only have power for three or four hours during daylight hours, but they are fighting to keep the lights on at night. I think the National Guard are the ones trying to keep the lights on. It would take some kind of military force to just stay alive at the power company.

"Remember how we would hear sirens from the time it started to get dark until the sun came up? Well, not anymore. We don't hear sirens around here at all. Police stopped showing up unless there was a murder, then they stopped showing up for murders as well. 911 has an 'all circuits are busy' message. We are completely on our own. The military came through. They were giving out MRE's and water on the first day. After that, they just started busting heads. It was some semblance of order, but I guess they were called somewhere else, because they pulled out of here.

"Grocery stores are closed up. It wouldn't matter anyway, we lost all of our money in the bank. Even if we do get our $5,000 on Monday like the White House says, the banks around here won't be opening. They are all busted up or burnt down. I wish I had paid closer attention to you. We should've got out of here when you did. I just had no idea things would deteriorate to this level. We don't know what to do, Matt."

Matt could hear Jack's voice cracking. He hated to hear his neighbor in such distress. "Well, we can work you into our group up here. You have a valuable skill set. The handyman is going to be king in the new economy. We won't be getting anymore cheap garbage from China, so folks are going to have to fix things when they break. Toasters and washing machines aren't going to be disposable anymore."

"Thanks, Matt," Jack said. "I just don't know how we would get up there. It is about 1,000 miles. We might have 5 gallons in the tank. With my van, that's probably about 100 miles. I have around $200 in cash, but there are no gas stations open around here. We could take a gamble and hope to find a station selling gas north of West Palm but, from what I am hearing on the radio, it's near $40 a gallon. $200 bucks will only get me another 5 gallons."

Matt replied, "Well, you might want to ask around and see if any of the remaining neighbors might want to sell the gas for less than $40 a gallon. Nobody has any cash unless they already had it out of the bank before the bank holiday. What about Trevor's car? Did the home invaders steal it when they killed him?"

"No, it caught a stray bullet in the back tire, so it is still sitting there," Jack answered.

Matt said, "Well, you should drain that tank before someone else gets it. He won't be needing it."

"That's a good idea," Jack said.

"At any rate, it sounds like you guys have to evacuate," Matt said. "It's a bad scenario. You don't have much to work with. Under normal circumstances, it's always better to shelter in place if you don't have the means to make it to a better location. There's a high probability that when you get on the road, you'll hit more trouble than what you have now. But it sounds like the gangs are picking people off one by one."

Jack replied, "That is exactly what it feels like. I feel like we're surrounded by predators, like sharks or wolves or something. It's just a matter of time before they come in for the kill."

"You both have bikes don't you?" Matt inquired.

"Yes," Jack stated.

"I would use some of that old PVC and rig up some type of rickshaw to carry your gear on a bike. Go as far as you can in the van, then ditch it and head out on the bikes," Matt suggested.

"Yeah, I think I can do that. I'll give you a call back in a day or two to let you know what we are able to do." Jack sounded relieved at the suggestion.

"Take care," Matt said.

Matt hung up and looked at Karen. She had a look of horror on her face. She was watching television. Matt looked to see what could be so awful, and he couldn't believe his eyes. The Texas local news affiliate was reporting from Fort Hood. The soldiers had just fired on the protestors.

The reporter in the studio of the Lexington, Kentucky, station broadcasting the coverage was speaking. "Folks, if you have young children in the room, you need to get them out. We are trying to maintain the live coverage and it is getting very violent."

Shots rang out and several protesters who had breached the deadline fell to the ground.

The reporter continued. "The soldiers standing guard at the main gate of Fort Hood just fired what looked to be shotguns at the wave of protestors who breached the barricades which are set up several feet in front of the actual gate. Some of those who were shot are running away. The ones who fell seem to be getting back up. We are going to listen in on coverage of the local affiliate."

The local reporter was speaking. "And it appears that the rounds fired by the soldiers were rubber bullets. They have also begun to fire tear gas into the crowd. The protestors began showing up by the hundreds this morning. They are blaming the governor and the military for benefit cuts caused by Texas through their defiant stance taken against D.C. President Howe said that states who would not cooperate in allowing federal agencies to enforce martial law will not receive government benefits until the governors resign and the military base commanders step down."

POP, POP, POP. Gun fire erupted from the crowd. The camera panned over to the main gate. Two soldiers lay on the ground in growing pools of blood.

The local reporter ducked down behind a concrete barrier. "There are people in the crowd firing back at the soldiers guarding the gate."

The cameraman found a safe spot and kept rolling. A huge segment of the crowd of protestors fell back, but there were still several armed gunmen left standing in the front. The gunmen continued to sporadically fire upon the guards. Two armored vehicles rolled out of the gate. Several soldiers came out on the sides of the armored vehicles using the vehicles for cover. They rained down a hail of automatic gunfire on the armed attackers. Once the armed men were dead, soldiers dressed in riot gear came out and began to take down the remaining protestors who would not disperse. They tackled them and restrained their feet and hands with plastic zip-tie restraints.

After they were all effectively hog tied, the commanding officer came out and began speaking to the captives. "You people have committed an act of terrorism against the sovereign country of Texas. The simple fact that you are here proves that you are not in agreement with our sovereignty. You people have come here because you think the government owes you something. I will agree that the way President Howe cut you off was criminal, but he is the criminal and not Texas. Your act of aggression is treason against Texas and the punishment is death. As Governor Jacobs is a merciful man, he is giving you the option of a suspended sentence if you agree to leave Texas tonight. If you accept this offer, you will be branded on your right cheek with the letter X. Anyone found in Texas with this mark in 24 hours from the time we set you free will be shot on sight. If you do not accept this offer, the other option is to assume room temperature. You will be shot right here in the road. This is a time of war, we do not have the resources to support prisoners, and you are no longer welcome in this state.

"I think you will find that if you treat the brand on your cheek with aloe and don't pick the scab, it will be hardly noticeable in a year from now. Of course you have to stay alive for a year for that to even be an issue. Now how many takers do we have for the brand?"

All of the prisoners began calling out for the brand.

The commander said, "I've never seen a bunch of folks so anxious to get branded. I wish my cattle liked it this much. Sergeant, get a nice hot fire going. We got some dogies to brand."

The reporter said, "Similar actions are being reported all over Texas. They have officially adopted the 'run the deadbeats out of town' policy. The branding seems cruel, but it ensures the trouble makers won't be back night after night."

Matt and Karen looked at each other. Matt was stunned by what he had just seen.

CHAPTER 19

"Dependence begets subservience and venality, suffocates the germ of virtue, and prepares fit tools for the designs of ambition."

-Thomas Jefferson

Matt and Karen got up early on Saturday to walk over to Adam's for breakfast. Miss Mae stayed boroughed under the covers of the bed on cold winter days and only came out briefly to eat and stretch her muscles. Matt patted the small bump in the covers which he knew to be Miss Mae.

The snow still covered the ground, but the sun was out. It was warm on their faces. It felt warmer to be in the natural light than staying cooped up in the house. The snow was just deep enough to make the walk a bit of a work out. The country road that wound around the hill to get to Adam's was completely covered by snow. There was no sure way to tell where the edge of the road was until it was either cleared or melted off.

As they walked through the countryside, Karen stopped to look around. The trees were topped with soft powdery snow. The ground was covered as far as the eye could see. The bright light of the sun reflected off the surface of the snow and made them both squint.

"It is so beautiful," Karen said. "So clean and pure."

"I knew you would get used to it." Matt smiled as he spoke.

"I didn't say I like being cold. I just said the snow in the country is pretty." Karen had dreaded leaving South Florida. She hated the cold.

"But we stay warm with the stove in the house, don't we?" Matt had done his best to keep her warm since they moved to the mountains of Kentucky.

Karen stopped walking again. She faced Matt and took his hand. "We did the right thing. I knew you were right when we moved. It was hard, but the call from Jack last night made me realize that we might not be alive if we had stayed. You are a good husband."

Matt pulled her close. "And you are a good wife."

When they arrived at Adam's, the smell of biscuits and coffee lured them to the kitchen.

"It smells great!" Karen exclaimed.

Mandy said, "I made the biscuits."

"I helped." Carissa added.

"She cut them out all by herself." Mandy tried to brush some of the flour off of her jeans.

"I can tell," Karen said with a laugh. Both of the girls were fairly well-dusted with flour.

Everyone sat down around the table and Adam prayed.

"Father God, thank you for this meal. We know that many folks around the country are not so blessed today. Our country has never known want like it's experiencing today. We pray for those who have less and hope you will provide for them and comfort them. We pray that you will guide our leaders to make the right choices. Your blessings made this country great. We pray that our nation will turn back to you so that you may heal her. Amen"

Everyone echoed, "Amen."

During breakfast, Matt had several questions about caring for the livestock during the winter. Adam and Wes had been doing this for a while. Matt was realizing just how little he knew. Adam learned most everything he knew from Mr. Miller, an old-timer he often traded with for honey, butter, cheese and livestock. Matt bought his goat and chickens from Mr. Miller when he first moved to the area.

Adam reminded him, "You know you can always go over to Mr. Millers. He loves to teach folks the lost arts of homesteading. He gets lonely over there by himself. I always try to stop by a couple times a month at least. It is mutually beneficial."

After breakfast, the adults gathered around the television. Howe was giving an address. They watched it on CNC.

Howe began, "Yesterday, rogue military bases around America fired on peaceful protestors that were only asking their state governments to comply with the law of the land. Citizens were murdered or evicted from their own states. These types of actions cannot be permitted. I will be sitting down with the Joint Chiefs on Monday and we will be developing a military response to be conducted at a time of our choosing. I am suspending all Federal aid to the states that have issued letters of rebellion to the Federal Government. This will include FDIC insurance monies to cover lost deposits from the derivatives situation. I am revoking the amnesty period for banned firearm confiscation in those states and enacting the portion of the firearms regulation order which will outlaw all types of firearms in those states. Anyone found to have firearms in rebellious states will be detained indefinitely and without bail. Responsible citizens may turn in their firearms to any Federal agency in those states next Monday, Tuesday or Wednesday. After that, you will be arrested and prosecuted under Federal law.

"The governors of Kentucky, Tennessee, North Carolina, South Carolina, Texas, Idaho, Wyoming and Montana will be tried for treason and, if found guilty, they will be executed. Military leaders on bases in those states who are supporting this seditious behavior will also be executed if found guilty. The state leaders of Northern Colorado, Eastern Washington and Eastern Oregon who are responsible for separating themselves from the compliant sections of their states will also be held accountable in a like manner.

"I am encouraging all citizens of those states and partitioned areas to leave. We will be setting up FEMA relocation camps in neighboring states to make sure you are kept safe from the horrific violence from the rogue madmen who have taken your states hostage. We will be announcing the exact locations of the camps early next week. I recommend you start making plans to get to the border soon. FEMA will have transportation available at the borders to take you safely to the relocation centers.

"Those citizens who are leaving the rogue states will be issued Federal Ration Notes for food and personal goods in the bank deposit amounts they lost due to the derivatives situation. We will be supplying MREs and several other types of essential items to get your lives back to normal. You will be able to pick and choose the items you would like at the commissaries inside the relief camps by paying for them with your new Federal Ration Notes. This will give you a sense of normalcy as you buy and trade in a safe environment.

"Folks who are relocating will not be permitted to bring any type of weapons. Even the restricted firearms that are permitted in the states you are traveling to will not be allowed until we have established your new residency in the compliant state.

"We are temporarily suspending all types of firearm and ammunition sales until this crisis is behind us. Effective immediately, ammunition and gun manufacturers and retailers will only be allowed to conduct business with the Federal Government or law enforcement agencies that have been cleared by DHS. This will ensure that much needed resources can be allocated to the men and women who are putting their lives on the line to secure our country.

"Thank you in advance for your support on this very important issue."

The screen switched back to the CNC news room.

Everyone sitting around Adam Bair's living room was in a state of shock.

Shelly was the first to speak. "What just happened? Is he declaring war on Kentucky and the rest of those states?"

Janice asked, "How can he just shut down firearms and ammunition sales to the public all over the country? I think he just announced that he is taking over the entire industry."

Wesley was a history professor prior to the crash. He said, "I have a pretty good idea what comes next after an announcement like this from a dictator. This is worse than the Soviet Union, China and Nazi Germany combined."

Statements like these had been made comparing America to these oppressive regimes for years now. Up to this point, they were just rhetoric, but now it was a very factual statement.

Matt was disgusted by the speech. "How did you like that part about 'peaceful protestors?' Every news station in the country has played the footage of the armed gunmen from the crowd opening fire and killing those two soldiers at the main gate of Fort Hood. That scene has been played over and over. I bet those gunmen were plants. The White House probably put them there or had something to do with arming them. No one, and I mean no one, can possibly believe anything this man says. It's all blatant lies. I guess the liberals have just decided to go along with the lies."

"Well, boys," Adam said, "sleep tight tonight and tomorrow, because training is going to get pretty rough Monday."

"Don't hurt 'em, Adam," Shelly said.

Karen gave a nod of agreement to Shelly's statement.

"I don't want to hurt them," Adam said. "I want to give them the skills they need to save their lives."

Matt and Wesley looked at each other. Matt knew Adam's training would be tough, but he knew it was all out of love and it was in their best interest.

Matt could see the look of concern in Karen's eyes. Not about the training, but about what would come after. He quickly tried to change the subject. "So I am curious to see what these Federal Ration Notes look like. They sound an awful lot like Federal Reserve Notes. Howe is going to issue them instead of the deposit insurance money to refugees of states considered to be in rebellion. It almost sounds like it could be an alternative currency."

Wesley agreed. "And, they're exchangeable for a specific category of goods. So in a way, they are commodity-backed notes."

Karen asked, "Think they're intended to compete against Paul Randall's gold and silver barter networks? After all, they're directed at the people coming from the states that are most likely to have been using gold, silver and other types of barter."

"Howe is a slippery devil," Matt said. "I'll bet you're right Karen."

"And it's the only way people from those states can get anything for the bank deposits they lost." Wesley spoke with contempt. "It's a perfect lure into Howe's concentration camps."

"Seriously?" Shelly said, "He's going to get those people into the camps where they will have nothing to do except sit around all day and consume the goods the government is going to steal. They'll buy it all with this fake money the government is just going to print out of nowhere."

Janice said sarcastically, "Sounds exactly like the system that just collapsed. What could go wrong?"

CHAPTER 20

"Is life so dear or peace so sweet as to be purchased at the price of chains and slavery? Forbid it, Almighty God! I know not what course others may take, but as for me, give me liberty, or give me death!"

-Patrick Henry

Paul Randall was making regular speeches to keep those standing against the White House up-to-date. He tried to inform them of the plans and progress of Texas and the other Coalition states. At first, FOX News was carrying some of the speeches. After the FCC threatened to take their license, they quickly folded and complied with the demands. They told Randall that they could no longer carry his speeches or any other news that may serve to aid in the secession movement. FOX continued to market their wares to the marginally conservative viewer, but did not dare get involved in any substantive conversations.

Paul Randall's speeches were now all via the internet. He had several people helping him with internet security and setting up proxy servers around the world. The servers were all connected in a decentralized network that was difficult to shut down. Every time Randall delivered a speech, the NSA went to work finding and shutting down the server which was propagating the feed. As each server shut down, viewers were automatically delivered a feed from a new server. Often, the broadcasts would go seamlessly, almost uninterrupted by the attacks. At worst, there would be a five-to-ten second delay. Paul knew his supporters were committed to getting the information; they would wait for hours if they had to.

The feed went live and Randall began his speech. "America, the President has announced plans to take military action against the Coalition States. As war has been declared against us, we must begin to prepare. We sought only to keep to ourselves and observe the laws of the Constitution, but we will stand to defend ourselves and our sovereign soil.

"The governors and state legislatures of the Coalition states and territories which include Idaho, Wyoming, Montana, Kentucky, Tennessee, North Carolina, South Carolina, Texas, Eastern Washington, Eastern Oregon, and Northern Colorado have unanimously appointed me to be the Commander in Chief of what they have agreed will be called the American Coalition. I humbly accept this appointment. I pledge to serve the citizens of the Coalition and defend the Constitution to the best of my ability.

"There are those living outside of those states who also support our cause. I encourage you to continue to let your governors and lawmakers know that you would like your state to join with the Coalition in defending freedom. If you see that goal is not going to be possible, we will do our best to make a place for you here. On the other hand, there are no doubt those within the borders of the Coalition States who oppose the decision. To them, I will quote Samuel Adams.

'If ye love wealth better than liberty, the tranquility of servitude better than the animating contest of freedom, go home from us in peace. We ask not your counsels or arms. Crouch down and lick the hands which feed you. May your chains set lightly upon you, and may posterity forget that ye were our countrymen.'

"We do not wish you harm, but there is no place for you here in the American Coalition. You will be uncomfortable and may be tempted to aid the enemy. To deter such temptations, the penalties for treason against the American Coalition will be brutal and swift. I implore you to take this opportunity to relocate to another area of the country where your views will be more accepted. There is no shortage of safe havens for those who hold socialist and communist views. These few states that have stood their ground to resist the abolishment of the Constitution are the last bastion of freedom in this once great country. We have been tolerant but not tolerated. This one-way street of compromise has created the dilemma in which we presently find ourselves. From this day forward we will dig in our heels and cling to our beliefs as steadfastly as the liberals and socialists who have demanded that we give up more and more ground while they, themselves have not budged an inch. From this day forth, we will meet force with force, intolerance with intolerance and violence with violence.

"I want to make a special appeal to the patriot men and women serving on military bases outside of the Coalition States. You should make every effort to make your way to a base located inside of a Coalition state. In doing this, you are not abandoning your post. We are the United States Government acting under the authority of the Constitution. It is the administration in the White House that are the rebels, they are the traitors. It is they who have seceded from the Union and asserted their sovereign will against the law of the land. Those of us in the Coalition States have never left. Our hearts are as true and loyal to this land and the principles represented by our flag as they ever were.

"I pray all those who are listening will stand together with us to defend this great land and the liberty given to us by our Creator.

"We know our days of communicating via the internet are limited, so we will be developing alternative types of communications to keep us all connected. We recommend that you begin to develop person-to-person contacts with which to bring your militias together when needed without conventional communications. The American Revolution was fought without cell phones or internet. The colonists had riders that went from farm house to farm house in a network to call people together to a predetermined position.

"While the enemy we fight speaks the same language as us, while he dresses like us and eats the same foods that we eat, nevertheless, he is a foreign invader. He has foreign ideas and seeks to destroy our way of life, our freedom, our ability to defend ourselves and our right to worship our God. He seeks to destroy America, our flag and all the things the American flag represents. Let us pray up, gear up, load up, train up and defend it to the last man.

"You will be in my prayers and I ask that you will return that favor by praying that we, your leaders, will make the right decisions and honor our God."

CHAPTER 21

"By failing to prepare, you are preparing to fail."

-Benjamin Franklin

Matt and Karen returned from Adam's house early Sunday evening. Matt still had to get his equipment ready for training the next morning. Adam would be picking him up at daybreak to rendezvous with their platoon.

Matt's phone rang. "It's Jack again," he told Karen.

"Hey, buddy," Jack said.

He was normally much more enthusiastic when he spoke, but to Matt it sounded like it took all the energy he had to just get out the few words.

"You guys able to get out of there yet?" Matt was concerned.

Jack replied, "I got about four gallons out of Trevor's car. I traded some hand tools for three more gallons from some of the folks around the block, but no one really wants to give up their gasoline unless it is for food. We barely have anything to eat, much less to trade."

"How is Tina holding up?" Matt asked.

"Not too good." Jack sounded even more discouraged. "We have both lost a lot of weight. I guess I had more to spare. She looks kind of sick. She is always kind of nervous. We're both on edge all the time. This is a very stressful situation. I suppose I always thought that everything would be fine, and if it wasn't, we would be dead. I didn't really think about things being like this. We aren't dead and things ain't fine."

Matt asked, "So what is your total for gas?"

Jack said, "I'd say about twelve gallons."

"Did you rig up any type of trailers for the bikes?" Matt inquired.

Jack answered, "I did. I took the wheels off the garbage cans and used some PVC like you suggested. We have everything we need in a backpack and a duffle bag. We don't have a tent, but I took the tarp off the top of my car canopy. It's waterproof. I just cut a tent-sized piece out of that. We can rig up that piece of tarp with some rope and a few pegs. It will be better shelter than nothing."

Matt asked, "Do you have a water filter? If you have to travel a distance on bikes, you won't be able to carry enough water for the journey. You'll need to collect it on the way."

"Didn't think of that," Jack said.

"Well," Matt replied, "get some bleach. It won't taste good, but it will keep you alive. Eight drops per gallon of clear water and sixteen drops per gallon of cloudy water. Find a few clean bottles to fill up and take with you. When you empty them, fill them up every time you come across a fresh water source. Take a clean cloth to drape over the bottle to filter out large sediment."

"We don't have any bleach," Jack said.

Matt said, "You are going to need something. Look around at Blaine's and see if he has any Pool Shock. I doubt the vandals would even know to take it. I don't know how much to tell you to use. I guess you'll figure it out. (It probably won't take much. If it's too strong tasting, let it sit over night with the cap off and some of the bleach from the Pool Shock should dissipate.) I don't think you guys will make it all the way up here on bikes. It's going to start getting pretty cold once you pass Daytona. I spoke with my buddy in Saint Augustine. He has a team that is going to be making their stand there. He said they could use a good handyman on their team. You would be expected to train with their militia and be ready to fight. You would also be expected to work hard. In exchange, they'll feed you and put you up in their garage. He said they have some extra furniture and will try to make the space livable for you."

Jack questioned, "Saint Augustine? Who do you know up there? Not that crazy Italian guy?"

Matt laughed. "Frank mellowed out. He gave his heart to the Lord and he is a totally different guy. Of course you still wouldn't want to get on his bad side."

Jack was silent for a moment. "Is he planning to fight against the government? I don't know about all that."

Matt replied, "He is planning to stand his ground like the rest of us. His group is not going out to look for trouble, but they are not going to be enslaved. You would be in the same situation if you were able to get up here. Everyone is expected to stand alongside the militias. I know you don't have internet right now, but Paul Randall gave a very good speech. He explained that the militia are the ones with the Constitutional authority. The present administration is the real enemy of the state."

"What about Tina?" Jack quizzed. "She can't fight in a militia."

Matt said, "The girls will have other tasks in the militia effort. Nurses, food preparation and such."

"Well," Jack said after a moment. "We're dead if we stay here, so I guess we'll take Frank up on his offer."

Matt said, "I don't know if twelve gallons will get you there or not.

It should get you close. I would leave early in the morning so you still have some daylight to travel by if you have to ditch the van. Keep your Sig in your waist and keep your Benelli shotgun in the duffel bag, on top where you can get to it quick. Do you think Tina would be able to shoot if it came down to it?"

"I don't think so," Jack said. "She has sort of froze up every time someone around here has been murdered. It takes her a day or so to even start communicating again."

"We'll be praying for you both," Matt said.

"Thanks, I appreciate it," Jack said. "I've never thought too much about spiritual things before all this happened. I hope we get some divine assistance. We'll need it to get us to Saint Augustine."

"He is always there Jack. All you have to do is ask." Matt didn't say it, but he knew Jack's chances were slim without God's intervention.

CHAPTER 22

"That the people have a Right to mass and to bear arms; that a well-regulated militia composed of the Body of the people, trained to arms, is the proper natural and safe defense of a free state..."

-George Mason - Father of the Bill of Rights

Matt was still in a zombie-like state when Adam and Wesley arrived to pick him up for training at the break of dawn on Monday morning.

"Will you have a cup of coffee with me, Cousin?" Matt asked.

"Just a quick one..." Adam looked at his watch. "We have to get on the road soon."

"I brought a thermos full of coffee," Wes replied.

Matt said, "Help me drink this pot and I'll take a few swigs of your coffee on the road."

"Sounds good." Wes smiled.

Adam did a pre-combat inspection of Matt's and Wes's gear before they left. He checked their walkies, extra socks, medical kits, rifles and magazines.

On this training, they would not be taking tents or food. They would have to forage and build their own shelters.

Adam asked Matt, "Do you still have your pellet gun?"

"Yes," Matt replied. "What good will that do?"

"We are going to be running silent," Adam answered. "If you take any game, it will have to be with a snare, bow or a pellet gun."

"How am I going to carry two guns?" Matt considered the logistical challenge.

"Bring your Pellet gun in here," Adam said.

Matt did as he was instructed.

Adam took out a length of paracord and quickly wove what looked like a spider web on the side of Matt's ALICE pack. "Just loosen these two slip knots when you are ready to take out the pellet gun and it will slip right out."

"That's ingenious." Matt studied Adam's contraption.

"It looks a bit more presentable when it's done on a MOLLE bag, but it still works," Adam said.

Matt went to the bedroom and kissed Karen on the head and pulled the cover over Miss Mae. Karen whispered, "Be safe," and went right back to sleep.

The guys loaded up the truck and headed out.

Adam told Wes and Matt, "Gary's place is big enough that the platoon can break up into squads and still have room to operate without stepping into one another's area of operation."

When they arrived at Gary's farm, they met up with the other men from Bair platoon. Adam went over the training activities for the day. He did a quick inspection and the platoon split up into squads. Adam would be leaving Gary's and making rounds all day to see how the other two platoons in London Company were working out.

Wesley and Matt were assigned to Bravo Squad with the men who were their closest neighbors. Gary Brewer was on their squad.

Gary whispered to Matt and Wesley, "I have a good idea where we're most likely to find wild edibles and game. I also have a good spot for a shelter. It has a bluff overhang that would help keep us warm."

Matt smiled slyly. "It's a bit of an unfair advantage to have the guy who knows all the good spots on our squad, but I'll take it."

Wesley was assigned as the Bravo Staff Sergeant since he had the most experience with the Eastern Kentucky Liberty Militia.

Bravo Squad found a good place in the woods with not too much snow to practice their individual and group troop movements. They practiced hand signals and the guys with earphones and headset mics practiced radio communications with as little peripheral noise as possible.

Adam returned to Bravo after making his rounds. He was spending the rest of the day with Bravo since this was the group he would be fighting with, if it came down to that. They spent the rest of the afternoon on camouflage and setting up ambushes. By late afternoon, they were all famished.

Adam said, "We're going to split up into groups of two or three and go foraging. Wes, Lee Jessup and Eddie Cooper, you guys head out to look for game using Wesley's bow. Matt and Gary Brewer, see what you guys can take with your pellet gun. JC Hunter, Bobby Mertz and Jeff Nolon, you guys team up and forage."

The last team were all avid hunters, but JC was the only one proficient with a bow. They headed out to see what they could find. Bobby was well versed on wild edibles. There wasn't much, but if there was anything to be had, Bobby would find it.

Adam, Michael Marino and Brian Mitchum stayed behind to get a fire going and to construct a shield out of branches to lean up against the bluff and block the wind.

Matt and Gary headed to the oak grove. They walked slowly and quietly. Matt hoped to find a squirrel. Squirrels don't hibernate, but they do stay inside to conserve heat in the winter. As they approached the oaks, Gary tapped Matt and pointed ahead. As Matt peered, he saw several black birds just ahead. Matt raised his pellet gun and took the shot. PING. The pellet hit the tree just beneath the bird Matt aimed for. That bird flew off, but the others were not overly disturbed. They settled back to the branches and Matt lined up another shot. Matt took a deep breath and squeezed the trigger slowly this time. POP. The bird dropped through the branches. The other birds must have found the sound of their comrade cascading through the branches to be more worrisome than the prior missed shot and flew away. Matt and Gary half-filled Gary's day pack with acorns and several walnuts. On the way back to camp, Gary pointed out a few small doves on the edge of the tree line. Matt found the biggest closest target and took the shot. POP. Its wings spread out and it fell, limp, on the frozen ground.

They were the first ones back to camp. Matt started skinning the birds and Gary started hulling the nuts and digging out the inside of the acorns.

Adam had several small fires built very close to the bluff.

Matt asked, "I thought we were going to sleep next to the bluff?"

Adam replied, "We are, and it will be radiating heat for the first few hours of the night."

"Smart thinking," Matt said. "Why are the fires all burning in the holes?"

Adam answered, "Those are Dakota fire holes. It keeps the flames lower, so they emit less light to be seen by the enemy. They also burn more efficiently and less visible smoke goes up to reveal our location. These small holes a few inches from the fire pit are actually tunnels that go into the pit underground. That allows the oxygen to feed into the pit as needed."

"Very cool." Matt was impressed with the fire pits.

Wes, Lee and Eddie were the next group to return. They had two very big rabbits and a dove. They each started skinning one creature.

When JC, Jeff and Bobby returned, they had a selection of small birds and one squirrel. Bobby had also found some wild garlic under the snow. He brought back more acorns as well.

The rabbits were pan-fried with the wild garlic. The squirrel and the birds were cooked on spits over the open flames in the fire holes.

Gary mashed up the acorns into mush with a bit of water and cooked it for a while. He threw in the few walnuts as well. He kept the pan drippings from the rabbits and fried small cakes of the acorn and walnut mixture in the drippings. He had a pinch of salt that he obviously snuck in. Adam had made a requirement that no food items were to be brought from home, but the salt made all the difference in the world for the flavor of the meal.

Once fried into cakes, the acorn mush came out like coarse, brittle pancakes. The men ate the wild garlic, tops and bulbs; both cooked with the rabbit and some raw on the side.

Everyone sat down and had a satisfying meal. Matt was sure that Adam could taste the salt. Adam didn't say anything. He was enjoying the flavor as much as everyone else.

Adam, Mike and Brian took the flames from the Dakota fire holes near the bluff and lit fires in holes that were already set up further away from the bluff, on the outside of their sleeping area. The heat would continue to billow up to the overhang and keep them warmer than they would otherwise be. Then, they extinguished the fires near the bluff. The men settled into the lean-to shelters that Adam had devised. The rock wall of the bluff acted as a radiator through the first part of the night and the men slept well that night.

CHAPTER 23

"Experience teaches us that it is much easier to prevent an enemy from posting themselves than it is to dislodge them after they have got possession."

-George Washington

Albert Rust finished gearing up just after sunrise on Tuesday morning. He double checked his weapons and ammo, then he and Trey Dayton stopped by Pastor John Robinson's small camper trailer.

"Trey, Albert, come on in and have a cup of coffee," Pastor John said.

"Thanks, Pastor, but we can't," Albert said. "The Governor is asking the Idaho Free Militia to assist the National Guard in evicting the federal agencies within the state. The other Coalition states will be using the soldiers that have been co-opted into their National Guards. As Idaho is a little short on military bases, the militia has agreed to assist in the mission."

"So all the Coalition states are evicting federal agencies today?" Robinson asked.

"Yes, sir," Trey answered.

John Robinson loved the idea. He had to know all the details. "Which agencies are on the eviction list?"

Albert answered "All of them. We are closing all the federal courthouses. We're taking over US Customs on the Canadian border. We are kicking out the FBI, IRS, DEA, FDA, DHS; basically the whole bowl of alphabet soup."

"Are you expecting resistance?" John sounded concerned.

Albert replied, "The plan is to show up with enough force that the agents will quickly capitulate. We want to try to do it all in one day so they won't have time to think about it or organize a response between agencies. Not that they have a habit of working together anyway."

Trey added, "We have assigned fifty armed men to keep Young Field secure. Bill Maxwell, Will Pender and James Macintosh will all be staying behind for security leadership."

Pastor John bowed his head and said a quick prayer over Albert and Trey. "Father, we ask that you watch over these men and bring them back to us safely. We pray that this may all be resolved peacefully and swiftly. If it is not to be solved in peace, grant us strength and courage. Amen."

Robinson looked up at the men. "May God keep you and make your plans succeed."

Trey and Albert thanked the pastor and headed out to meet their platoon. They were to meet up with several guardsmen from the Idaho National Guard. The guardsmen would be taking the lead on this mission.

Trey and Albert were assigned to the eviction team handling the DHS/ICE Field Office in Boise. This would be one of the most aggressive evictions, but the team Albert and Trey were on also had the highest number of troops.

Everyone loaded up into the vehicles that they were taking to the field office. There was a wide array of vehicles. The convoy consisted of a couple of Humvees that belonged to the Idaho National Guard, one armored personnel carrier that had been sent as part of an assistance package to Idaho from a military base in Texas and several private vehicles belonging to the individual militia members. Those were mostly SUVs and assorted pickup trucks. It was a short forty-five-minute drive to the Boise DHS field office from Young Field. This was good as it didn't give the team too much time to start worrying about the outcome of the operation. Everyone was apprehensive. No one knew for sure how the federal agents would react.

The team arrived at the field office in force. Guardsmen and militia poured out of their transport vehicles and stormed the building. The DHS agents were caught completely off-guard and quickly put their hands on their heads. The eviction team went from room to room and cleared all of the stragglers. Everyone was herded into a large open meeting room and briefed on the eviction.

Idaho National Guard First Sergeant Nick Powell, The lead officer on the eviction team, addressed the federal employees. "The State of Idaho considers you to be an occupying force in our sovereign state. We are making two options available to you. You may choose to take an oath to never fight against a Coalition state and leave the state or, you can choose to be imprisoned until you're put on trial for treason."

The DHS agents seemed to be in disbelief. They were well aware of the politics, but they were shocked by the decisive action of the eviction. When asked to choose their fate, every federal agent elected to take the oath of non-aggression and leave the Coalition States.

The federal employees were relieved of their weapons and escorted to their cars. The team split into two groups. One group was assigned to escort the federal agents to the border and the other half went to evict an IRS field office nearby.

Trey and Albert were on the escort detail.

As they were driving down Interstate 84, Trey and Albert discussed how smoothly the operation had gone.

Trey said, "A lot of these federal employees that are being evicted from the state lived here for a long time. Some have probably lived in Boise all their lives. Now I guess they will be living in the FEMA camps."

"They knew the battle lines were being drawn," Albert said. "They have had ample opportunity to leave their jobs and show their loyalty to Idaho and the Coalition."

"You're right about that," Trey agreed.

"I understand they needed a job to feed their families, but that doesn't justify continuing to work for a criminal organization like the Federal Government," Albert stated.

"Well," Trey said, "Now they'll get their new Federal Ration Notes in the relief camps. Won't life be grand?"

The two men laughed as they drove down the road, escorting the federal employees down the road toward the Utah border.

CHAPTER 24

"If you know how to spend less than you get, you have the philosopher's stone."

-Benjamin Franklin

Matt stopped by Adam's early Wednesday afternoon. He brought by a bag of rice to trade for a can of coffee.

Matt inspected the can. "That was a good call, buying a pallet of coffee when you saw the crash coming."

Adam sat the rice on top of some buckets in the corner of the barn. "You gave me the idea to get out of dollars. I figured this would be one of the commodities that we couldn't produce ourselves, so why not. It has certainly held its value better that the money I used to buy it with."

Matt headed toward the door of the barn. "Mind if I check out The Liberty Mill online before I head back?"

"Help yourself," Adam said.

Matt found his own way to the computer and scrolled through the headlines of the news-aggregation site, The Liberty Mill. He took the time to read an op-ed piece on Zero Hedge entitled The Unstable

State of The Union.

"It has been nearly two weeks since the derivatives bubble brought down the entire financial system. Gold has skyrocketed over the past two weeks. It shot through its key resistance level just under $10,000 per ounce to nearly $30,000 by the time it was no longer priced in US dollars. In fact, nothing is priced in dollars anymore. Gold is now priced in SDRs, the common currency of the IMF, or Brics, the trade currency used by Brazil, Russia, India, China, and South Africa. The spot price in both basket currencies soon found a market equilibrium for the gold price that is the equivalent of $15,000 in US dollars, given the value of the dollar prior to the derivatives collapse. As the astronomical gold prices quickly push most people out of the gold market, silver quickly rose to take its place as the money of choice. The silver to gold ratio closed from 25 to 1 prior to the derivatives bubble, to now just over 15 to 1. If the white metal were still priced in US dollars, it would be roughly $950 per ounce when exchanged for Brics or SDRs. Speculators expect the ratio to get even smaller as silver is only being mined at a ratio of 9 to 1.

Like all other commodities, oil and gasoline are no longer sold at homogeneous prices. The markets have all become local. In areas where oil is produced and gasoline is refined, 2 gallons sell for a tenth ounce of silver. In areas where there is no oil production or refineries, a tenth ounce of silver might get you half a gallon or less. The disparity in prices is caused in part because of the massive looting of trucks on the highway by gangs and bandits. The truckers are on their own for security. Most police officers are no longer getting paid. The majority of those that were getting paid, were receiving a currency that is now worthless. Most have decided to stay home and protect their own families.

Truckers have taken to travelling in long convoys of ten to fifteen rigs. They are often escorted by two security vehicles, one in the front of the convoy and one in back. Each escort vehicle typically has two or three designated shooters. Truckers and the private security teams that escorted the convoys take payment in the goods they are hauling, ammunition, silver, gold or some combination thereof.

In states where the truckers are not allowed to defend themselves, commerce has all but ceased. In states where gun rights are respected, the farmer still tills his soil, the baker still bakes his bread and the market is finding a way. To say that small towns have adjusted to the collapse much better and more quickly than the cities, would be an extreme understatement. While life in small towns resembles something from the great depression, the cities, depending on their size, resemble nuclear waste lands. In many small rural communities, the town's people are coming together to figure out ways to compensate their police forces with silver, food or other commodities. The first green sprouts of economic activity have begun to emerge from the charred remains of the burned down financial system in the Coalition States.

In the states that stamped out the second amendment long ago, it is the government coming to the rescue. Howe has begun to pay Federal and State employees of those states with the new Federal Ration Notes. This effectively puts the state employees on the federal payroll, making them de facto federal employees. This shows Howe's magnanimous side in providing for them, and it accomplishes his goal of concentrating manpower under the control of Washington, D.C.

Howe has semi-nationalized all food production and storage warehouses in the states that have not joined the Coalition. Those states are now being referred to as the Federal States. Private owners of farms and warehouses were told they are now partners with the government. They were put on government payrolls and are being paid in Federal Ration Notes. The offers were made to the private business operators in person by DHS representatives flanked by four heavily armed DHS agents. The representatives cited Executive Order 13603 as granting the authority for the action. Though it was not verbalized, it was heavily implied that turning down the proposal could be hazardous to one's health. The Federal Government gave them an offer they couldn't refuse."

The piece was posted by a writer who was using the pen name, Daddy-O.

CHAPTER 25

"Over grown military establishments are under any form of government inauspicious to liberty, and are to be regarded as particularly hostile to republican liberty."

-George Washington

Secretary of Defense Scott Hale walked into President Howe's office in the underground facility at Mount Weather.

"Mr. President," Hale said, "you wanted to see me, sir?"

Howe looked up from his computer. "Scott, it is time to start weeding out the traitors. I want you to give an amnesty period of twenty-four hours for any military personnel who are not willing to fire on the rebels. Tell them that they are free to go if they will lay down their weapons and agree to leave the states that are remaining loyal to the democracy."

"So we are just going to let them go?" Hale asked.

"No, Scott." Howe's eyes had a sinister glare. "We are going to load them up in transport vehicles and take them directly to detention centers. We'll tell them it is a processing center. Tell them it is just a formality and that we'll drive them securely to the border as soon as everyone is debriefed of access codes and current assignments. Anyone who has specialized warfare training will be executed as soon as they arrive at the detention camps. There's not a snowball's chance in hell that I will let these traitors walk away only to have to fight against them in two weeks' time. But what better way to identify the traitors than to give them a one-shot chance at amnesty?"

"I think it is an ingenious plan, sir," Hale complimented.

"Now, what can we do about disrupting the Coalition?" Howe asked. "I understand that Texas is sending heavy equipment to the Northwest Coalition."

Scott Hale responded, "Yes, sir, they are sending lots of armored vehicles that way from depots located in Texas. There's also a heavy stream of resources such as food, ammunition, oil and gas flowing back and forth. I think we should shut down their supply routes."

"Do you have a plan?" Howe asked.

"We are developing one," Hale responded. "Hill Air Force Base is in Utah near Salt Lake City. It's not that big, but just across the lake is the Utah Test and Training Range. It's hundreds of square miles where fighter pilots and bombers train. Hill has a large air field to bring in troops and equipment. We can move everything to the training range in Tooele County and use it as a staging area. From there, we can launch attacks on The Northwest Coalition and clamp down on Interstates 80 and 84. This will significantly hamper the ability for Texas and the Northwest Coalition to resupply each other. They will still be able to maintain trade and mutual resupply by air, but we can set up a significant no-fly zone. They can fly around it, but it will cost them more valuable fuel."

Howe nodded his approval. "Sounds like a solid plan, Mr. Secretary. Make them deplete their resources. We'll have plenty of space in the training range for large prison and relief camps. Get started right away. I would like to launch our first assault this Sunday morning. That preacher up in Boise was sowing the seeds of dissent even before the election. I would like to make an example out of him.

Get some intel and find out where he is. I want that to be our first assault. Hit them while they are in church. We'll see how much they trust their God then."

CHAPTER 26

"No government ought to be without censors; and where the press is free no one ever will."

-Thomas Jefferson

Matt acquired a mild case of frostbite on the tips of his toes during militia training Monday and Tuesday. Karen tried to dissuade him from walking.

"Really, it is not that bad. It doesn't hurt much today. I think it was only the surface of the skin," Matt said.

On Tuesday when he arrived home, his toes were a bit itchy and burning as he soaked them in warm water. Now, there was a small blister on the tip of one toe. Matt was learning how brutal February could be in the mountains of Kentucky.

"If we are going to go, we'll drive," Karen insisted. "Besides, it's too cold to walk over there anyway. I don't want to get frostbite on my toes."

Karen won the debate and they drove over to Adam's. They arrived just in time for lunch. Janice and Shelly were cooking a nice pot of venison stew. Wesley had bagged another big buck the day before, during militia training. Fortunately, this time he was able to use his .308 to take the deer. He could have never made the shot with a bow.

Mandy and Karissa were bickering with each other.

"Both of you! Knock it off!" Janice yelled.

Karen and Matt looked at each other. They had never heard Janice raise her voice at the girls before. They two girls quit arguing immediately and went into separate rooms.

"Oh, I'm so sorry," Janice said to Matt and Karen. "We're all getting on each other's nerves a bit. This weather just makes it impossible to get outside. I've been trying to keep projects going for the girls, or keep them playing games and working puzzles, but I guess I'm getting a little cabin fever, too."

Karen said, "Why don't the girls come stay at our house tonight. It will give you a break and it will be a change of scenery for them."

"I won't argue with you on that one," Janice said.

Karen called out to Mandy and Karissa, "Hey girls, do you want to come over to my house and play with Miss Mae?"

The two girls came running back into the kitchen.

"Yes, please, can we, Mom?" Mandy asked.

"I want to go, too!" Karissa added.

"OK, but you better be good for Aunt Karen and Uncle Matt," Janice answered.

"We will be!" Mandy insisted. "I can't wait to see Miss Mae."

Miss Mae, like many cats, was not particularly fond of visitors, but for some reason she was more tolerant of children than other houseguests. She especially liked Mandy who would slip her a bit of food from her plate when she came to visit.

Everyone gathered around the big table for lunch.

Karen said, "You know, this is not the best of circumstances, but we're all growing so close together as a family."

Adam said, "I love having everyone here all the time. It feels like the way things are supposed to be."

Shelly added, "Times like these force us to focus on what is important."

"We are blessed. Not everyone's families can get along this well." Wesley winced as if he wished he could take back what he had just said. Shelly had not gotten along very well with her parents. They were polar opposites from the Bairs, and even from Shelly. They had come from Louisville for Wesley and Shelly's wedding two months ago. Shelly had not been able to reach them since the wedding. No one said anything, but most assumed they were carjacked and possibly murdered on the way home from the wedding. Gangs had taken over Louisville and these types of crimes were common in the city.

Wesley gave her a warm squeeze on her leg to let her know he was sorry. Shelly was tough though. She choked back the sadness and said, "I am very blessed to be part of this family."

She gave Wesley's leg a squeeze to let him know it was OK.

The days of watching the mainstream news channels at Adam's were over. Howe had clamped down on them and they were state-run stations now. They had gone from the puppet show that kept up the façade of independent reporting to the grossly obvious propaganda machines that operated in communist countries like China.

Matt, Adam and Wes went into Adam's office to watch some alternative news stations on the internet. RT was reporting on the amnesty being offered to the US troops who were not willing to fight against the Coalition States.

A female reporter stated, "This video footage sent to us by an anonymous soldier seems to be of a detention facility. The troops who elected to accept the offer to leave the military were told they would be brought to facilities like these to be debriefed and processed out.

"From what we know, thousands of conscientious objectors were brought to this facility yesterday, and we have had no reports of any soldiers who have been processed out. All of the footage we have received indicates this facility is very heavily secured. It's not at all what we would expect from a processing center.

"Our source told us they witnessed thousands of body bags being brought to this facility as well. The soldiers who did not defect to the Coalition States are becoming very suspicious of the government now. If the reports turn out to be true, if President Howe has indeed detained all of the soldiers he vowed to release, it may have a very negative effect on the military men and women who are still with him."

Adam went to Prison Planet Nightly News to see what was being reported there.

A caller was on the air. The caller was in the middle of his sentence. "….was dumping what looked like body bags into mass graves. I saw four bulldozers covering up the graves."

The reporter replied, "And you're patrolling the site? We don't want you to get in trouble for calling. Are you sure your phone is safe?"

"I just finished my patrol," the caller said. "I had permission to leave the base after my patrol finished prior to this evening. I stopped and bought a burner phone just to call in. I'm ditching it as soon as we hang up. Then, I'm headed to Texas. I suggest your listeners, not already in Coalition states, get to one as soon as possible. Yesterday, I didn't even agree with the Coalition, but what I saw today woke me up."

"Thanks for your call. Be safe." The reporter disconnected from the call.

Matt looked up from the computer. "Are they killing everyone that took the offer to opt out?"

Adam said, "I don't know what's going on. It doesn't sound good."

Wesley added, "Howe may just be getting rid of the high-risk individuals, like anyone who has been in any type of special forces training. Then again, he may not have the food to feed the prisoners and he may be gassing them all. He is probably using gas chambers disguised as showers or waiting rooms. He doesn't strike me as a very original thinker."

Matt was disturbed. "I wish there was something we could do."

"We're pretty much powerless on this one," Adam said. "We have to take this information and recognize who we are dealing with. Howe is ruthless. But mark my words, this is going to back fire on him."

The men continued to look for any information they could find on the processing centers.

CHAPTER 27

"Pride goes before destruction, a haughty spirit before a fall."

-Proverbs 16:18

Secretary of Defense Scott Hale and President Howe were meeting with the Joint Chiefs Saturday morning to finalize the plans for the action being taken against Pastor John Robinson's compound on the following morning.

One of Scott Hale's staff members burst through the door. "Mr. Secretary, I'm sorry to interrupt, but the soldiers being held in detention at the camp outside of Biloxi are taking over the camp as we speak."

Scott Hale looked at President Howe without speaking.

President Howe said, "Scramble jets out of Kessler and light the camp up. Make a surgical strike and eliminate all life forms within a half mile of the camp. This is war, Scott. Don't look at me to do your job. If you can't make these decisions on your own, you need to step down. There are plenty of men in this room that can do your job if you can't."

"Yes, Mr. President," Hale said. He had just been embarrassed in

front of all the Joint Chiefs. This President was a tyrant. Maybe the
Coalition was right, but Scott Hale was not the type of person to rock
the boat, particularly when he was in it.

"You heard the President, scramble the jets," Hale said to his
staff member who was still standing there.

The men reconvened their meeting.

"Gentlemen," President Howe began. "I think we need to
eliminate this threat. All of the soldiers presently being held around
the country are deserters and guilty of treason against the United
States. I feel I have been too soft on these traitors. The punishment
for treason is death. I have a soft heart for these men and women
because of their prior service to our country, but the reality is that we
do not have the resources to dedicate to guarding them and caring
for their nutritional and medical needs. I feel the humane thing is to
put them down."

Howe paused. There was a look of shock among the Joint Chiefs
at his recommendation to exterminate the prisoners. After Scott
Hale's reprimand for not being more proactive in his brutality, they
didn't question him.

Howe raised his voice, "Anyone who is not on board with the
Federal States is free to hand in their resignation and leave!"

It was obvious to the Joint Chiefs what that meant. If they
resigned now, they would likely not make it out of the room alive.

They all muttered somewhat in unison, "No, Mr. President, we
are with you, Mr. President."

"Very well," Howe said. "Since we are all in agreement, you
gentlemen come up with a plan to carry out this mission. I think we
should postpone the attack on Pastor John Robinson's compound
until after we have put our own house in order. One week should be
plenty of time for that to be handled. Scott, you should coordinate
with Jared Campbell to make sure this gets to the media in the right
light. Don't make us look like monsters."

Howe walked out of the room.

Scott Hale took the reins and started off with his suggestions. "What type of chemicals can we use in the food supply or water supply to get rid of the prisoners?"

The Vice Chairman spoke up. "If we use a weaponized virus, we could eliminate them all through the food supply. The downside is that all of the guards will be eradicated along with the prisoners. The upside is that we could say the food supply came from the Coalition."

The Chief of The National Guard Bureau spoke next. "That could work to our advantage. The casualties among the guards would be proof that we did not initiate the biological attack. We could simply say it was fate that caused us to distribute the food among the prison camps first. We will claim the reaction time was such that we were able to destroy the contaminated food supplies prior to it being fed to our troops."

"I like it," Scott Hale said. "Feel around and see what the rumor mill is spitting out about other bases that may be considering siding with the Coalition. We could send them contaminated supplies as well. That would make the story more credible and eliminate potential future threats. The proverbial two birds with one stone."

Hale and the other finalized their plans to infect the prison camps.

CHAPTER 28

"We are persuaded that good Christians will always be good citizens, and that where righteousness prevails among individuals the Nation will be great and happy. Thus while just government protects all in their religious rights, true religion affords to government its surest support."

-George Washington

Matt said to Adam, "Venison steaks and baked potatoes, what a feast." The potatoes were the last ones remaining from the previous fall. There would be no more until this spring's crop came in.

A couple of the men from the militia, Eddie Cooper and Franklin Johnson, attended the same church as the Bairs. They came over to Adam's for lunch Sunday afternoon.

Matt's phone rang. He got better reception at Adam's than on his own farm. He wasn't sure where the cell tower was, but it must have been closer. It was his friend Frank in Saint Augustine.

"Hey, Frank. Still no word from my buddy, Jack?" Matt inquired.

"They just got here a couple of hours ago," Frank answered. "They don't look good man."

"Wow," Matt said. "Two weeks to go 300 miles?"

"Jack said they got robbed at a road block in West Palm Beach," Frank explained. "The bandits took everything they had, then beat the heck out of them. He says they just beat them for the fun it. They are both very dehydrated and malnourished. They wouldn't have made it much further. Jack has a really bad infection on his arm from the attack. The girl isn't talking. She looks catatonic."

Matt shook his head. "That's rough. I guess they're blessed to be alive. Did they get any of their clothes or anything?"

"Nothing," Frank said. "The only things they arrived with were the clothes on their backs and the things they scavenged on the way here. They had a shopping cart he picked up in Vero Beach. It was full of every kind of thing you could imagine. They had cardboard they used for making a bed, trash bags tied together to make a shelter, plastic bottles to get drinking water from creeks and streams. I don't think they were purifying the water. We've got them eating some soup and drinking hot tea. It's in the 60's here, but they're cold because they didn't have the right clothing.

"We're going to try to get them to clean up after they eat. I can't tell you how bad they smell. Angie is taking a collection from the rest of the group for clothes and personal items. When they get back to normal, I'll dig up that little cache we buried last fall when you came through here."

"Oh man, I forgot all about that. You still have those buried?" Matt asked.

When Matt and Karen had left South Florida to head to Kentucky last fall, Matt was robbed at a rest station while filling up the gas tank with gas cans from his trailer. As soon as his assailants showed their weapons, Matt drew his Glock and shot them. In his panic, he picked up the bandits guns and threw them in the trailer. He then went to Frank's to lay low for a while. Frank buried the guns in case anyone came around to ask questions. Matt killed the two men in self-defense, but the stuff had just hit the fan and he had no intention of getting caught up in an investigation.

"I'll give that Berretta to Jack," Frank said. "It only has one magazine, but it beats the heck out of the broken broom handle he's been carrying for a weapon. We have plenty of 9mm ammo for him. If the girl comes around... what's her name again?"

"Tina," Matt said.

"Tina," Frank said. "If Tina comes around, I'll give her the .357. No one has ammo for it, but it still has the six rounds it had when you brought it here. After what they've been through, the guns will make them feel safer."

"I don't know how to thank you Frank," Matt said. "You came through for me again."

Frank said, "Everything I have belongs to the Lord. If He sends someone in need by me, I have to do what I can to help out. Besides, you supplied the guns."

"Yeah, don't remind me." Matt didn't like to remember the event.

"Brother, you did what you had to do. It was them or you," Frank reassured him.

"I still feel bad about it." Matt fought with what he had done.

"You wouldn't be human if you didn't," Frank said. "I'll give you a call in a couple of days and let you know how they're doing."

Matt came back into the room and gave Karen an abbreviated version of what had happened.

She didn't say anything. A single tear fell from her eye. She had not been very close with Tina, but they had been neighbors for several years.

Wesley and Shelly listened in as Matt told the tale of Jack and Tina's ordeal. It was shocking how far downhill things had slid.

Everyone except the kids crammed into Adam's study to listen to Paul Randall's internet address. They brought a few extra chairs and a couple of people sat on cushions on the floor.

Franklin Johnson had a notepad to take notes. As Commander of the Eastern Kentucky Liberty Militia, he was using ham radio to coordinate with militia and military units in other Coalition states. This internet address was his only method to get direct communication from the Commander in Chief himself.

Paul Randall began his address.

"America, we have just received intelligence reports that a severe outbreak of a deadly disease has swept through the prison camps in the Federal States. President Howe had granted amnesty to any US troops who wished to leave bases located in Federal States. Those who took him up on that offer were detained in prison camps, and we now believe that they are being executed with a biological weapon.

"We think it may be a weaponized version of Ebola. Intercepted radio communications indicated severe flu like symptoms running rampant in the camps. The typical incubation period for Ebola could be up to two weeks, but we believe these prisoners were infected in the last twenty-four hours. This would indicate a genetically modified strain of the virus. It leads us to believe the soldiers were infected on purpose. There have already been several deaths reported. The Federal States have quarantined the infected camps allowing no one in or out.

"It is obvious that Howe has ratcheted up his savagery. We must be ready. No atrocity is below him if he is willing to do this to his own soldiers."

Adam got up and left the room. Janice followed him.

Matt looked at Wesley. "Is he OK?"

"He had a couple buddies that were supposed to leave Quantico during the amnesty period," Wesley said somberly.

Everyone else remained in the office and turned their attention back to Paul Randall's address as he continued.

"While we are deeply hurt over the loss of the lives of these brave men and women, we will not be drawn into an offensive position. With that said, we will defend the Coalition States to the last gun, the last bullet and the last man. We have drawn our line in the sand and we will surrender no further liberties. All those in the Federal States who wish to keep their liberties are free to join us here in the Coalition States.

"On a more upbeat topic, all federal agencies have been evicted from the Coalition States. Likewise, the employees of those agencies that did not see fit to resign from those agencies but decided to remain loyal to this criminal regime occupying Washington D.C. were also thrown out of the Coalition States.

"As of today, any federal employee or agent attempting to enforce any taxing authority or federal law within the Coalition will be shot on site; the same as any other traitor. Therefore, it goes without saying, there will be no banned firearm collection at any federal agency or anywhere else in a Coalition state.

"This is my last plea for liberty-loving patriots outside the wire to join us here. Your future is certain bondage and unimaginable tyranny if you stay where you are. I know many of you hope to fight and win freedom for your states as well, but without state-level leadership and military support in your state, your struggle will be very difficult. I realize it's hard to walk away from your homes and all you have worked for, but it may be stripped from your hands by Anthony Howe anyway.

"I ask for your prayers patriots. Know that I will be praying for all of you in return. God bless and God speed!"

Wesley was the first to comment on the speech. "Yahoo! No more IRS!"

Eddie Cooper was right there with Wes for a high five.

Shelly asked, "Won't the Coalition start their own IRS?"

Matt said, "They'll have taxes, but I don't expect it to be anything that resembles the IRS. Paul Randall was running on dismantling the IRS slowly over time. I suppose the present situation just sort of fast-tracked that objective for the Coalition."

The conversation quickly turned to what the government would look like in the Coalition. Matt loved the subject, but he excused himself to go check on Adam.

He found Adam and Janice sitting quietly on the front porch swing. The sun was just setting and the air was turning cold.

"You gonna be Okay, big guy?" Matt asked.

Adam had a solemn expression on his face. "I'm just thinking about all those American heroes that survived countless firefights and attacks overseas only to be murdered by their own president."

Matt said, "Especially your buddies at Quantico?"

"Especially them," Adam said. "Their death will not be in vain. It will strengthen the resolve of this Marine to fight like I have never fought before. I don't mean to brag, but I arranged many meetings between Allah and his jihadists when I was in the sandbox. I'm good at what I do, Matt."

Even during militia training, Matt had never really seen the killer inside Adam before. When he looked into Adam's eyes as he made his vow, Matt saw it and it spooked him just a bit.

CHAPTER 29

"If we desire to avoid insult, we must be able to repel it; if we desire to secure peace, one of the most powerful instruments of our rising prosperity, it must be known, that we are at all times ready for War."

-George Washington

Pastor John Robinson had just walked to the pulpit Sunday morning when Albert Rust ran to the stage. The Security protocols had been put in place weeks ago, so there was no need to get permission from Pastor John before Albert began his announcement.

"Folks," Rust began, "I want everyone to take a deep breath and remain calm, but we have to dismiss church right now. Our observation post on State Road 55 has reported several armored personnel carriers headed this way. We think an attack on Young Field is imminent. Militia, you know your positions for an attack from the south. Everyone who is assigned to the north, east and west borders, hold your positions unless we call you to the southern border. We don't know if we're going to get hit from multiple directions. Ladies, you know where you are supposed to be hunkered down, let's get there right away. The ladies who are responsible for the medical aid tent, let's get everything set up just as if you have injured already coming in. If it turns out to be nothing, it will be a good drill. If the worst happens, you'll be ready to start saving lives."

Pastor John stopped everyone. "Before everyone runs out, I want to say a quick prayer. I know we have to hurry, but I feel the Holy Spirit asking us to give God one minute even though it goes against everything in our being."

The congregation fought the urge to run out anyway. They all stayed for Pastor John's quick prayer.

Pastor John quickly bowed his head and began praying from the third Psalm. "But you are a shield around me, O LORD; you bestow glory on me and lift up my head. To the LORD I cry aloud, and he answers me from his holy hill, I lie down and sleep; I wake again, because the LORD sustains me. I will not fear the tens of thousands drawn up against me on every side. Arise, O LORD! Deliver me, O my God! Strike all my enemies on the jaw; break the teeth of the wicked. From the LORD comes deliverance. May your blessing be on your people. Amen.

"Now go fight for your families, fight for your liberty and fight for your freedom to worship your God."

The congregation's fear melted away with those few short words inspired by God's Holy Book. They were supernaturally charged with courage and faith as they took their battle stations.

Albert Rust and several of his men were the first to arrive on the southern side of Young Field. They saw hundreds of federal troops rolling out of their personnel carriers quickly and orderly. The Federal troops formed up into squads and began to take defensive battle positions.

Several pickup trucks and a few more Humvees provided by the Idaho National Guard were still taking their defensive positions inside of Young Field as the commander of the Federal troops called out to them from the other side of the fence. "If you throw down your weapons and surrender, you will be given quarter. There is no reason to lose your lives today. We have you completely outnumbered, out trained and outgunned. You have five minutes to comply or your blood will be on your own head."

Trey Dayton told the men near him on the line, "Don't listen to him! That is the same thing they told those soldiers that were infected with the Ebola virus. If we're going to die, let's die right here and die with our dignity."

Albert Rust looked at Will Pender and said, "I'm going to go down the line and give everyone a heads up. Wait two minutes and blow all the mines on the south side."

The militia had fragmentation mines buried outside of the barbed wire fence. They were hard-wired into four detonators. One for each side of the camp. Will Pender was holding the detonator for the south side in his hand.

Albert started up the left side of the line to tell them to open fire after the detonation. He was trying to avoid using the walkies in case the federal troops were listening in on their frequency. He sent James Macintosh up the right side of the line with the same message.

Will looked back and forth from his watch to the detonator. The adrenaline coursing through his veins was making his hand shake. The seconds counted down slowly. There were 20 seconds before he was to light up the enemy line. The enemy was oblivious to the fact that they were sitting right on top of the mines. 10 seconds. Will focused on the watch and the toggle switch. 5, 4, 3...

"Don't blow it!" Will's walkie screeched out. It was Albert Rust's voice.

Will's shaking hand was on the toggle. The sound almost made him hit the switch.

"Don't blow the mines yet Will!" Rust reiterated. "There are a bunch of soldiers surrendering to us."

More than a hundred soldiers had thrown down their weapons and were walking quickly towards the militia's line.

Bill Maxwell was right beside Albert Rust and Pastor John Robinson. Bill said, "I think it's a trap. I think we should shoot."

Pastor John said, "Let's put some men on them and see what they have to say. If it is a trap, we'll mow them down."

Rust said, "I agree Pastor, but you should be in the shelter. These people need a spiritual leader."

Robinson replied, "God is their leader. If He sees fit to bring me home today, He'll raise up someone else to fill the gap."

Albert Rust called over the walkies, "If your last name begins with an S, escort the prisoners to the meeting barn."

The federal commander shouted out over the loudspeaker, "Open fire on the deserters. Kill the deserters!"

The federal troops that had not walked off the line seemed confused by the number of their fellow soldiers who were walking away and hesitated to follow the command they were given.

"I said fire!" the loudspeaker rang out. The commander ran up to the line and began firing with his side arm. The men walking off the line began to run towards Young Field.

The commander hit the soldier beside him and screamed, "Fire!"

The trooper began to fire on the deserters. Soon the entire federal line was shooting. Many of the federal deserters began to fall. Many more reached the safety of the Young Field line.

"Hold your fire," Albert Rust said over the radio.

They moved two Humvees and propped up the bottom strand of barbed-wire to make a space for the defectors under. Once they were all inside or shot down, Albert Rust called to Will Pender on the walkie, "Blow the mines, Will."

Will immediately complied. He hit the main toggle switch which was labeled "fire all".

The militia watched as thirty separate mines blew up. Four armored vehicles flipped over. One flipped up in the air and fell right on a fire squad of federal soldiers. The federal commander was three feet away from one of the mines when it blew. He was blown to pieces. The explosions caught the federal troops completely off-guard. Hundreds were killed or injured beyond being able to continue the fight.

"Fire at will," Rust called over the radio.

The militia began cutting down the federal troops as they spun around in confusion. Many of those not killed or severely injured by the blasts were temporarily deafened or blinded by the explosions. All of them were confused and disoriented by the quantity and quality of the eruptions, but that didn't last long.

The federal troops began to organize and return fire. One soldier fired a stinger missile into one of the Humvees being used as a shield for the militia in Young Field. The Humvee exploded and killed several men in the vicinity. Five more stingers were fired into the militia's line killing many more.

Albert Rust called to the two Bradleys positioned in the tree line. They were manned with Idaho national Guardsmen who had been given strict orders not to fire on federal troops unless Young Field was fired upon. "Bradley Alpha, Bradley Bravo, I think this qualifies under your rules of engagement. We could use a little support."

All Rust heard back over the radio was, "Roger." Seconds later the 25mm shells from the Bradleys began tearing through the armored vehicles of the federal troops. Once again, the federal troops were caught off-guard. Hundreds more were cut down in the cross fire of the Bradleys and the militia.

The militia's line was not unscathed. Their dead were piling up. Others were injured and some were unable to continue in the battle. Pastor John took his rifle and stole away to the meeting barn where the defectors were being held.

He grabbed one of the defectors and asked, "Why did you men cross over?"

The man replied, "A bunch of us decided to leave the Federal States after we heard about the prison camps. They told us it was the Coalition that had sent in the contaminated food, but we knew better. This was the only hope we had of defecting. We were just hoping you all wouldn't shoot us."

"Will you fight with us?" Pastor John asked.

"We'd be honored, sir," The soldier replied.

Pastor John called out, "Militia, defectors, follow me. We need every man on the line. Defectors, take off your shirts bearing US insignia so we don't have any friendly fire issues. You'll find rifles on the ground by the fallen militia. Just grab one and start firing. If you can't find one, I'll try to get some side arms from some of the men. That will at least make some noise. Let's go!"

They all returned to the line.

Albert Rust called out to the northern border, "North border, if your last name ends with a letter between A and R, we need you on the south border. We are taking casualties. East and west, if your last name ends in A through L, we need you on the southern line. Everyone else, hold your position.

The six men from the observation post were just arriving from the two mile hike on foot since they spotted the vehicles approaching Young Field. They arrived directly behind the federal troops. They took up positions in the tree line at an angle so their stray bullets would not end up hitting the militia inside the camp. They were able to take sniper shots without being noticed as the Bradleys were making so much noise.

It soon became obvious that the federal troops were not going to win the day. The man who stepped into command after the original commanding officer was killed called out over his radio "Cease fire!"

The few remaining federal troops laid down their weapons. They were rounded up by the militia. The prisoners were held under heavy guard. They would be transported to an Idaho National Guard facility the following day.

CHAPTER 30

"He who is void of virtuous attachments in private life is, or very soon will be, void of all regard for his country. There is seldom an instance of a man guilty of betraying his country, who had not before lost the feeling of moral obligations in his private connections."

-Samuel Adams

Anthony Howe poured a bit of whiskey into his coffee. He had never been a morning drinker but, then again, he never had such a shocking defeat as the one in Idaho yesterday.

The phone rang and rang but he didn't pick it up. Finally his Chief of Staff came into his study.

"Sir," Alec Renzi began, "we missed you at the briefing this morning."

"I am sick, Alec," Howe said.

Renzi inquired, "Would you like me to have the physician come take a look at you?"

"I drank myself to sleep last night, Alec," Howe answered

matter-of-factly. "No one else needs to know about that, so no, I don't want to see the doctor."

"Mustafa Al Mohammad is on the phone for you sir. He has been calling all morning. He insists that you speak with him," Renzi stated.

"Give me five minutes and I'll call him back," Howe said.

"I'll let him know, Mr. President." Renzi let himself out of the room.

Howe's staff cleared out when he was like this. He put the coffee down and took a gulp of the straight whiskey instead. He felt his stomach flip and the saliva began to flow into his mouth. He fought back the vomit and breathed. Howe poured himself a glass of whiskey and mixed it with a bit of water to cut the strength so he could get it down without getting sick. He took out his cell and called Al Mohammad.

The former president answered on the first ring. "Anthony! What are you doing? If it gets out that you had these troops exposed to the Ebola virus, they'll have you beheaded! What happened in Idaho yesterday? You took your first military action against a Sunday school class? And lost?"

Al Mohammad's voice got louder with each question. Howe finally lost control.

"Shut up, Mustafa!" Howe screamed. The liquor kicked in just in time for him to let it rip. "You're not going to control me by hanging that video recording over my head anymore. Do you think the country cares that I had a couple of underage hookers in Brazil when the economy is tanking? I control all of the mainstream media. If they run that story, I'll have the FCC pull their license. Do you think Jenna will care? She's along for the ride. I'll call her right now and tell her myself!"

Al Mohammad was silent. He may have assumed he had Howe on a leash, but evidently he didn't. Mustafa said, "I'm sorry you won't take my counsel, Anthony. I only wanted to help. I am afraid you're going to find out that you're not the emperor sooner than you think."

Howe shot back, "What is that supposed to mean?"

Al Mohammad said, "Ask your father." Then, he hung up.

Howe finished his whiskey and water then called Scott Hale. The Secretary of Defense was there within fifteen minutes.

"Mr. President I am very sorry about the way things turned out yesterday." Hale said as he walked in. He looked nervous.

Hale continued to explain himself without being asked, "We sent a thousand men in there. We didn't get the intelligence that they had Bradley fighting vehicles, and we had no way of knowing that over one hundred of our men would walk off the line, sir. They had mines buried right underneath the positions our troops took. It was just really bad luck. Any one of those things, we could have worked around, but all together, sir, it was more than we were prepared for."

"You're forgiven, Scott." Howe said. "Do you want a drink? You look a little shook up."

"No, sir, I'm fine," Hale answered.

"I insist," Howe answered. "I am having a drink. Don't make me drink alone, Scott."

"If you insist, sir," Hale said.

"Good." The President responded. He poured them both a neat shot of whiskey.

"Neat?" Howe asked.

"May I have a little ice?" Scott Hale asked.

"Get it yourself. I'm not your waiter," Howe said.

Hale dropped the subject of ice and drank the whiskey neat.

"Scott," Howe began. "I think there may be a conspiracy inside Mount Weather to eliminate me. I think Paul Randall has people inside of the Secret Service. I need to get out of here and I need a black ops team for my security detail. I don't know who in the Secret Service is conspiring with Randall."

If Hale thought the President was drunk or perhaps delusional, he didn't voice his concerns. He didn't oppose him in any way.

"I can have a team together by tomorrow morning, Mr. President," Scott said.

"Get a team together to move me by tonight," Howe responded. "Just me. Jenna can stay here. No one needs to know about this but you. I'll handle my communications through you and you alone. Can I trust you with this?"

"Yes, Mr. President," The Defense Secretary conceded.

CHAPTER 31

"Not all the treasures of the world, so far as I believe, could have induced me to support an offensive war, for I think it murder; but if a thief breaks into my house, burns and destroys my property, and kills or threatens to kill me, or those that are in it, and to 'bind me in all cases whatsoever' to his absolute will, am I to suffer it?"

-Thomas Paine

Paul Randall was focused on the mission at hand. He joined Larry Jacobs, Sonny Foster and Allen Jefferson in Larry Jacobs's large study early Tuesday morning. After the assault on Pastor John Robinson's compound in Idaho, all the leadership within the Coalition States pushed for strict border security. Randall and the others were meeting to come up with a standardized protocol to secure the borders of the Coalition.

"I want to try to have a balanced approach to this," Paul Randall stated. "I wish there were a way to let the patriots who have been dragging their feet into Coalition states."

"We have to have hard borders, Paul," Jefferson replied. "We can't risk a repeat of the Idaho incident. If you insist on not launching a counter strike, the borders are going to be our battle ground. We have to have an asset and troop buildup all along the borders. We need air patrols. The Northwest is especially going to have to utilize air patrols. There is no way they have the manpower or equipment to cover their borders. We have no way of getting more ground assets up there. Howe's no-fly zone and massive troop buildup in Utah, Nevada and Southern Colorado have them cut off from Texas."

Texas Governor Jacobs suggested, "Can we have hard borders and still check in patriots looking to relocate?"

"What is the vetting process, Larry?" Jefferson asked.

"I don't know," Jacobs said. "Ask for their voter registration card?"

There were a couple of lighthearted chuckles at the suggestion.

Jefferson objected, "Being a registered Republican is a poor litmus test for being a patriot."

"That's true," Larry answered. "But being a Democrat is a sure sign of being an enemy of the Constitution."

"Point taken," Jefferson conceded.

Randall said, "We don't really have the resources to open up the states for people who are wishing to be uninvolved and enjoy freedom in the Coalition without sacrifice. I recommend that we require a period of military service from anyone who wants to come in from an outside state. That will deter freeloaders who think we're going to have a better economy."

"Are you going to require women to serve on the battlefield, Paul?" Jefferson asked.

"Not on the battlefield, but there are other capacities." Randall was adamant about this. "We're going to need support personnel and lots of nurses. If Idaho was any indicator, this is going to be a bloody contest."

"We still have no means of weeding out spies," Jefferson said.

Paul Randall responded, "We have no means of weeding out spies that are already here. We don't know which soldiers could still be loyal to D.C. Who could have stayed behind with the intentions of trying to disrupt our efforts? I think the best form of deterrent against such actions are coarse punishments."

Sonny Foster spoke up, "Harsh punishments will no doubt reduce spying and treason, sir, but if you are viewed as being too rough, the patriots may think of you as a dictator."

Paul sat quiet for a moment then said, "That's a good point, Sonny. How do we deal with that issue?"

Sonny answered, "You could put it to a vote. Let the people decide the punishment for spying and treason. Who knows? They may come up with a worse method of dispatching the enemy than you would have. Then they can say nothing about cruelty."

Larry Jacobs said, "That is a fantastic idea Sonny. What would you say to letting each state have its own form of punishment?"

"If it were up to me, I would require each state to come up with their own punishment," Sonny agreed. "State sovereignty is one of the main issues in our movement. Each state should be responsible for coming up with their own laws. I don't want to overstep my boundaries as I'm not a leader in the capacity of the rest of you gentlemen."

Paul Randall said, "You're here because I value your opinion, Sonny. You have become a very trusted advisor to me personally. You have never overstepped your boundaries in all the years I've known you. Please continue."

"In that case," Sonny continued, "perhaps we should be wary of stepping into the role of the Federal Government. Unfortunately, I think the entire process of federalism has become deeply ingrained into our way of doing government. Our present conflict will tempt us to strive towards a strong leadership role among the Coalition States. I don't think we want to become a scaled-down version of Washington, D.C. It would be far better to start out on the right foot, working towards a constitutional republic made up of sovereign states."

"Sonny," Jacobs said, "I can't thank you enough for that reminder of who we are and what we're fighting for."

"Of course," Sonny continued, "we have a common enemy, and it will serve us all well to have a strong military strategy for all the states to combine their efforts."

Allen Jefferson said, "You are a man of wisdom, Sonny. Paul is very blessed to have had your counsel over the past few years. We are all fortunate to have you advising us.

"I'll formalize my military recommendations and send them around to all the states. They can ratify as is or modify them to the specific state's needs."

Larry stated, "Texas will adopt your recommendations as soon as they are formalized. We should start the initial buildups on the borders within the hour."

Paul Randall added, "I'll put together a recommendation for the states to begin drafting their individual punishments for treason and spying. The only guidance I'll give is that they should be sufficiently harsh to effectively deter such activities."

The men concluded their meeting to begin their individual tasks.

CHAPTER 32

"The spirit of resistance to government is so valuable on certain occasions that I wish it to be always kept alive."

-Thomas Jefferson

Matt heard Adam's truck driving over the gravel and walked up to the drive to meet him early Wednesday morning.

"You're already up and at 'em?" Adam asked.

"I don't want everyone around here knowing I'm a city boy. Gotta get up early to keep my cover intact," Matt joked. "Something got one of my chickens last night."

"Let's have a look at your coop," Adam said. "That thing is in shambles. You need to build a new one."

The two men walked towards Matt's chicken coop.

"I spoke with Franklin early this morning," Adam said as they walked. "General Jefferson has made recommendations for all the Coalition states to start patrols on the borders."

"Okay," Matt said. He wasn't prepared to hear this. He knew about the attack on Pastor Robinson's compound and assumed something like this would be coming. Everything was happening too fast.

Adam continued, "London Company has been assigned to the Virginia border. We'll be maintaining a checkpoint on State Road 421. We'll be rotating with Manchester Company; one week on, one week off."

"Alright," Matt said. He wondered how serious it was, but didn't feel right asking. He felt he should just do his duty and not voice his concerns. All the things Adam had been through, this probably wasn't a very big deal for him, but to Matt, this meant he would be responsible for defending a line with his life. He was up for it, just not excited about it.

Adam paused when they got to the chicken coop and looked around. "This is where they are getting in." Adam pointed to a tunnel under the wood. "Probably a coon. You need to put in a floor or do something to keep predators from being able to tunnel under the wall and into the coop."

They filled in the hole. Matt said he would set a trap later for when the critter returned.

On the way back to the house Adam explained a bit more of his thoughts about the mission. "I wish I could tell you what to expect, but I don't know. Virginia is heavily contested territory. There are a lot of folks on the extreme left, and a lot of folks on the extreme right. For now, it seems like Howe is focusing on disrupting the flow of trade and supplies between Texas and the Northwest states. That's good for us, but who knows how long until he turns his attention toward Kentucky and the rest of the Southern Coalition.

"421 is a country road. I doubt we'll get hit with a massive troop movement, but we could get called to back up Tennessee if they get hit from I-81. That's all mountains as well. Federal military hates moving through mountains. They still have a bad taste in their mouth from Afghanistan. The military mostly used private contractors to move stuff through the mountains. They avoid it at all costs.

"That being said, Howe has no reputation for acting rationally, so there is really no telling what he might do. It's like we got our own personal Kim Jong. If they try to hit us in the mountains though, we'll crush them.

"We're going to be responsible for deciding who comes across the border. Virginians who want to join the Coalition are going to be required to volunteer for military service.

"Folks who chose to leave won't be allowed to return. It's a one-way ticket. Same thing coming in. One way, no turning back. I suspect they will shut the border permanently in a couple of weeks."

The explanation made Matt feel better. He was glad Adam had volunteered to tell him. Matt did not look forward to telling Karen. She was not going to take this well at all.

CHAPTER 33

"The tree of liberty must be refreshed from time to time with the blood of patriots and tyrants."

-Thomas Jefferson

Pastor Robinson finished the memorial service for the fallen militia men at Young Field. Several of the men had died. Many more were wounded. The wounded had been taken to the hospital in Boise.

After the service, Pastor John and Albert Rust walked over to Will Pender's camper. Pastor John said, "Will held on for a few hours after he was hit, but eventually expired. Will told me that he wanted everything he owned to go to the church. Will had a nice camper with a full-size bed and another sleeping area that could be made by folding down the kitchenette table and pulling out the bench. What would you think about putting a couple of the men who defected in Will's camper?"

Albert thought for a moment before responding. "Those guys who defected had nothing but the clothes on their backs, so they would be very well served by utilizing the camper. I think we should try to select two guys that were close to Will's size. He was a big burly fellow. This way whoever we put in there could also wear Will's clothes."

When they arrived, they straightened up the camper and took a few personal items to distribute according to Will's last requests.

Albert and Pastor John selected two young soldiers to put in Will's camper. Harry Wilder from Oklahoma and Oliver Stillwell from upstate New York.

As the two soldiers were settling in, Harry said, "Like the other defectors, we're dead set against what the government is doing. We came to the party a bit late, but like folks all over America, we're finally waking up to the tyranny that's quickly growing out of control. We signed up to defend America against threats foreign and domestic."

Oliver added, "We bought the lie being told by the White House and the puppet media for years."

Pastor John patted Oliver on the back. "At the last minute, you did the right thing. All of you defectors risked being shot by both sides to cross that line. I know it was hard watching your friends being shot before they hit the other side."

After Pastor John got the two soldiers moved in, Ron White came to give him an update on the burials. Ron said, "The ground is frozen and it makes for hard digging, even with the backhoe. The graves for the militia members are being dug to a depth of four feet. Fuel is a limited resource and it has to be conserved. Manually digging enough graves would have been impossible to accomplish in a timely manner. The freezing air is buying us a little time as it keeps the corpses from decaying. I guess it's the next best thing since there is no embalming services available.

"The enemy soldiers were buried in a mass grave away from the camp. They were stripped of all useful items before being disposed of. We took all of their body armor, weapons, ammunition, radios, boots, assault packs and state-of-the-art optics."

Pastor John nodded his approval. "All of these items can go to the militia members who are being assigned to secure the Southern Idaho Border."

Pastor John and Ron continued talking about the other business of Young Field.

CHAPTER 34

"Even peace may be purchased at too high a price."

-Benjamin Franklin

Paul Randall picked up the phone to call North Dakota Governor Mickey Abrams. "You have to quit dragging your feet and put this to a vote with your state legislature. South Dakota is waiting to see what you do. They don't want to stick out like a sore thumb with borders on three sides to defend."

Mickey replied, "You have to understand Paul, the Marines have already built up defenses around Minot. Howe has no intention of letting you have Minot Air Force Base. That is the last ICBM site still under D.C.'s command. Siding with the Coalition will make North Dakota a war zone."

Paul said angrily, "Then get in the cattle car and go die in peace, Mickey. Do you think being passive will save you from a violent end? North Dakota will be a battle zone. The only question is which side you'll be on. You'll either be a border state of the Coalition or you'll be a border state of the Federal States. If you choose the latter, know that Howe will use your state as a launch platform for attacks against the Coalition."

Mickey said, "Paul, we do not have the manpower to hold the borders, even if we could take Minot."

Paul responded, "I'll promise you all the support of the Coalition in taking Minot Air Force Base. It's a strategic base. Besides the ICBMs, Minot houses a large cache of nuclear warheads and a fleet of B-52Hs that can make delivery of those weapons.

"As far as holding the borders, you'll only have your eastern border to defend if you join. South Dakota will follow your lead. Montana will have no borders with the Federal States if you join the Coalition. I'll broker a deal to have Montana's militia and National Guard assist you in securing your eastern border if you'll sign on. They'll assist upon your invitation and leave when you ask. What more can you ask for? Do you think Howe is going to make you a deal like that?"

Mickey said, "Paul, we support what you are doing. I don't want a deal from Howe. I am just trying to do what is best for my state."

Paul said, "If you want to do what is best for your state, then present my deal to your legislature. Get it on the floor tonight and let me know before I go to bed so General Jefferson can start positioning assets to evict the Federal forces from Minot. Either way, North Dakota is going to be a battlefield. You just have to decide what side of history you want to be on, Mickey."

Mickey Abrams agreed to take the proposal to the North Dakota House of Representatives and call an emergency session.

As soon as Paul hung up, his phone rang again. Paul recognized the number. "Ryan! How are you, son?"

"I'm working hard, Dad," Ryan replied. "Boot camp was rough, but I did a lot better than most of the guys. I have you to thank for that. All of the outdoor activities and chores on the ranch paid off I guess."

"I hear you already started pilot training." Paul was proud of his son.

"Yes, I think someone pulled some strings and got me bumped

up," Ryan said. "All the guys in my class were riding me about it."

"I had nothing to do with it," Paul replied. "Allen Jefferson knows your character and he may have given some specific directions, but the military is his department and there is nothing I can do. Besides, your mom would kill me if she knew I was doing anything to get you in the air faster."

Ryan asked somberly, "How is Mom?"

"She has good days and bad days," Paul said. "She misses you. She is proud of you, but she doesn't want to lose you, too. She misses your brother a lot. We all miss Robert, but you not being here makes her miss him that much more."

Ryan said, "I'm doing what I have to do, Dad."

"I know it, Son," Paul Randall replied. "Your mom knows it, too. Nobody thinks you should be anywhere other than where you are. We just miss you. I know the Air National Guard is tough, especially when you're first starting out, but try to call Mom once in a while. It'll do her good."

"I will," Ryan said. "I guess it reminds me that Robert is gone when I call. I'm not hiding my pain in my training, it's just keeping me busy; keeping me focused. We were twins, we did everything together our whole lives. I don't feel like a complete person without him."

Paul Randall could hear his son start to sob. Tears began running down his own face as well. It had only been three months since his son had been murdered by the kill team sent to assassinate Paul.

Ryan said, "I am doing this for him." He paused as he regained his composure. "I'll call a little more often. Tell Mom I'll call every Sunday."

"We would like that very much, Ryan," Paul said.

Paul hung up and went back to work, trying to get more support for the Coalition.

CHAPTER 35

"Three can keep a secret, if two of them are dead."

-Benjamin Franklin

Anthony Howe was getting settled in at his new fortress just north of Tupper Lake, New York. He thought to himself, *I love this part of the country. It's close enough to Albany to still get in touch with my friends that supplied my questionable entertainment habits when I lived in the Governor's Mansion. I like to have a good time, but this is about garnering a friendship with the private security team.*

The men Scott Hale had found to watch the President were among the most ruthless in the industry. Prior to his arrival, Scott told Howe, "Raven Thorn is at the apex of private military contractors. The Pentagon and CIA have used these men for every type of unsavory mission in the book. Whenever it was imperative that no US footprint be left behind, these were the mercenaries that incited the riots, kidnapped the heir or planted the evidence. Likewise, they take care of reporters and whistle-blowers who don't know when to shut up. Their dark craft has been behind many car accidents, heart attacks and apparent suicides that we read about in the headlines."

After a week of keeping the men well entertained when they

160

were off-duty, Howe finally tipped his hand to Darren King, the CEO and company commander of Raven Thorn. Darren was a beast of a man. He was 6 foot 4 inches with a bald head. He was well over 300 pounds, and all muscle. While he looked like a mafia enforcer, he spoke very eloquently and was highly educated.

"Darren," Howe began, "Your country is very indebted to all you have done to keep America safe. I would assume that I can always count on your loyalty?"

"Mr. President," King replied, "America is our best client and we consider our fiduciary duties in that relationship to go beyond what most would call loyal. Trust has always been our highest priority."

Howe looked straight into Darren's eyes and said, "We have an issue within our government. It is a conspiracy that has penetrated the very fabric of our government. I'm not talking about Paul Randall and the Coalition secession. I am speaking of someone in our own ranks that is trying to undermine my administration. We have a mole that has access to very high level information and is abusing that information for his own gain. Because of this man's previous position, we cannot prosecute him under normal procedures. The scandal would be more than the American people would be able to bear. The best course of action would be to remove him quietly."

"How can Raven Thorn help, Mr. President?" Darren asked.

"I'm glad you asked." The President smiled.

Anthony Howe took out a picture of Mustafa Al Mohammad and showed it to Darren King. Darren looked at the picture and then looked away. Howe took out a lighter and lit the picture and let it burn in the ashtray. Darren took out a pen and wrote on a cocktail napkin. He picked it up and showed it to Howe. It was a number. He had written 25 M.

Howe was shocked. His thoughts raced. *Is he asking for $25 million dollars? I knew it wouldn't be pro bono, but I had never anticipated such an astronomical number.*

He carefully kept his expression neutral as he nodded in agreement. At this point, it could just as easily be blackmail money against Howe himself. Howe had taken a huge risk trying to put this together, but he had to get Al Mohammad out of the picture. He had become an unbearable pain in the neck.

No matter, Howe thought. *$25 Million isn't going to bankrupt me, but I don't like the idea of spending that much. This isn't coming out of my pocket. I could fund the operation through black box spending allocated for CIA and NSA spending. That money is tossed around pretty loosely and no one really knows where it all ends up. Perhaps the most efficient method of payment would be to double their regular fees for ongoing operations. Darren would certainly appreciate the need to keep the funds transfer as discreet as possible.*

Howe said to Darren, "We can discuss payment details at a later date. For now, we have an agreement and nothing else needs to be discussed. I don't need to know any of the gory details. In fact, the less I know, the better."

Darren nodded without saying a word. Knowing Raven Thorn's reputation, Mustafa's death should appear completely natural. Foul play should never even be considered.

CHAPTER 36

"For a people who are free, and who mean to remain so, a well-organized and armed militia is their best security."

-Thomas Jefferson

Matt only had two more days to finish his week of guard duty on State Road 421 coming into Kentucky from Virginia. The militia outpost was set up on a side road that turned south off 421 right at the border, just feet away from a sign that said "Welcome to Virginia." The gravel road led to three farms.

On the corner of 421 and the gravel road was a small farm house where a gentleman repaired trucks out of his garage. He was kind and helpful to the militia and offered to let them use his water and even gave them access to the repair shop in case they needed to get out of the rain.

The side road made a convenient turnaround point for folks who arrived at the checkpoint. Folks who didn't have adequate documents to cross the border were turned around and sent back to Virginia. People who didn't wish to stay in Kentucky or leave permanently once they crossed, had the opportunity to return the way they came.

The farmer who owned the truck repair shop offered to let the militia set up camp in his open field, but Adam wanted the men in a more concealed location. The camp was set up on the north side about 300 feet off the road and about 1200 feet back from the checkpoint. A thick line of trees and heavy brush contoured the north shoulder of 421. The camp was close enough for reinforcements to arrive quickly, but far enough to not be spotted from the road. Just over the hill from the camp, sniper positions were available if the checkpoint was attacked.

Adam had two Listening Post Observation Post, or LPOPs set up on the north side of the road and two on the south side of the road. One LPOP was set up 1000 feet on each side of the road along the border. The next LPOP on each side was 1000 feet from the first. Matt was at the northernmost LPOP.

Gary Brewer was the second man at the northernmost LPOP. Gary said to Matt in a voice just above a whisper, "Your wife is a jewel. This ham, deviled eggs and cornbread she brought out here for you makes for a spectacular lunch. I appreciate you sharing it with me."

Matt nodded. "You always share everything with me. Besides, when she or Janice makes their mid-week run to the checkpoint, they always bring more than we can eat."

Gary said, "That's thoughtful of them. You tell them I said thanks. I noticed Shelly always rides along with whoever drives out."

Matt said, "Yeah, it's tough on a new wife to not see her husband two weeks out of every month."

Gary finished chewing the cornbread. "My wife tries to come out when I'm here, but you know gas is scarce. Everyone's family doesn't get to come out every time we're out here."

Matt said, "That's part of the reason Karen and Janice always try to bring a little extra.

"After five days of sitting in the woods and seeing nothing, it's getting hard to stay alert. Why don't I stand guard while you go back to camp and make a pot of coffee to bring back to the LPOP."

Gary stood up. "You don't have to twist my arm. I'll be right back."

Matt sat beneath the crudely constructed lean-to made of fallen branches and leaves from the forest floor. He kept watch from the opening which faced east so he could watch for people moving in their direction from Virginia. Anyone who did not have proper identification or did not consent to the one-way passage mandate would likely try to evade the checkpoint by walking around it through the woods.

The one-way passage mandate was enforced with a ledger. The person coming in to Kentucky or deciding to leave had their name, description and ID information recorded in the ledger. The record of all those using their one-time pass to cross the border was sent to Lt. Joe who was maintaining the database at his cabin near Wood Creek Lake. Lt. Joe had a very impressive ham radio set up with which he could send and receive information to the separate checkpoints along the Kentucky-Virginia border. The information was passed by hand-held transceivers that operated on ham frequencies.

The State Road 421 checkpoint used two Baofeng UV5RA radios to communicate with Lt. Joe. They could also communicate with the Middlesboro checkpoint to the south and the State Road 23 checkpoint to the north with the radios. The State Road 421 checkpoint sat low in-between some hills, so the militia ran antennae up into the trees to be able to communicate at the longer distances. One Baofeng radio was kept at the checkpoint and the other was kept up the road at the camp. The men had simple walkie-talkies for communicating between base camp, the checkpoint and the LPOPs. If the need to communicate with a checkpoint further than the ones directly to the south or north, then Lt. Joe would act as a relay as his system could transmit at much longer distances than the hand-held Baofeng radios.

Matt didn't hear Gary return until he made the militia alert click with his mouth. Adam had taught them to roll their feet to minimize the sound of the crunching dry leaves in the woods. The militia used a simple two-click sound, similar to calling a dog, to let other members know they were approaching the camp. World War II paratroopers had used a hand-held clicker to make clicks when the Allied Forces had invaded France. The click with the mouth was a natural sounding click that would be more easily confused with wildlife by the enemy, and it required no special equipment. The simple two clicks reduced the odds of a friendly fire accident by alerting the other men standing guard that someone was approaching. Additionally, it did not require them to speak in loud human tones that could give away a position.

Matt smiled as Gary filled his cup from the thermos of hot coffee.

"Thanks Gary," Matt said softly. They were permitted to speak as long as they kept conversation at a whisper.

"This is just a little too serene up her for me," Gary whispered in reply. "I was fighting sleep. I feel better just walking to camp and back."

"This cold weather doesn't help, either," Matt added as he took his first sip of the strong black coffee.

The sun had peeked out a couple of times throughout the day, but it was still cold winter weather. March was here. They had made it through the worst of it, but spring still felt miles away to Matt.

Matt and Gary had a small Dakota fire pit right at the opening of the lean-to. It kept a little warmth in the shelter, but not much as the front was completely open to give them a wide view to the border.

Matt's walkie was the only one with an earphone, so it was the only one turned on. Gary had a walkie as well, but he would only turn it on if he needed to call out.

Matt's walkie chirped in his ear. Gary had been speaking so Matt put a finger up to let Gary know he was receiving a message over the radio.

After a few seconds, Gary asked, "What's up?"

Matt replied, "We've got some guys walking up the road toward the border from the Virginia side. Wesley said there are quite a few of them and wants us to move up to the tree line to cover them."

Matt and Gary moved quietly to the tree line on the north side of the checkpoint. When they arrived, Jeff Nolon and JC Hunter were already in position. They had been called to the tree line from the northern LPOP closest to the checkpoint. Everyone got into a firing position. Jeff had a Barrett .50 caliber rifle configured in a bullpup design so it could be shoulder-fired as well as utilized for long distance shots. Even with the bullpup configuration, it took a big guy to effectively hold such a heavy weapon. Jeff filled that description well. He was a towering 6'7" and just over 300 lbs.

There wasn't as many good cover options from the south side of the checkpoint, so the men from the southern LPOPs joined up with the guys standing guard as an extra show of force. Adam and a few of the guys from Alpha squad came running up the road to the checkpoint. Adam had excellent night vision and pulled night duty at the checkpoint. He and the other night shift guys were just waking up when the call came into the camp that a large group was approaching.

By the time Adam and the others arrived at the checkpoint, it was obvious that the group approaching the checkpoint on foot were military soldiers. Matt's heart started racing. His thoughts raced. *Are we being invaded? Why would they be approaching on foot? None of this makes any sense.*

Matt felt guilty to be in the tree line. He was well hidden while Adam, Wesley and the others were exposed with only the vehicles for cover. Matt took comfort in the fact that his position was necessary. He knew if something went down, he would be able to pin down the enemy while the others took better cover.

The more Matt thought about it, the less this made sense. He whispered to Gary, "If we're getting hit on foot, it seems like the men would've hit us at night. Maybe this is a trap. Maybe other forces are circling around from the north or south to hit us from behind while we are occupied with the men walking up the road." Matt began scanning the woods to the north. He began having second thought about leaving his LPOP. "This isn't right." He whispered, "That post should not have been abandoned."

Adam called out to the soldiers, "Lay down your weapons and continue to the checkpoint with your hands on your heads."

A voice from the approaching group called back, "Identify yourself."

Adam returned, "Lay down your weapons or we will cut you down where you stand!"

The man who appeared to be in charge made a gesture with his hand and the men in the group melted into the shrubbery and woods along the side of the road. The man in charge however, did not. He complied with Adam's command and laid down his rifle. He placed his hands on his head and began walking very slowly towards the border. Everyone at the checkpoint had found solid cover and had their weapons trained on the man walking towards them or the roadside where the others had disappeared.

Adam tapped four militia men to turn around and watch for approaching people or vehicles from the rear. Matt felt better about not getting ambushed from the rear while everyone's attention was on the border. But he continued to scan the woods to the north for other soldiers.

The man stopped just short of the border and called out again. "I want to speak with the person in charge."

"State your business," Adam called out.

"May I have the courtesy of knowing to whom I am speaking?" The man called back to Adam.

Adam called back, "My name is Adam Bair. I am the Captain of London Company of The Eastern Kentucky Liberty Militia. Kentucky has asserted her sovereign right as a free and independent state under the authority granted by the Tenth Amendment. We do not recognize the authority of the government in Washington, D.C., as the present administration has violated the laws set forth by the Constitution and is currently a rogue occupier of the Capitol. We do not wish you harm, but we are prepared to kill and die to defend this sovereign soil."

Matt smiled at Adam's explanation. Matt considered that, just as the liberals had taken great liberty in interpreting the Bill of Rights to destroy them, the Coalition had taken great pains to look to the founders in interpreting the Bill of Rights to preserve them.

Matt recalled the text of the Tenth Amendment. It was very short and sweet. It read "The powers not delegated to the United States by the Constitution, nor prohibited by it to the States, are reserved to the States respectively, or to the people."

Matt kept up with the politics of the Coalition States. The Coalition looked to the original Articles of Confederation to help interpret the Tenth Amendment. The Articles of Confederation were written in 1776 and served as the defining law of the land until the Constitution was ratified in 1789.

The provision in the Articles of Confederation used for guidance on the Tenth Amendment stated "Each state retains its sovereignty, freedom, and independence, and every power, jurisdiction, and right, which is not by this Confederation expressly delegated to the United States, in Congress assembled." Furthermore, the Coalition found that D.C. was in breach of contract in adhering to its obligations under the Constitution and thereby nullified any requirement of the Coalition States to be bound by obligations to D.C.

The man called back to Adam, "We do not recognize the authority of Washington, D.C., either. I am going to instruct my men to lay down their weapons and we are going to surrender ourselves to you."

Matt was sure this was a trap. He could see the confusion among the other militia men at the checkpoint.

Adam called out, "Okay, line up single file with your hands on your head. We'll process each man through the checkpoint one at a time. We'll search you and remove any dangerous objects. We'll place wrist restraints on you until we clear you or determine where you are to be held. If you are cleared and accepted as citizens of the Coalition, you will not be allowed to leave. Doing so may be considered desertion. You will be required to commit to military service in the Coalition. I want this to be very upfront, so you know what you are consenting to by entering Kentucky. Any of your men that do not consent to these terms are free to turn around and walk away. I give you my word that you will not be fired upon if you go back the way you came."

The men who had come to the checkpoint from Virginia slowly started to come out from their cover with their hands on their heads. Matt kept his rifle sights trained on them as one by one, Adam and the other militia men searched them, placed zip tie restraints on them and sat them to the side.

Matt continued to scan the woods to the north while the men were being processed through the border. He looked across the road and could see the man who lived in the farmhouse looking out the window at all the commotion. Matt wondered if the man realized he lived on the edge of tyranny and freedom?

Several militia members inside Virginia had launched small scale assaults against federal government buildings and ambushed federal agencies over the past few weeks, but Howe had sent massive responses and locked down the towns where the attacks had taken place. Virginia was now under a tighter lockdown than any other state. Matt thought that Howe probably saw its proximity to the capitol as being too important to tolerate any resistance. This left Kentucky and North Carolina on the border of the most occupied state in America. Right now, London Company was assigned to guard perhaps the most volatile piece of real estate in the world.

Matt's shift had ended during the event. He came out of the tree line, walked up to Adam and said, "I'll be milling around to be sure everything is going to be alright."

Adam nodded as he continued to clear each man. Once all the men were processed and counted, their number was 27. Adam sat down with the man who led them here. Matt stood nearby to keep watch while Adam interviewed the young man.

"So, how did you Marines end up on our border?" Adam asked.

The young man explained, "We were part of a supply convoy out of Quantico. The Marines had commandeered a dry food storage warehouse in Blacksburg, Virginia. Our convoy went there to make a pick-up. While the trucks were being loaded, we had two hours to go around town, get a bite to eat or whatever. The 27 of us had predetermined to make a run for it. We headed straight for the hills. We kept moving that night, then laid low for two days. On the fourth day we started toward this border."

"Why did you abandon your post?" Adam asked.

"You don't know what's going on there," The young Marine explained. "My First Sergeant tried to get a bunch of us to leave and join up with the Coalition. He told us what was going on. It was very different from what we were getting from most of the brass and the news. I don't think we really believed him. He took the amnesty offer to leave the Federal forces and was supposed to go to the Coalition States. He said he was coming here to Kentucky to make a stand. He said he had a buddy that he served in Afghanistan with who was in the militia.

"They were sent to a processing center where they were supposed to be debriefed and let go. The center turned out to be a prison camp. They were all poisoned and died in the camp. I was part of the Hazmat team that had to clean up the corpses."

The young man was starting to get choked up. Adam let up on the questions for a moment, then asked, "What was your First Sergeant's name?"

"Hammer," The young man said.

"What was his first name?" Adam asked.

"Carl. First Sergeant Carl Hammer." The man answered.

Adam jumped up and called out to his brother. "Wesley, cut these men loose."

Matt could tell Adam was upset. He thought he had seen a tear forming in his eye as he walked away.

The young man looked at Matt and asked, "Did I say something wrong?"

Matt replied, "On the contrary, I think you just passed the test. Adam served in the Marines with Carl in Afghanistan. Adam is the one Carl was coming here to link up with. He's just a little sad right now. He'll be fine in a few minutes."

Matt pulled out his Kiowa folding-blade knife and cut the plastic wrist restraints off the young man's hands. Matt and Gary walked them back across the border to collect their weapons.

Wesley took the initiative to get the Marines set up in an area adjacent to the militia camp. Wesley said to the men, "You guys set up your camp right over here. There's drinking water inside that tent. You guys have been hiking a while. Is there anything else you need right now?"

The lead soldier said, "We are out of food. We had four days' worth when we set out. We stretched it because we knew we wouldn't be able to hunt or resupply. We made a forced march and covered about 30 miles per day."

Wesley whistled. "That's quite a feat. Most of that area is through mountains."

The soldier nodded. "We wanted to avoid being seen on the roadsides. It took six days to get here, we have been burning a lot of calories."

Wesley called out to JC and Jeff. "Can you guys go around and take up a collection from the militia members for food to give the Marines?"

The two gave a quick affirmative nod and got right to it.

Matt said, "Gary and I will get a fire going. Then, these guys can start cooking whatever they receive from the collection."

The militia all chipped in enough to feed the Marines well. The men who had finished their watch were curious to hear all about the Marines' journey. Adam radioed Franklin Johnson to send several trucks out to pick up the Marines the next day. They would set up a camp at Lt. Joe's until they found them more permanent places to live.

CHAPTER 37

"One man with courage is a majority."

-Thomas Jefferson

Paul Randall sat his bags by Larry Jacobs' front door.

Larry said, "Paul, I hope this isn't about you being afraid you're wearing out your welcome. If there is anything I can do to be a better host, let me know."

Randall took Kimberly's day bag off his shoulder and sat it near the other luggage. "You could write a book on hospitality, Larry. You have made us feel right at home. I feel it isn't wise to have too many high value targets in one place."

"I see your point, Paul," Larry said, "but we have a very good security plan here at the ranch. If you return home, you're going to have to make some serious modifications."

Randall replied, "The general said he will take care of all that. We have to think about continuity of leadership. The security here at your ranch is fantastic Larry, but nothing is impregnable. Do you think Howe wouldn't hit us with a drone strike? One missile from a reaper could eradicate all of us."

"We can catch a reaper with our radar," Larry said.

"Can you pick up a RQ-180?" Randall asked.

"Those are just for surveillance," Larry answered.

Paul continued to build his case. "How hard would it be to put a payload on it? You could strap one AGM 114 Hellfire to the RQ-180 and hardly increase the radar signature. If you stripped out the interior of all the surveillance equipment, you could put in a bomb bay and not increase the radar signature at all. It only takes one, Larry."

Larry nodded in agreement. "Well, you'll be missed. It has been nice having you around. Promise you won't be a stranger."

"You won't miss me, Larry," Randall kidded. "You are at the halfway point between the general and me, so the face-to-face meetings will all be here. You'll be charging us rent by the time this conflict is over."

Larry laughed but insisted that it was no trouble.

Larry and his wife, Allison, walked them to their SUV. General Allen Jefferson had arranged for a military security motorcade to escort the Randalls back to their ranch. Sonny Foster accompanied them back to their home.

The ride home was pretty exciting. Part of the security protocol was to drive quite fast. This made it difficult for a planned attack to time an impact or explosive device.

When they arrived home, Kimberly stated, "This house is a mess."

Military contractors were all around the property. The lead contractor approached the Randalls. He greeted them and began to explain what was being done. "We're installing ballistic glass in all the windows. A safe room has been installed as well as a below-ground bunker. The bunker has been placed adjacent to the house. We dug a short tunnel under the concrete footer of the garage. It's accessible via a trap door in the garage. The bunker also has an exit tunnel that leads out to the cattle barn. General Jefferson instructed us to spare no expense in making you safe."

Paul said, "We sure do appreciate all of the hard work."

It was the first time Kimberly had been home since Robert had been killed. She walked into his room, sat on his bed and began to cry. Paul followed and sat down beside her. He pulled her close to comfort her. After several minutes of crying, Kimberly took a deep breath, looked at Paul and smiled softly as she embraced him.

Sonny came to the doorway. "I am so sorry to interrupt, but there is a phone call for Paul."

"I'll take it, Sonny," Paul said. He kissed his wife on the forehead and got up from the bed to answer the phone.

"General," Paul said, "the house looks great! This is fantastic. The contractor showed me the door to the bunker. We just got home, so I haven't had a chance to check it out yet, but it's the next thing I'm going to do."

"I'm glad you like it, Paul," Jefferson replied. "I'll be by in a few days to point out some of the extraordinary features. The below ground bunker has its own oxygen source so you can't get smoked out or have tear gas injected into the ventilation system. There is enough oxygen to last you about a week. The airlock feature has to be engaged for the oxygen to kick in. There's enough food and water to keep eight people alive for three months. I took the liberty of placing a pretty serious weapons cache down there as well. I know how you like to shoot. Hopefully you'll never need any of it, but if you get bored and decide to shoot your way out, you'll have that option.

"Before I get sidetracked here, that's not why I'm calling. The House Judiciary Committee is pushing to have the President impeached and subsequently detained. It couldn't get any traction because all of the representatives from the Coalition States have dropped out of Congress to serve in their states. It's really just a fistful of establishment Republicans from both houses that are trying to let the President know they still have a say. Howe isn't having it.

He's had them all detained. This might be a good time to see who else we could get to make a commitment to the Coalition. There are still a lot of red states out there that are trying to stay neutral."

Paul joked, "Well, the Ides of March is next week. I suppose if anyone is trying to proclaim themselves 'Emperor for Life,' this is a good time to be locking up any dissenters in the Senate."

General Jefferson laughed. "Put out your feelers and see who is interested in joining the Coalition. Arizona had a few representatives detained. West Virginia had one very popular Senator locked up. Don't make anyone any promises about dedicating military support to evict federal offices or take over military bases in their states. We are going to be focusing all of our attention on taking Minot Air Force Base. Once that is out of the way, we can discuss what's next on our agenda."

"Sounds like a plan, General. I'll call around and see where the leadership is at. The more the merrier. Take care." Paul finished and hung up the phone. It operated via encrypted VOIP. His next calls were to the Governors of North and South Dakota. They had just joined the Coalition and there was much to discuss with them. Paul need to speak about border security, shutting down federal offices and taking control of the military bases in their states. Unfortunately, they were not yet set up with the encrypted VOIP software that the rest of the Coalition leadership was using.

Paul told the governor of North Dakota, "Governor, I'll be sending a delegate from the Coalition to meet with you this week."

This "delegate" was actually the Coalition security IT specialist that would be getting them set up with the encryption software so they could have private conversations. Traveling across the Federal States was too risky for leadership, but communication was vital to the effort.

The governor of North Dakota agreed to receive the delegate just as the governor of South Dakota did.

Next, Paul Randall called the governors of Arizona and West Virginia.

The governor of Arizona said, "We're sympathetic to the Coalition, but we're just not ready to make a commitment."

The West Virginia Governor said essentially the same thing. "The state legislature is just unsure at this particular juncture. I'm sure you understand."

Paul understood alright. *I understand that you are choosing tyranny because you are a bunch of cowards,* he thought to himself.

CHAPTER 38

"The trifling economy of paper, as a cheaper medium, or its convenience for transmission, weighs nothing in opposition to the advantages of the precious metals… it is liable to be abused, has been, is, and forever will be abused, in every country in which it is permitted."

-Thomas Jefferson

Matt sat on his porch and drank his coffee quietly in the cool mountain air. He considered how much life had changed all over America. Nothing about it looked the same as six months ago. The decline had been coming steadily for years, but the past few months brought about a sharp crash that changed the living standards of every American. Even the rich felt it. They could no longer go to their favorite restaurant in the hot part of town. Restaurants were nonexistent. The restaurants that had clientele who could absorb the rapid increases in prices held on until the dollar completely failed, but after that, they locked the doors.

The news told stories of home invasions that had erupted in upscale neighborhoods. The days of picking up the phone and calling 911 were long gone. Those who had the foresight to have items available for barter could hire former police officers or former military personnel for security. There was a growing market for security work among the affluent who had something to pay with. Unfortunately, before the crash many of the so-called upper class were living above their means to keep up appearances. A large portion of those who were truly wealthy prior to the collapse had all of their wealth tied up in the stock market or in cash. (Those with vast sums of cash in the mattress were no better off. If they hadn't converted their dollars to hard assets before the dollar bit the dust, their money was useful only for kindling or wallpaper.)

Then Matt considered the working class like Karen and himself. The middle class was entirely wiped out. There were no more jobs and suburban landscapes had been transformed into wastelands run by gangs and criminals. Those that had somewhere to go, left. Those who didn't, weren't able to survive. Food was pretty much gone in all metropolitan areas. The last remaining bits of food in warehouses and convenience stores were stripped out by gangs and looters.

The news showed that the military was doing everything it could to keep the soldiers fed, but millions of civilians were dying of starvation. The gangs turned to cannibalism and were feeding on other humans to survive.

Rural areas were a different story. Those fared much better depending on whether they were in the Federal States or the Coalition States.

According to reports on alternative media sites, in the Federal States the military had begun going house-to-house to collect supplies to distribute to the needy. The needy ended up being the military. Cattle, pigs, poultry, eggs, and stored food were commandeered for the "good of the country." Farmers were left enough to survive on so they could continue to produce goods. They were promised compensation once the new currency was established.

In the Coalition states like Kentucky, barter networks were developing. People pitched in to help each other out. Many folks had taken Paul Randall's advice and converted their dollars into silver, gold, ammunition, tools, storable foods, toiletries and the things they would need to get by until manufacturing and trade with other nations could be reestablished. In London, Kentucky, and many other small towns, people were setting up flea markets in the abandoned parking lots of Walmarts and other big box retailers. Few people had enough stored fruits and vegetables to trade, but spring was just around the corner. With the high demand for canned vegetables at the flea markets, you could be sure lots of farmers would be devoting large plots of land to produce.

Meat was priced high, but was available if you had the right currency. Many cattle farmers, like Adam, killed cattle to feed their own families. They would often end up with more than they could store, so the flea markets made a good outlet to get rid of the extra meat. They would typically sell it to someone at the market with a booth. As this trend continued, entire booths became dedicated to butchers. Butcher booths were often run by the very butchers who lost their jobs at the big box grocers and retailers. Besides beef, the butchers regularly carried venison, rabbit, chicken, pork and various other wild game. There was no FDA to regulate the butchers, however the free market quickly weeded out anyone who sold foul-smelling meat or failed to keep a tidy workspace. Customers simply chose another vendor.

At the flea markets, large transactions typically took place utilizing gold. Gold coins were common, but gold jewelry was accepted by merchants who had scales and the time to figure out the value of the pieces. Jewelry traded at a very slight discount to gold coins. The coins were standardized and weighing wasn't necessary, so the jewelry was viewed as an inconvenience by merchants.

Midsized transactions were most likely to be made in silver one-ounce coins. Fractional silver had also become popular after the price passed $50 per ounce. In the years leading up to the crash, private mints produced one-half, quarter, and tenth ounce silver rounds. This made silver available in the same denominations as gold. While fractional silver had been around for a while, the premiums were too high to bother with until the price shot up. Pre-1965 US silver coins were used as well. (While not quite a tenth ounce of silver,) pre-1965 silver dimes would buy the same as a tenth ounce silver round. Matt figured that it was a convenience factor, or it may have been the fact that the dimes were old and would never be minted again. Silver dollars, quarters and half dollars were subject to the merchant. Some accepted them at the value of a quarter ounce, half ounce or ounce, but most discounted them to their actual silver content.(One dollar face value of pre-1965 silver coin contained only seven-tenths of an ounce of silver.

Smaller transactions used ammunition for a standardized currency. Different caliber shells held differing values. Other popular barter items were soap, razors, deodorant and makeup.

Utility services varied widely across the country as well. When payment for utilities became impossible because of the dollar collapse, military personnel were assigned to keep them operational. The boards of the utility companies signed them over to anyone who could take care of them as they were completely useless as profit centers without a currency.

Franklin Johnson told Matt that the services in Texas were uninterrupted. Texas had their own power grid and were completely energy independent and capable of producing all of their own water. The Texas State government assumed operation of the utilities until order and trade could be reestablished. Texas promised to hand control back to the utility companies as soon as they felt they were ready to take over.

The eastern electrical grid initially had major problems when maintenance workers and operators began not showing up for work. Many large cities had intermittent service or regular outages during the day despite military personnel keeping the plants open. Some northern cities were completely dependent on electricity for heat. Matt read that over one hundred thousand people froze to death that winter.

An alternative news source reported that President Howe was looking for ways to have the Coalition States cut off while keeping the power on for the Federal States, but the interconnectivity of the Eastern Grid made that impossible.

Matt learned from a Kentucky National Guardsman that the Southern Coalition States were working frantically to tie together a centralized grid of their own. The Northwest Coalition States worked hard at building their own independent grid as well. They had a bigger challenge as most of their states were part of the western grid, but the new members of the Coalition, North and South Dakota were connected to the eastern grid.

Matt finished his coffee as he recounted the recent events that were creating the new landscape of America. It was barely recognizable as the same nation it had been only months ago.

CHAPTER 39

"For our struggle is not against flesh and blood, but against the rulers, against the authorities, against the powers of this dark world and against the spiritual forces of evil in the heavenly realms."

-Ephesians 6:12

Howe returned to Mount Weather after sealing the deal with Raven Thorn. He assured Secretary of Defense Scott Hale that he received bad information and there was no plot inside the White House or Secret Service to assassinate him after all. It was obvious that something wasn't right about the story from the beginning, but Hale was not the type to question the President.

The week after his return, Anthony's father, Porter Howe called him.

"Dad," Howe answered, "how are you doing?"

"We're fine, Anthony," Porter replied. "You could call once in a while. I know you're busy, but your mother may not be with us much longer. She hopes to see you sometime soon."

Anthony had never been close with his parents. His mother had been a socialite when he was a child and he had been raised by his nannies. As soon as he was old enough for boarding school, he was sent away. He was brought out at parties and paraded around on occasion, but they never spent any substantive time together. Anthony Howe didn't resent his parents for it. It was just the way things were for people in his social echelon. While he did not harbor a grudge against them, he also did not feel particularly compelled to call or visit. Even now, when his mother was dying from lung cancer, he didn't call. Now, more than ever, the conversation would be awkward and uncomfortable. He didn't really know the woman and didn't quite know what to say.

"Are you safe?" Howe asked his father.

"We are. We have private security. They're pretty top-notch and they're well connected," Porter replied.

"What firm?" Howe asked.

"KBR," Porter said. "With the loss of so many US military contracts for logistics and security, they're venturing into international personal security. The supply and demand curves being what they are, high net worth individuals are seeing the value that justifies the fees KBR charges. Ten years ago, the only way you could afford them is if you had a printing press. Well, things change."

"I bet Halliburton would like to patch things up with KBR about now," Anthony commented. His father and he could always talk about business together. It was the one thing they had in common. "Halliburton is hiring all of these rookies to work at the camps. Rookies can run the FEMA camps, but the prison camps are giving these guards a run for their money. Paul Randall really stirred up a hornets' nest for me. I'm filling up the prison camps as fast as Halliburton can build them."

Porter said, "Son, I would love to chitchat, but there is something really important that we need to discuss."

Anthony replied, "I know Mom is sick, but I have a lot of responsibility right now."

"That's not it," Porter said. "It is something you need to know.

It's something you'll want to know."

"What is it, Dad?" Howe asked. "You can say whatever you need to say. This phone is about as secure as any phone in the world."

"I need to tell you in person," Porter said. "I am going to take a helicopter down there. My pilot is with KBR. He has clearance to land at any military installation. Tell Secret Service I'll be there this afternoon."

Howe stammered for an excuse. He was usually so good at that, but he knew this must be important for his father to even call, much less fly down from New York.

"Okay," Howe finally said.

Howe thought to himself as hung up the phone. *What could this be?* He was puzzled more than anything.

Several hours later, Anthony Howe got the call that his father's helicopter was arriving. Anthony Howe rode the elevator to the surface. It was the first time he had been exposed to natural light since he returned from New York. The Mount Weather physician had encouraged Howe to get up to the surface at least once a day to get some fresh air and keep his spirits up. The doctor was worried that Howe's drinking was affecting his health, but Howe was sensitive about the subject.

Even with his sunglasses, the light made him squint. Howe thought to himself. *I suppose I rather like the darkness. It seems to suit me better than sunlight.*

The helicopter landed and Howe greeted his father. While not close, he did like the old man. He had a great amount of respect for him. He admired the way his father had built a financial empire from the ground up. Porter had always made sure Anthony had the best of everything and a good education in all things business and politics.

Porter Howe said, "I can't stay long."

Howe had grown to expect it. *Even when I'm President, he doesn't have time for me*, he thought. It was a matter-of-fact thought. Anthony Howe had learned not to let that get to him emotionally many years ago.

"Anthony," Porter said, "you have crossed a dangerous line. I know that you think you're the supreme being of the universe, and why wouldn't you? No one has ever told you any different."

Howe wasn't quite sure what his father was saying. He asked "Is this about the prisoner extermination rumors?"

"No, Anthony," Porter said, "it isn't. And we don't have to pretend they're rumors. You did what you had to do. The simple fact is that you have been groomed for this position from birth. Before you were born, it was determined that you would be brought up with a certain education, certain connections and a certain path would be laid out for you."

"I knew you had aspirations for me." Anthony still didn't know where this conversation was going.

"Not me," Porter said. "We. When I was a young man at Yale, I made a pact with my fraternity that my first-born child would be brought up into the position of President of The United States. Many men have worked diligently to make certain that this would come to be."

"A lot of presidents have come from The Skull and Bones fraternity. All of my fraternity brothers knew we would have influential positions," Anthony said.

His father continued "Yes, many of them knew they were to become president. After Kennedy, the men in power decided that it was best to let the elect think it was destiny that brought them to their positions. In his speech in April of 1961, Kennedy threatened to expose the very men who had brought his entire family to their glory. Of course they backed off when he threatened to expose them. For a couple of years anyway. But these men are patient. Two years later, as you know, Jack Kennedy learned to keep his mouth shut.

"After that, no one else was to know the plans the men in power had for them. I shouldn't be telling you this, but you are very close to being eliminated; just like Jack Kennedy."

Howe just listened. His father had always been very level-headed. Anthony Howe knew that being in the Skull and Bones guaranteed a prominent position, but he had never thought it meant elections would be decided for him or that there were men behind the scenes pulling the strings and pretending to be gods. Howe thought, *maybe Porter is just getting old. Perhaps the strain of mother's sickness is getting to the old man. Maybe he has Alzheimer's or is on the wrong dose of some medication.*

Porter continued, "It's this business with Al Mohammad. He is a protected member. He served the men in power well and his reward is a long life. You cannot put yourself in the place of a god. It is not up to you if he lives or dies."

Anthony Howe's heart dropped to his stomach. *How does my father know about this? Who said something? It had to be Darren King. No one else knows anything about this.*

"I don't know what you're talking about," Howe covered.

Porter took a stern tone. "This is not a game. This determines if you live or die. Your life is in the hands of these men, Anthony!"

The President retorted, "Al Mohammad isn't in the Skull and Bones. I've never seen him at the Grove, I don't know how he ever made it to where he is."

Porter spoke with a whisper as if he thought the very wind might hear him. "These men are not the Skull and Bones, Anthony. They are much higher. They are the Masters. It is not necessary for him to be a Skull. The three presidents before him were Skull and Bones. At some point, they have to change it up a little. It starts to look a bit odd when you have five presidents in a row from the same Yale fraternity.

"To make up for this indiscretion, it would be wise of you to take Al Mohammad's counsel on occasion. The Masters would like to help you with one of your problems. They have come up with a solution to the defectors from your military." Porter took out a small RFID device. "This chip can be a great tool to get control of your armed forces and government employees."

Anthony Howe sat stunned as his father continued speaking. He thought. *I've seen some very peculiar things during rituals at Bohemian Grove and of course at Yale, but I never believed in God or any other higher power. There are men in stations of power that I did not even know about an hour ago. These men are like gods and I am a mere mortal.* The misfortune of not being the apex predator was a crippling disappointment.

Howe took the chip from his father, but he was still stunned by the information. His father stayed only an hour then boarded his private helicopter and left Anthony alone again.

CHAPTER 40

"Rightful liberty is unobstructed action according to our will within limits drawn around us by the equal rights of others. I do not add 'within the limits of the law' because law is often but the tyrant's will, and always so when it violates the rights of the individual."

-Thomas Jefferson

Eddie Cooper's sister had just come to live with Eddie from Louisville. She told Eddie the horrors of what it was like there. Eddie relayed the information to the rest of the guys from Bravo. At a group meeting days prior, Eddie told everyone the story. "Louisville has a very ethnically diverse population. There were gangs prior to the meltdown, but now the ethnic gangs really stick with their own kind. The city is being divided up into strict territories. The Vietnamese hold the south end, black gangs control the west end and a new violent Mexican gang is running rampant in the east end of town. The east end had previously been the most affluent, but the Mexican gangs now occupy several neighborhoods through systematic home invasions.

"My sister stayed in Louisville for so long because she lived in the east end and thought she would be safe. Her husband was killed two days ago, and she left. She told me all about the conditions around town when she finally left. There was no economic activity aside from the gangs. There were no flea markets that she knew of. She had heard from a neighbor that there was a small barter network in Okolona, a suburb south of the area held by the Vietnamese. Okolona is the more redneck area. Most everyone there has a gun and from what my sister said, they organized their own security.

"No one goes downtown. All the shops, bars, restaurants, offices, condos and stores have been looted and it is a ghost town. The Louisville municipal bus service known as TARC has solar panels on the top of every bus stop for safety lighting. My sister said that none of the panels had been taken from her neighborhood, which makes me suspect that they would still be on the bus stops downtown. It seems like the gangs are not paying any attention to the politics that are heating up over the power grid and have not thought of taking the panels for backup power yet."

With this information, Adam devised a plan to go in and get the panels since that area of the city was completely abandoned. Adam's plan was to drive straight into the center of downtown, get as many of the panels as they could carry and get out fast.

Matt, Wesley and Adam loaded into Adam's truck. Adam said, "We'll stop near Shelbyville to gear up and put on our tactical gear."

It was 4:30 in the morning and most of the gunfire would be dying down. Adam briefed the team "We'll arrive in downtown Louisville right around 7:00 a.m., the calmest part of the day. I'll pull my work trailer to load up with solar panels. JC will follow me in another truck. Gary and Eddie will ride along with JC. Jeff and Lee will follow in a third truck which is pulling a flatbed trailer."

Matt said, "JC's truck has no trailer. We could use the old beat up horse trailer that I used to haul everything from Florida."

Adam answered, "I think it would be too much of a target. We are a big enough target just because we have fuel. A horse trailer would make folks assume we have livestock. When people are starving, even honest men may consider making a bad move if they think we have something to eat in that trailer."

Adam's truck was full of gas. Matt and Adam had stocked up fuel back when the ration cards first went into effect last year. Every member of the family could get a card, so they took cards for everyone in their group, even Mandy and Carissa. Jeff also stocked up on fuel when it was more available. Conserving fuel was a way of life now.

JC's truck was marked 'flex fuel' which meant it would run on E85. Gary was producing several gallons of fuel grade alcohol every week to sell at the flea market. Prior to Gary dedicating his life to Christ, as a teenager, he had helped his grandfather make moonshine. Kentucky had lifted the prohibition on distilling for personal use after the crash. The state was not encouraging drunkenness, they were encouraging people to be able to take care of themselves. The state recognized the usefulness of moonshine for a fuel alternative and for an antiseptic. Seeing as there were no more federal laws in Kentucky prohibiting it, Gary's conscious was free to produce it for fuel and medicinal purposes.

Adam continued, "Three trucks running 300 miles round trip is going to dump a massive amount of fuel, but the payoff could be great. Gasoline and diesel are still available at the flea market, but both fuels are very expensive. If we can get enough solar panels, the amount of energy we will harvest from the sun will far surpass what we will be expending to retrieve it. Solar panels won't fuel trucks, but they will keep us from having to burn more fuel to run generators if the grid does go down. We all know the risk of it going down is pretty good. The load being sucked out of the grid by the cities could cause a cascading failure. Besides that, Howe has proved that he's a hothead. If he could shut down our grid without turning off his own power, he would've already done it. Who knows how long that will stop him? He's already proven that he'll kill his own in order to inflict pain on the enemy."

The men loaded up and rolled out. All three trucks reached Shelbyville without incident. They pulled off at the exit and met up at an abandoned gas station. Adam gave the last minute instructions. "Everybody, gear up. You six are going to be working security, Matt and I will be removing the panels and JC will be loading them into the trucks and trailers.

"Matt, JC and I will be wearing blaze orange vests and white hard hats. This will at least make us look like city workers, even though there hasn't been a city worker for months. The security team will wear all black which makes them look more official. Matt, JC and I all have our side arms in case we need to engage an enemy.

"I know everyone just finished their checkpoint duty yesterday and haven't had a chance to rest up. I wanted to get this done before everyone got a chance to get home and relax for too long. Right now, your minds are still in militia mode, you're still sharp. After a week off from checkpoint duty, we all get relaxed and lose our edge."

After the men geared up, Adam did a precombat inspection to make sure everyone's gear was up to spec.

During the inspection Jeff asked, "Is this stealing?"

Matt answered, "Do you mean when the Republican congressman from that district took an earmark for these solar panels so he would sign off on the Democrat's common education bill? Yes, Jeff. That was stealing. Money stolen from the American people by the IRS, went to buy solar panels for bus stops in one congressman's district. As a representative of the American people, I know I will never be made whole for all the wealth that has been stolen from me through egregious taxation and federal money printing, but I am willing to accept these solar panels as partial concession."

Matt wasn't smiling when he said it, but the rest of the group burst into laughter. Wesley applauded and mimicked a cheering crowd.

The men mounted up and drove on to Louisville. They got off on 9th Street and decided that would be the western border of the operation. It was just as Eddie's sister had said. The glass was busted out of every single shop. There was no one around because there was nothing left to loot. It was an eerie scene, like something out of a sci-fi horror movie. They came to the first bus stop. Adam and Matt quickly jumped on top of the shelter and assessed the tools needed to remove it.

Matt looked at the connectors and said, "These are standard

MC4 solar connectors which just pop out. The screws have a special tamper-proof head. It's a Torx, a six-pointed star head. Adam do you have a driver for that?"

Adam answered, "I have a driver with multiple attachments, it has a Torx that will fit, but I only have one. I'll work on the screws while you disconnect the connectors."

JC said, "I'll start taking apart the lighted display." This held a very cheap 10 amp charge controller and a 200 watt inverter.

JC showed them to Matt, who said, "They only served to light the advertisement in the bus stop shelter, so they didn't need be high-powered. Nevertheless, if we can get several of these, it would put out a lot of juice. That battery is even more of a joke. It's only an 18 amp hour cell. On a positive note, it is 12 volt and several of them could easily be wired together to produce a higher capacity."

They quickly moved on to the next bus stop shelter. There was no one around, so two of the six guys working security got involved with removing the panels to make things go faster. It would have helped to have another Torx head driver to remove the screws.

When they got to the fourth bus stop, Adam said, "You guys are getting the hang of this. We are moving along pretty fast."

By 8:30 am they had cleared five bus stop shelters of the panels, inverters, cables, charge controllers and batteries. It was going to be an all day job. Adam reminded everyone, "Regardless of what we have at 4:30 p.m., we're going to pull out. I want to make sure we can drive through Lexington well before sundown. As far as cities go, Lexington is in about the best shape of any of them, but that isn't saying much."

The first part of the day went pretty smooth and no one bothered them. They saw a few solitary stragglers move by on occasion, but none were in a hurry to take on a well-armed militia. The team took turns eating lunch and using the screwdriver to remove the specialized star screws. At roughly 2:30 p.m., they stopped at a bus stop in front of an old building on Broadway. They came face-to-face with several Mexicans exiting the building. The

Mexicans looked as startled as the militia. The security team quickly raised their battle rifles to a ready position. The Mexicans lifted their hands as they came out of the building. The Mexicans had several lengths of copper pipe that they let fall to the ground as they raised their hands. The Mexicans slowly backed away and the security team slowly lowered their weapons without a word to one another.

Adam said, "Okay, that's a wrap. We're heading home."

JC said, "I don't think they are much of a threat. I think they are just scavenging like we are."

Adam replied, "Yeah, but we don't know who they are scavenging for. They may be getting that copper for a gang that uses it for building stills to make liquor. We could be seen by them as a threat. I don't want to take that chance. We're rolling out."

Everyone nodded and loaded up. The two trailers were fairly full and one truck bed was half full of cables and batteries. It was a good haul and well worth the trip; if they could get home safely.

They passed through Lexington at just after 3:30 in the afternoon. As they turned from I-64 east to I-75 south, two Kentucky Highway Patrol cars pulled in behind them with their lights on.

Adam picked up the walkie and alerted the other two drivers. "There is no way these guys are real cops. We weren't even speeding. They have no reason to pull us over. Besides that, have any of you seen a cop in the last month? If they were real cops, they would have something to do besides pull over random drivers. I think this is a robbery. Jeff, you're in the rear. See if you can tell how many are in the front car."

Jeff radioed back a few seconds later. "Looks like two. Lee says they are in uniform."

Adam said, "They would be. It wouldn't be believable if they weren't. I don't think they'll just let us keep rolling back to London. I think if we don't stop, they'll pick a target and start shooting at the tires. The best thing we can do is make a coordinated stand. Okay, let me think for a minute."

Everyone was quiet. No one wanted to do this, but there were no good options. There were only bad options and worse options.

A minute later Adam called back on the radio to everyone. "Jeff, slow down a bit and back them up off the trailers. We will jump up ahead and then pull over. When you get to us, pull over behind us slowly to give us time to get ready. When you pull over, cut your truck sideways. We'll all jump out and run up to your truck. If we have to engage, we'll have the truck for cover."

No one said a word.

Adam called back, "Is everyone on board with that plan?"

JC called back, "10-4."

Jeff called back, "Roger."

The two trucks pulling the trailers shot forward then pulled over. Jeff slowed down then pulled in sideways behind the trailers. Jeff and Lee both jumped out of the passenger side so they were behind the cover of the truck. Adam, Wes, Matt and the others were at the truck by the time the men in the Highway Patrol cruisers got out.

Adam called out, "We're on a mission from the Kentucky Liberty Militia. I am ordering you to stand down."

The first man yelled, "You men are all under arrest. Come out from behind the truck."

Adam said softly, "Everyone pick your target."

The militia members in the rear raised their rifles over the bed of the truck. Those in the front raised their rifles over the hood.

The man who appeared to be in charge raised his shot gun and yelled, "Drop your weapons!"

Adam called to his team, "Fire!"

The militia men fired. The front man in the Highway Patrol

uniform fired one shot then crumbled to the ground. The man near him fell before he pulled the trigger. The two in the back ran back toward their patrol car. One limped as he had been shot in the leg.

The militia ceased fire except for Adam who yelled, "Keep firing!"

The rest hesitated, but then resumed firing. The man who was limping fell to the ground after several shots hit him in the back. The other made it to the car. As soon as he pulled out from behind the other patrol car, Adam had a good shot at the man's head through the windshield. He took the shot. The windshield shattered, the driver slumped forward, and the vehicle rolled to a stop.

Adam kept his rifle sight on each downed man as he went to kick away their weapon and put two extra rounds in each of their heads as he passed.

The rest of the militia men watched as he moved with cold indifference. To the other men, it was frightening. To Adam, it was work. He took no pleasure in it, but this is the way he had been trained. Like it or not, this was the best thing for his men.

Adam's brother, Wesley, was the only one who had the courage to say what many of them were thinking. "What if they were real cops?"

Adam's reply was sharp and without remorse. "If they were real cops, they violated their duty by pulling over a convoy of trucks for no reason. They then violated their duty by not complying with a military order. Lastly, and most importantly, they violated their duty by trying to arrest us without cause. I'll bet you a weeks' worth of cow milking that those badges don't have matching photo ID's, but even if they do, they were rogue cops turned highway bandits, and that's worse that a regular highway bandit. Either way, there is no place for their kind in this world. We are at war, gentlemen."

Wesley hated milking cows. Not that he detested the chore itself, but he hated getting up so early. He was tempted to take the bet, but he knew Adam was probably right. Besides, he had no desire to go rifling through a fresh corpse's pockets.

Adam said, "Collect their weapons. Lee, Jeff, check the cars for ammo and anything useful. Wesley, Matt, pop a hole in their gas tanks and let's get that gas in our trucks."

Matt and Wes looked for some containers. Matt found a few empty water containers the men had used throughout the day. They saved their empty plastic bottles to refill and reuse. (Six months ago everything was disposable. Now, nothing was.) Wes slid under the first car and very slowly poked a small hole with his knife in the bottom of the gas tank. He was careful not to create a spark that could blow them all to kingdom come. Once the hole was there, the fuel began to trickle out. Matt bent down to hand Wes an empty bottle and take the full bottle. While Wes caught the fuel running out of the tank, Matt ran the filled bottles to the trucks.

When they finished, they had about eight gallons from the first car. Gary and Lee were already working on the fuel from the second tank when Matt and Wes finished. This process took longer than the other task of clearing the vehicles of useful supplies.

The cars yielded a couple boxes of 12 gauge shot gun ammo, a 50 round box of .40 caliber pistol ammo and two 50 round boxes of 9mm pistol ammo. When the weapons were collected, they had a .40 caliber S&W, a .45 caliber Colt 1911, a 9mm Springfield 1911 and a 9mm Sig Sauer. The shot guns also ran the gamut. There was a Remington 870, 2 Mossberg 500s, and a Winchester Pump. This wide variety of weaponry was certainly not consistent with real police officers. Adam checked for ID and badge wallets on the dead men.

The men loaded up and headed home. Matt felt the familiar calm as the adrenaline wore off. His body became tired and he fought sleep on the ride back. No one talked much. Matt wondered if the men had really been officers. Adam didn't volunteer the information and Matt didn't ask. He supposed Adam's reasoning had been sound. The men laying on the side of the road back there were criminals, regardless of what their job had been prior to the crash.

CHAPTER 41

"The Constitution is not an instrument for the government to restrain the people, it is an instrument for the people to restrain the government - lest it come to dominate our lives and interests."

-Patrick Henry

Howe convened his first meeting with his cabinet since his father's visit from New York.

Howe started by addressing the Attorney General of The United States Corey Erikson. "Corey, the DOJ needs to prosecute these traitors from the House and the Senate. As you know, we can hold them indefinitely and without filing charges under the 2012 NDAA indefinite detention clause, but I want the American people to know what these men are guilty of. They have determined to side with the insurrectionists by moving to have me impeached for simply acting expeditiously in a time of war. We have to do whatever it takes to hold this country together."

Howe smiled as he paused to think. His smile turned into a suppressed chuckle.

"Is something funny, Mr. President?" Erikson asked.

"It just struck me," Howe replied. "All of the establishment Republicans that we detained today under the indefinite detention clause voted against the Smith-Amash Amendment."

The Smith-Amash Amendment was legislation introduced years ago by Congressman Adam Smith and Congressman Justin Amash to nullify the indefinite detention of American citizens under the National Defense Authorization Act. The NDAA was an annual spending bill passed every year to approve military spending for the year. The indefinite detention clause had been stuffed in the back door of the spending bill. Smith and Amash had fought to have the clause banned, but most Democrats and establishment Republicans had shot down the effort.

Anthony Howe continued addressing all of his cabinet. "We're facing two major challenges right now. Paul Randall has poisoned the minds of our military and we are seeing mass desertions. The second major issue is resource scarcity. We are having trouble procuring the amount of commodities we need to sustain the military and welfare recipients. The best solution seems to be to allocate three-quarters of the resources to the military. If people are starving, they will be more likely to join the military. I have also devised a plan that will pay additional family benefits to those serving in the military so they won't just run out after their belly get full. This will be a way for families to still receive assistance if one member joins DHS.

"We are going to have to implement this right away, so it is up to you, Jared, to make sure we present this to the press as an opportunity and not a punishment. Scott, would you like to explain what we have come up with to deter desertion?"

"Yes, Mr. President," the Secretary of Defense said. "DARPA has developed a tracking chip that is completely free from GPS. This ensures the satellite feeds can't be tampered with or disabled by those wishing to desert. The chip is encapsulated in a mercury envelope. The mercury acts as an antenna to ensure soldiers are still traceable in deep subterranean structures and deters tampering. If the chip is tampered with, the mercury is released into the blood stream. Mercury poisoning is a horrific death."

"Thank you, Scott." The President was pleased. "We will be rolling out the new recruitment campaign on Monday. New recruits will be joining the DHS rather than the traditional branches of the armed forces. I feel the recruits will complete training faster through DHS and the agency is not so ingrained with this culture of patriotism. That's a big part of the problem we're having with the other branches. They think it's unpatriotic to detain or fire on American citizens. A terrorist is a terrorist, regardless of where he was born. The existing armed forces branches will be subordinate to the DHS, at least throughout this civil conflict.

"About the chip, it's not entirely negative. It has a lot of positive elements built in to it. We're able to connect it to the NSA database in Utah. With that amount of computing power, we'll be able to keep medical records, bank account information, driver's license information, education documents, and deeds to property and automobiles. It will be able to store all of the data that we have to keep track of these days. This will revolutionize information. We'll have the ability to have all of our important information with us twenty-four hours a day. Imagine having your credit card, your college degree, prescriptions, allergies and all of your online authentication codes embedded in your hand. DARPA has already licensed Lockheed Martin to produce keyless entry systems for all DHS and military structures and vehicles that will work with the chip. The public will love it.

"Obviously, we won't be promoting the fact that it is enveloped in mercury. It's completely safe unless it's tampered with or in the instance that a soldier goes AWOL. If that happens, we can remotely trigger the mercury to be released into the blood stream. As long as you're not doing anything wrong, you have nothing to worry about.

"People who receive government benefits will be transitioning to payments that will utilize the chip in the next few months when the new currency units are finalized. This will prevent the misuse of government benefits like we have seen in the past. This chip is going to cut out everything from EBT benefits being traded for drugs to tax evasion.

"We will make the chip available to the rest of the public on a voluntary basis by the end of the year. To instill a sense of trust with the public and to help spread hope in a time of despair, I would like all of you to take the chip at a press conference on Friday. The new technology will give Americans something to focus on besides the internal conflict."

Everyone nodded their heads in agreement. No one looked particularly thrilled to have a chip with a mercury kill switch embedded into their bodies, but Howe did not tolerate dissent. Many of them sitting in this room had often used the saying "If you're not doing anything wrong, you have nothing to worry about." Now, the shoe was on the other foot and it was quite a poor fit.

CHAPTER 42

"None but an armed nation can dispense with a standing army. To keep ours armed and disciplined is therefore at all times important."

-Thomas Jefferson

Paul Randall's head security officer said, "We're ready when you are, sir."

No one called him anything more than "sir." While Paul had been elected as Commander in Chief of the Coalition military forces, no one called him Mr. President. There was a formal agreement between the militaries of the individual Coalition states to co-labor in this mutual objective of resisting Anthony Howe. Beyond that, there was nothing declaring the Coalition, as a whole, a new government entity. The States saw themselves as individually sovereign and committed to each other as the Constitution prescribed.

"Give me five minutes, First Lieutenant," Randall replied.

Paul grabbed his shoulder bag and walked into the kitchen where Kimberly sat looking out into the field behind their big Texas home.

"I'll see you when I see you." He kissed her forehead.

She pulled him close and hugged him.

"Say you'll be home by tonight," She pleaded.

Paul stroked her cheek with his thumb. "I'll try, but I can't make any promises. We have a lot of details to get ironed out on this thing. A lot of men will be risking if not sacrificing their lives on this engagement. I owe it to them to not rush through the planning. You understand don't you?"

Kimberly sighed. "Yes, I understand."

It pained Paul to leave her alone. He knew she was used to him being gone a lot. During the last months of the presidential campaign, they hardly saw each other. The twins had always been there when Paul was running for office. Now Ryan was in the military and Robert was dead. The security team would be at the house with her, but there would be no family around.

Paul knew she was still grieving the loss of their son. This wasn't a good time to be alone. "You know I would take you with me but security says it is too risky," He said.

Kimberly smiled to let him know it was okay, but didn't say anything.

Paul's transport team drove two black SUVs with tinted, bullet resistant glass. The doors were reinforced with ballistic plates to make them more impervious to an attack. Sonny was ready to go and waiting in one of the vehicles when Paul arrived.

The two vehicles looked identical and switched back and forth from the lead position on the road to Governor Jacobs's ranch. Sonny sat silently and looked out at the landscape as it raced by. Paul thumbed through his Bible on the way. He needed all the divine wisdom he could get. Over the next several hours, he, Jacobs and Jefferson would be planning the raid to take over Minot Air Force Base in North Dakota.

When they arrived, Larry came out on the porch to greet them.

"Paul, Sonny, come on in." The salutation was more subdued

than Larry's typical welcome. These men were here to discuss a heavy subject and Larry's somber greeting reflected the weight of the topic.

On the way to his study, Larry said, "General Jefferson already has the maps and photos hung on the walls."

Arriving at the study, the men sat down and got right to business.

General Allen Jefferson began, "I have a few thoughts on the general direction of the planning. If you men have no objections, I'll lay that out first and then open up to your recommendations. Sonny, you are included in that invitation. Your counsel is respected by all of us."

"Thank you, General," Sonny said.

Jacobs and Randall gave affirmative nods.

Jefferson pointed to the map. "The topography of the area surrounding Minot supports a preliminary air strike to soften up the target before we go in with troops. Because there are no mountains between Minot and the border, we can fly F-22s in at about 300 feet. That will put them overtop of most any water tower or grain silos in the area. We can map out a path around any wind turbines taller than 150 feet. The F-22 Raptor is already a stealth fighter; this altitude reduces the odds of getting picked up by Minot's radar even more. There are a few little foot hills just past Tioga and these hills right before Minot." Jefferson pointed to the rings on the topography map as he spoke.

He switched to an aerial view of Minot Air Force Base that showed several massive B-52 bombers sitting on the tarmac as he continued to lay out his plan. "I recommend we go in and eliminate the B-52s and light up all of the hangars on the base. We'll avoid the nuclear missile silos. Howe won't launch the ICBM's. Even he respects mutually assured destruction. We'll fly multiple sorties and take out the runways next. This will keep them busy until we can get ground troops in there. We'll send the personnel transports across the border prior to the air assault."

Jacobs pointed at the first map "Can we preposition some troops in Williston, North Dakota? Maybe we could camouflage them as oil field workers. It would keep us from having a massive buildup on the border."

Jefferson shook his head. "No, Howe has troops in Williston. We're going to have to deal with them sooner or later, so I suggest we hit them on the way to Minot. By the time Howe can respond to the call from Williston, we'll already have ground troops in Minot."

Sonny asked, "Are there a lot of troops in Williston?"

"No," Jefferson answered. "It's a bit larger than a normal border patrol. Howe is protecting his interest in the Bakken oil fields. Williston has a lot of infrastructure for drilling and moving oil."

Paul said, "An ounce of prevention could have avoided all of this if the Dakotas would have jumped on board at the beginning."

"Yes," Larry agreed, "but better late than never. Minot is a big deal. Strategically, it's a game changer."

Paul thought for a moment then said, "You're right, Larry. I'm glad they came around."

Larry asked, "How are we going to position jets up there? We don't have much to work with in the Northwest."

Jefferson said, "We'll send the Raptors we have sitting in Corpus Christi to Malmstrom. We can launch the attack from there."

Paul asked, "Are those the jets the Oath Keepers from Holman Air Force Base brought with them when they decided to join the Coalition?"

"That would be them." Jefferson smiled.

The men continued their planning well into the early morning hours. Paul knew he was not going to be home and felt bad about leaving Kimberly alone overnight.

CHAPTER 43

"For lack of guidance a nation falls, but many advisers make victory sure."

-Proverbs 11:14

All of the men who had gone on the scavenging run to Louisville got a few of the solar panels. Matt helped everyone to get their panels set up as he had some experience with them. Matt added his panels to his existing setup on his metal work shed. The shed was exposed to more direct sun than his house. He connected a couple of the small batteries together in parallel to increase the capacity of the overall system.

On Thursday afternoon, Matt, Adam and Wesley took several panels up to Lt. Joe's cabin. His cabin was the communication hub for the Eastern Kentucky Liberty Militia and the point of contact for the surrounding militias. It was imperative that his ham radio have an alternate power source.

Commander Franklin Johnson was at Lt. Joe's when they arrived.

"Hey, fellas," Franklin said when they pulled into the drive.

"How's it going?" Adam asked as he shook Franklin's hand.

Johnson told the men, "Sounds like the Coalition is about to do something big up north."

"Like what?" Wes asked.

"Not sure," Franklin said. "The details are on a need-to-know basis. All we need to know is that we need to be on high alert in case of a retaliatory strike from Howe."

Matt said, "So we can assume it is something big enough to ruin Howe's breakfast. I wonder if they are going to try to evict the federal forces from the Dakotas. They have to address that issue sooner or later."

Johnson said, "We'll know soon enough. We are getting Franklin set up with some digital communication software. The protocol is called PSK-31. It allows us to send text messages over the ham radio. The main benefit is that once it is in digital format, it's very easy to encrypt. The secondary benefit is that it can transmit over a much longer distance using less power."

"Sounds complicated," Matt said.

"Not to use," Johnson said. "There is a free program that you can download from the internet called FLDIGI. Once the program is on your computer or laptop, you just type in the message and it will send out the signal in digital through your speaker. You can just hold your mic up to the speaker and it will transmit. Of course we have some cables to connect directly to the ham radio, but you could do it without them. You could even use it with regular walkie-talkies. You could broadcast the message with one walkie and hold the receiving walkie up to the mic of another laptop running FLDIGI and converse over longer distances than voice."

Adam added, "So we could use a book cypher for that since it uses written messages?"

"Absolutely," Franklin answered. "A book cypher is low tech, but very effective. Here is a flash drive with the FLDIGI program, so you guys can get it installed on all your computers. Make sure every

TEXT MESSAGE OVER HAM RADIO

squad has it installed on a tablet or some portable device that you can take in the field. Where did you guys get all of the solar panels?"

Adam rolled his eyes. "That's a long story, why don't we go in and I'll tell you all about it."

Once inside, everyone greeted Lt. Joe. They sat down in Joe's living room as Adam told the story of the run to Louisville. Lt. Joe agreed that Adam had made the right call on the way home. Franklin didn't question him as he had not been there and could not say what he would've done in the situation.

After the adventure briefing, everyone headed outside to get the solar array set up on Lt. Joe's roof.

"Thank you, boys," Lt. Joe said. "This is real nice. This will power the system just fine if there is ever an outage. No use letting the power go to waste in the meantime, though. I'll keep my icebox running on it for now."

Adam asked Joe, "Would you mind if we cache the firearms we took from the road bandits in your backwoods?"

"That'd be just fine, Adam," Joe said. "As long as I know where they are in case I ever need them."

Adam and the rest of the men worked together to get the weapons and ammo airtight and waterproof. They oiled and sealed the guns in Food Saver vacuum bags then sealed them in twelve-inch PVC pipe with end caps. Finally, they headed out to the woods to bury them several hundred yards from Joe's cabin.

CHAPTER 44

"Precious in the sight of the LORD is the death of his saints."

-Psalm 116:15

Pastor John Robinson kissed his wife goodbye and went to meet up with Albert Rust and the other militia men who had been assigned to Operation Rocket's Red Glare.

"Pastor!" Rust said with surprise. "What are you doing?"

"I am going with you, Albert," Robinson replied.

"No, you're not. I don't mean to usurp your authority, but the people need you here to head up security," Albert replied.

Trey Dayton and several others had left Young Field to defend the southern Idaho border. Two-thirds of those who remained at Young Field would be heading to Minot, South Dakota, to participate in the Coalition effort to take command of Minot Air Force Base. Operation Rocket's Red Glare was as close to a secret mission as they could get. The only men who were going on the mission were established militia, National Guard and Coalition Military. Newcomers were not part of the assault, both because of their lack of training and to reduce the odds of a spy getting a hold of intelligence.

Robinson said, "I stood in the pulpit preaching fire and brimstone against the government in the years leading up to this conflict Albert. I won't miss it for the world.

"These folks will be fine. We have plenty of security personnel staying behind. The southern border is very well secured. There is little risk of a second attack on Young Field. Especially while we are gone. I think Howe is going to have bigger fish to fry after he hears from us in Minot."

"You're a grown man. I guess you can make your own decisions," Rust said.

They jumped into Albert's jeep and headed out in front of the militia convoy. Their first stop was to be in Kalispell, Montana, to meet up with two other militia battalions. Today would be a slow steady roll over the 500 miles from Young Field to Kalispell. The two men had a lot of time to consider the outcome of the operation as they drove through the mountainous terrain between Boise and Kalispell.

Once in Kalispell, they were led to a staging area outside of town. The two local militia groups they joined were staying in a nearby farmer's field.

Albert said, "It's nearly dark, we better get these tents up right away."

That taken care of, they headed to the chow line.

Pastor John said, "The folks from Kalispell are very supportive of the militia. That fellow over there told me church groups and neighborhoods had organized to bring out this food."

Albert and Pastor John sat down to eat with some of the other men from their group. The local folks had contributed a potluck dinner.

Albert said, "I'm going to try shepherd's pie, chicken pot pie, and a bit of lasagna. I don't want to be a pig, but everything looks so good."

Pastor John agreed. "I know, I want to try everything, but I am going to save a little room. The dessert table has some pies that look very interesting."

The next morning they were up early and the convoy moved out toward Malmstrom Air Force Base.

Albert commented, "This will be a short drive compared to the journey we made yesterday."

When they arrived at Malmstrom, several high-ranking military officers laid out the plans for the individual battalions; both those of the state militaries and militia. They were all on the same team for this operation. With the combined forces of the militia, National Guardsmen and other state military personnel, this was a real army. Each battalion was given a grand overview of the objective and a detailed plan of the exact timing and mission objectives they were to achieve.

After the overview, the men broke for dinner. Pastor John said "These aren't bad for MRE's. They don't compare to what we ate in Kalispell, but they're probably on the top of the list for MREs."

Albert said, "I'm grateful for what we have, but this is nothing like what we ate in Kalispell. On the upside, we get to sleep in the empty hangars tonight. Winter may be over, but that wind can pull the heat right out of you. They have large space heaters inside which should keep the hangars fairly warm."

After dinner they were assigned to their space in the hangar. Pastor John said, "These cots are going to be a lot better than sleeping on the ground. I have to say they are pretty big; it's a perfect fit for my sleeping bag. I think the generals have put together a solid plan. What do you think about it?"

"I believe it'll work, Pastor." Albert Rust agreed. "It sounded like General Allen Jefferson may have devised it. It utilizes all the military resources we have up here."

"Too bad we'll lose those B-52s in the air raid," Pastor John said. "They could've come in handy."

Rust said, "They could've, but if they get airborne before we take the base, then we would have a real problem."

"I hope I can live up to the honor we've been given in this battle, Albert," the pastor said.

"You've already been tried in battle, sir." Albert patted the pastor on the back.

The men went right to sleep. They knew the next night would be full of apprehension about the coming engagement.

The next morning, the convoys rolled out in staggered groups toward the border. Everyone had a set place to stop somewhere in between Wolfe Point and ten miles from the North Dakota border. Wolfe Point was about fifty miles from North Dakota. This strategy spaced the camps out over a forty mile stretch of US Route 2. It made the camps harder to spot and reduced the chance of them all being taken out at once if they were discovered while approaching the border.

Pastor John and Albert woke early the next morning and rolled out.

"We don't have much driving today," Albert said. "Our camp is about fifteen miles from the border. No fires are permitted and tents have to be in earth tones."

Pastor John grinned. "Mine was blue, so one of the fellows at the base gave me one of those old military tents. Otherwise, I would have had to sleep in the truck."

Albert said, "It's supposed to get down in the 40s tonight, so make sure you sleep with lots of layers."

When they arrived at the camp, Albert pulled his Jeep under a thick cover of trees several hundred feet from the road. That night they ate MREs and then prayed for God's blessing on the mission. Several other men from Young Field joined them as they prayed. Pastor John prayed a special prayer of protection over each man. God's peace came over the men and they slept much better than they expected.

The next morning, the advance team shot by the roadside camp. Several hundred Coalition State military soldiers went in hard and fast to eliminate the federal border guards and secure the town of Williston, North Dakota.

Williston was easily taken and the town's people were very happy to help locate federal officers for elimination by Coalition troops. Most of the inhabitants of Williston had come from somewhere else to work in the oil fields. When Howe partially nationalized the oil fields, they were forced to accept whatever form of payment Howe decided was fair. Worse than that, they had been conscripted to stay and work the oil fields. They were not allowed to return to the towns from which they had originally come.

A few militia men stayed behind in Williston to keep it secure and watch out for other federal troops crawling out of the woodwork. No doubt at this point, the federal troops had radioed for backup and the posse was on the way. The clock was ticking now. Everyone barreled down US Route 2 at breakneck speed.

It was about 140 miles from Williston to the base, but the first wave of soldiers left Williston as the advance team was killing off the federal troops in the town.

Pastor John looked at Albert's speedometer. "115 miles per hour. We can make good time on this long straight road. We just left 30 minutes ago and we are already halfway there."

They heard a sonic boom to the left and saw the F-22 Raptors zooming over the tree tops.

"Wow!" Pastor John exclaimed. "I've never seen anything like that in my life."

"How fast do you think they are going?" Albert asked.

"I don't have any idea. 500 knots, maybe 600." The pastor replied. "I couldn't even see it. It was just a blur."

Minutes later, they heard muted booms and saw clouds of smoke rising over the horizon.

Just before they arrived at the base, another sortie of F-22 Raptors caused a sonic boom as they passed directly over their heads. The closer explosions sent up flashes of brilliant light and bloodcurdling rumble.

Pastor John commented, "I could feel that explosion from my teeth to my stomach."

Their squad finally arrived at Minot Air Force Base. Black smoke filled the air.

Albert said, "The smell of burning jet fuel makes it hard to breathe. It looks like the element of surprise paid off big time. I don't see any resistance at the main gate. We should be able to roll straight through the base."

Albert was the team leader for their squad. He called out over the radio, "This is the building they were supposed to search. It was marked as an administrative building, but I think it may be more than that. Those doors look pretty heavy duty. Everybody stay sharp. I don't know what we're walking into."

The team pulled straight up to the doors and jumped out of their vehicles.

Albert gave instructions over the radio. "The door is locked. We are going to blow it. Everybody take cover."

Albert proceeded to place the explosive charge on the lock. As soon as he detonated the explosion, he called, "Go! Go! Go!"

The team was through the door before the smoke cleared. Albert called out, "Alpha, go left, Charlie squad, you take the right corridor. Bravo, we are taking the center hall."

They meticulously cleared each room. As they approached the end of the hall, automatic machine-gun fire began to rain down on them. They took up positions in the doorways of other rooms in the hall. They exchanged fire with the hostiles at the end of the hall for several minutes.

Albert called for help over the radio. "We are pinned down in the center hallway of building 2-G. Repeat! Coalition forces are pinned down in the center hall of building 2-Golf. We need assistance to take this building."

"We're right beside you." The radio came back. "Our building was a residential building. We can send 20 of our guys to you. Be there in 5 minutes. Hang tight."

Pastor John, Albert and their team continued to lay down suppressive fire, but they could not get a clear shot.

Minutes later, they heard gunfire come from behind. The backup team was shooting into the enemy from the outside of the building.

The other team that came to assist called over the radio. "Two hostiles are down and the others have retreated into the room they were firing from."

"Roger," Albert called back. "We'll enter the room and start clearing. Follow us in and back us up."

Albert led the team to the doorway. They opened the door and poured into the room. Gunfire erupted from several directions. The team scrambled for cover.

Pastor John found cover behind a row of crates. The room they entered was a warehouse space behind the administrative offices. Pastor John found a small space in between the crates and started to scan for a target. He saw a muzzle flash come from behind a wooden crate.

He prayed, "God make me accurate." He then made his best estimate of where the center of mass would be behind the crates and took a single shoot. The man fell from behind the crate and his weapon went skidding across the floor.

Unfortunately, Pastor Johns muzzle flash had broadcast his position. He was drawing fire from two different assailants. Albert Rust took the opportunity to stand up from his cover and take a shot. He took out one of the men shooting at the pastor, but the bullet from another hostile found its path to Albert's head. He fell silent. Instantly, without pain or suffering, Albert was transported from this life to eternal glory.

Pastor John did not hear nor see Albert get shot, but he felt it in his spirit when he fell. Pastor John thought to himself the words Albert must be hearing from the lips of the King at that moment, "Well done, good and faithful servant." A single tear trickled down the pastor's cheek.

Pastor John went back to the crack between the crates. Three hostiles ran out from behind their cover toward the positions being held by the pastor and his team. The pastor took a shot as did others from his team. The three men were taken down, but so were two more of Pastor John's team members.

A grenade flew from the other side of the room and landed right by another one of the Coalition force members, taking him out as well.

The assisting Coalition team pushed into the back room. They were a well-trained Special Forces team.

As Pastor John saw the effectiveness of the team he thought, *It's a shame that they had not been assigned to take this building. The casualties would have been much lower. Our team did very well, but we're not trained for this sort of thing.*

The team turned out to be Navy SEALS. They cleared the rest of the hostiles in seconds. When the smoke cleared, it was obvious that the room was a weapons cache. This building had been labeled as offices which was the reason it had been assigned to militia instead of the regular military. It turned out to be a stash of Hellfire, Maverick, and Harpoon Air to Ground Missiles.

One of the SEALs explained to Pastor John, "These are missiles that would typically be fired from a jet or a chopper and not the standard stockpile that would be dropped from the B-52s stationed at Minot. The only reason they would have been here is that Howe must have been planning to launch and attack from this position."

Pastor John was glad that Albert had not died in vain. He said to the SEAL "So this was an important building to take."

"Very important," The man replied.

The base was secured and the prisoners were held on the base. Many of them would be interviewed over the coming days to gather intelligence.

Pastor John and the other survivors from his team collected Albert's body and the bodies of the other men from Young Field and headed back. It would be a long, sad drive home.

CHAPTER 45

"The alien who lives among you will rise above you higher and higher, but you will sink lower and lower. He will lend to you, but you will not lend to him. He will be the head, but you will be the tail. All these curses will come upon you. They will pursue you and overtake you until you are destroyed, because you did not obey the LORD your God and observe the commands and decrees he gave you."

-Deuteronomy 28:43-45

President Anthony Howe sat with the Joint Chiefs, Secretary of Homeland Security Rosa Ortiz and Secretary of Defense Scott Hale.

"The bad news, gentlemen," Howe said, "is that Minot Air Force Base was to be our launch site to invade the Northwest Coalition. We are also losing control of the Bakken oil field. We really needed those resources. I am less concerned with the loss of the missile silos as neither party wants to be the guy who pushes the button and turns the entire continent into a radioactive wasteland.

"Of course, the public doesn't know that, and we can certainly use the fear of a nuclear attack from the Coalition to justify all of our future actions against the Coalition States. What we lost in the assault can quickly be converted into political capital both for the opinions of the American people and those of the international community. Our national sovereignty has been attacked and the UN will sign off on any action we take.

"We have to secure the loose cannon states that have not taken sides yet. I think we all know by now that 'neutral' means 'future Coalition state.' We need to get a thick presence of DHS troops in all the towns and cities of the so-called neutral states. I want DHS agents overseeing every state and local law enforcement agency in those states. We can't afford to have disloyal people working in those jobs. The towns where the police are being paid by the residents through barter networks need to have that system replaced. If law enforcement are paid by the people, they'll get the idea that they work for the people. They need to know they work for us, so they need to be compensated by us.

"Start with West Virginia. I hear entirely too much about militia activity in that state. It is practically our own backyard. Anyone caught displaying any militia, revolutionary or Coalition insignias are to be sent straight to a work camp. In West Virginia, I want the DHS and Department of Energy to begin to convert the FEMA camps into work programs that mine for coal. We need every bit of energy we can get.

"Next, we need to take the southern states of Louisiana, Mississippi, Alabama, and Georgia. Convert all the relief camps and prison camps into food production work camps in those states.

"I don't think Florida is worth dealing with right now. The population far outweighs the agricultural production in Florida. We'll put up a fence from the northern suburbs of Jacksonville to Apalachee Bay. The rest of the panhandle can be annexed by Georgia. There is enough militia activity down there to declare it a hostile territory. That will protect us from political fallout from the decision. 90% of the population will die off in a couple of years without support from the rest of the country. Two years from now, we will be in a much better position to go in and take over after we have dealt with the Coalition. Mother Nature will take care of most of the dirty work for us while we wait.

"New Hampshire is another rabble-rouser. Fortunately for us, they're completely isolated from the rest of the rebellious states. Because of New Hampshire's location in the heart of our Northeastern stronghold, we cannot afford to have them spreading this anti-government cancer. I want to fence off the entire state and turn it into a work camp. Start the fence west of I-95. That will allow commerce to flow from Maine to the lower states. Make sure the areas of the state east of I-95 are very well patrolled. At the first sign of disrespect for a federal officer from a resident east of the fence, immediately process them to the work camp.

"We have to do all of this with an iron fist. The people are going to learn that they cannot just declare themselves free from their federal obligations. They will respect this government or they will be sent to a work camp. If they can't get along in the work camps, we'll execute them."

Secretary of Homeland Defense Rosa Ortiz voiced her concern. "Mr. President, you are talking about thousands of miles of fence."

"It's fence, Rosa!" Howe yelled. "It is a metal pole in the ground with some metal wire. I'm not asking you to build the Great Wall of China. The relief camps across the nation are full of able-bodied laborers. Order the materials from wherever you need to get them. We are in a global depression, I am sure someone will be willing to sell us some material to build a fence.

"All of you need to start thinking outside of the box about how to get things done. I don't want excuses, I want action. We have plenty of resources. We have military equipment. We still have the country's gold reserves in the New York Federal Reserve.

"That reminds me, as soon as we lock down West Virginia, I want to launch an invasion to occupy Kentucky. It's relatively vulnerable as it only has its southern border that it can rely on for assistance. I want to take back Fort Knox so we will also have that gold reserve. Kentucky is a key state strategically for us to have the ability to break up the Southern Coalition.

Any more questions or excuses?" Howe glared at each person around the table.

No one said a word. They simply nodded and prepared to get out of the meeting room as quick as possible.

"Good," Howe said. "Let's get to work."

Minutes later, Howe's phone buzzed.

It was California Congressman Juan Marcos. Marcos had run against Howe and Paul Randall in the previous election. Marcos was a Republican, but had not proved to be a troublemaker… yet.

Howe looked at his phone. "I wonder why he would be calling me. I'm in no mood to be putting up with any more dissenters. There is plenty of room in one of our black site political prisons if Marcos feels the need to rock the boat."

"Juan," The President answered. "It has been a while since we spoke."

"Yes, Mr. President," Marcos replied. "We have not spoken since I called to congratulate you on your presidential victory."

Howe liked the tone in Marcos' voice. It wasn't apparently disrespectful.

"What can I do for you, Juan?" the President asked.

Marcos said, "The California State legislature has asked me to try to broker an agreement between the State of California, the White House and a Chinese company called Hangyun Hong.

"Hangyun is a globally integrated conglomerate that is willing to donate vast amounts of relief to California in exchange for control of the Ports of Los Angeles, San Diego and San Francisco.

"The breakdown in the American economy is hurting the entire country of China. The lack of security in the ports make it difficult for them to do business in the west. They are offering to bring in their own security that will both secure their interest and lock down those major ports from outside terrorist threats to the United States. This deal will allow them to branch out to do more business with Canada as well as Central and South America.

"For California, it will mean much needed nutritional aid as well as other needed forms of aid. They have pledged to assist in getting our infrastructure back up and running and to do everything they can to get California back on line economically.

"This would greatly reduce the burden to Washington, D.C. as you would no longer be obligated to provide nutritional supplements to the state. DHS would have resources freed up as they would no longer have to keep the ports secure. I don't have to tell you that those ports are currently shut down because of the riots and instability. The Port of Los Angeles isn't even functional in its present condition. It is essentially a burned-out shell. Everything has been looted from all of the containers in L.A., and people are living in the containers. It looks like a scene from a movie.

"As I see it sir, we have nothing to lose."

Anthony Howe sat quietly for a moment after Congressman Marcos laid out his case. Howe knew it was a threat to the sovereignty of the country, but California was a wasteland right now anyway. This deal would keep it out of the hands of the Coalition and signal to the international community that Howe was a team player.

Howe didn't need to look into Hangyun Hong to find out if it was a shell corporation operated by the Chinese government. He just assumed it was. He had never heard of them before, and if they were a company large enough to do everything Marcos was claiming, he would have heard of them. Even if, by chance, they weren't a shell corporation, any international company this big based in China would have the state as a partner.

After pondering his response, Howe said, "Send over the specifics of the deal. It sounds like something we could work on. I want to have Corey Ericson over at Justice comb through it. You can tell the representative from Hangyun that we will consider the offer very carefully. Thank them for their generosity and casually mention that there will likely be a licensing fee from the Federal Government that will need to be paid in gold due to the current instability of the currencies market. Of course we can structure the fee to be set for twenty years before it can be increased."

Congressman Marcos and President Howe finished their conversation.

Howe was happy to have someone from the other side of the aisle treating him with respect. With all of the recent house cleaning that had been done in Washington, there was a seat at the table for a Republican who knew how to play ball.

For Howe personally, having someone like Marcos involved in the affairs of the country would show the public that he wasn't the socialist tyrant the alternative media tried to make him out to be.

CHAPTER 46

" 'For I was hungry and you gave me something to eat, I was thirsty and you gave me something to drink, I was a stranger and you invited me in, I needed clothes and you clothed me, I was sick and you looked after me, I was in prison and you came to visit me. Then the righteous will answer him, 'Lord, when did we see you hungry and feed you, or thirsty and give you something to drink? When did we see you a stranger and invite you in, or needing clothes and clothe you? When did we see you sick or in prison and go to visit you?' The King will reply, 'I tell you the truth, whatever you did for one of the least of these brothers of mine, you did for me.'"

-Matthew 25: 35-40

Matt and Karen were busy getting their garden planted. They had several small seed trays that they germinated in the covered back porch area of the farmhouse. The mountain nights had the potential for frost until the middle of April. They had to get a head start with the seedlings indoors because the growing season was short.

Matt said to Karen, "If we can get the lettuce, cabbage, corn, peas, potatoes and tomatoes in the ground this week, we'll be doing great."

Karen said, "I think we can handle that. This is going to be a big garden plot. If we have even a mediocre year, it should be plenty to sustain us until next year with a little left over to barter with."

Matt heard Adam's truck pulling up and went to meet him.

"Hey, Cousin!" He yelled.

"How y'all doin'?" Adam asked.

Matt smiled. "Very good. Karen is happy that winter is finally over. I feel less anxious since I can get out and start getting some crops in the ground. I'm finished with your tiller. It helped a lot. I could've never completed all that by hand."

Adam said, "Hopefully that foal will be born soon and you'll be able to use a plow in a couple of years. Smokey is getting big. It shouldn't be too much longer before she gives birth."

Matt said, "That's exciting."

Adam had a solemn look on his face and Matt knew he wasn't here to talk about gardening and horses.

"So, what's up?" Matt asked.

Adam answered, "I spoke with Franklin this morning. We're getting hit with a wave of militia and refugees from West Virginia.

DHS are moving into the state in force. They have completely locked down Huntington. It looks like something from the holocaust from what the refugees are saying.

"I don't know what that means for us, but it ain't good. The Kentucky National Guard is setting up a militia camp just across the river from Huntington. I-64 runs right across the river from Huntington to Kentucky. If Howe was going to invade Kentucky, it would probably be through there.

"They are trying to incorporate the refugees into the militia camp up there, but there are too many and they just can't handle it. Franklin told them we would take twenty or so.

"I hate to impose, but do you think you could give up your extra bedroom to a couple? Keep in mind, it could have just as easily been us hoping our state would do the right thing. If the Kentucky legislature would have dragged its heels the way West Virginia did, we might be refugees somewhere. It ain't over, either. We could still end up being overrun and having to bug out."

Matt sat silent for a moment. He just realized how selfish he was as he hesitated and tried to think his way out of it. There was the obvious inconvenience of having to share. That side of it was pure selfishness. But there was also the issue of not trusting people. Many lesson over the years had taught him not to trust everyone he met. As he counted the times he had been let down after giving folks the benefit of the doubt, he quickly ran out of fingers. As he thought deeper, he soon ran out of toes as well.

Matt finally answered, "I have to talk to Karen. Who are these people? Are they militia? How do we know they aren't DHS spies?"

Adam replied, "The two that would be staying with you is a young couple, early 20's, from West Virginia. Franklin has already prescreened the twenty people he is accepting from up there. They are all staying out at Lt. Joe's. He is letting them all use his facilities and they're sleeping in tents.

"This young man is going on patrol with us next week. I'll put him with you and Gary for the week. If you get along with him, that'll be great. If not, we'll find them somewhere else to go."

Finally, Matt said, "Okay. If Karen approves and he checks out during patrol, I'll give it a shot. What else do you know about this invasion? Who are the refugees? Are they all able to volunteer for the militia?"

Adam answered, "About the refugees, they range anywhere from well-armed, well-trained militia, to single moms with two or three kids who have nothing more than a backpack, to elderly people. It's a cross section of society. The thing they all have in common is that they would rather die free here in Kentucky than live under oppression in West Virginia.

"About the invasion, it happened all of a sudden. Franklin says thousands of DHS agents in armored vehicles are flooding into the ports by ship in Savannah and Mobile. Sounds like Howe is going to choose for the states who had trouble making up their minds. He can't afford to lose any more oil refineries after North Dakota sided with the Coalition. If he can lock down the Gulf coasts of Louisiana, Mississippi and Alabama, he can get his filthy little fingers on the oil coming out of the Gulf of Mexico.

"The refugees said the West Virginia Militia tried fighting the first wave of DHS, but they were outnumbered and under-equipped. The West Virginia National Guard wouldn't lift a finger. Franklin says the National Guard is probably under federal command at this point.

"A lot of the militia are unaccounted for according to the ones who got out. They don't know if they have been captured or if they are staying behind on purpose to try and fight an insurgency battle. At this point, there is no getting across the border. DHS has them all locked down. I suppose we'll be having staring contests with DHS at our checkpoint. They're setting up hard roadblocks all along the Virginia border as well.

"The only good news is some intelligence we got from a couple veterans. They said the DHS agents look like they're made up of mostly nineteen and twenty year old kids. They said they're undisciplined and appear to have little or no training. I bet they've all been recruited in the last month or two. If you have to fight against somebody, these are the type of people you want to fight. They're not physically nor mentally ready for a fight and their heart is not in it. Even if they outnumber us ten-to-one, we can whip 'em.'"

Matt said, "They probably all signed up after Howe cut the assistance programs. He gave them the choice of fight or starve. The enslavement of the poor through entitlements is paying off quite well for the left, isn't it?"

Adam chuckled. "Yes, it is. All of a sudden free isn't so free. Well, I'm going to head home. I'll let you get back to your garden. Might be nice to have a young buck around to do some of this heavy farm work. Make sure you talk it over with Karen."

"I will." Matt waved to his cousin.

Matt went back to the garden where Karen was still working. He explained the situation. She had a big generous heart, but she also had enough bad experiences with people to not trust them further than she could spit. Matt explained that he would check the young man out during the patrol.

"What about the girl?" Karen asked, "How will we know if she's going to be a good fit?"

"I don't know," Matt answered. "I guess we'll just have to hope the boy made a good choice when he got married."

"And they are at Lt. Joe's sleeping in a tent right now?" Karen inquired.

"Yes, with all of the others," Matt said.

"Why don't you have the girl come stay with me for the week while you are out on patrol with the boy?" Karen kept working as they talked.

"It'll be that much harder to say 'no' after she's already in the house." Matt continued planting the row of corn he had started.

"I know," Karen replied. "If we were homeless refugees, I would want someone to take us in. If they can't abide by the rules or if they are disrespectful, they can leave just as fast as they got here."

Matt smiled. "That's very true, my love."

CHAPTER 47

"As our enemies have found we can reason like men, so now let us show them we can fight like men also."

-Thomas Jefferson

Before breakfast Saturday, Paul Randall had his morning security briefing in his own study. The IT team which General Jefferson put together were among the best in the world. They linked all of the Coalition leadership through a secure network so they could communicate through encrypted video conferencing.

All of the governors and the commanding officer of each military base inside the Coalition States attended the briefings every Monday through Saturday.

Governor Simmons of Kentucky started his segment of the briefing which updated every one of the situation on the Kentucky-West Virginia border. DHS troops were building up on every road that crossed over into Kentucky.

Governor Simmons said, "We are sending armored personnel carriers and more troops from Fort Campbell and Fort Knox to back up the militia who are guarding the border, but this leaves the bases weak. Additionally, we don't have much in the way of heavy munitions."

Tennessee Governor Sam Richards asked, "What about the stuff you have at Blue Grass Army Depot?"

Simmons replied, "We have used most of the MRAP transport vehicles out of there. We have .50 calibers mounted on top of all those. We have some Gulf War stingers scheduled for demolition and some mines sent there for disassembly and recycling, but most of the weapons stockpiled there are nasty stuff. The vast amount of the US chemical weapons stockpile is stored at Blue Grass Army Depot. In fact, it was all supposed to be destroyed next year, which is when the chemical destruction facility is scheduled to be completed. If we use any of that junk, we'll lose public support. Those stingers look pretty rough. I would ask the general to speak to their viability."

General Jefferson said, "You're right, Governor, we don't want to use sarin gas or any chemical weapons if we can avoid it. The Gulf War stingers should work. Worst case scenario, you pull the trigger and it doesn't fire. That might be the case with one or two out of a hundred. I'd hand them out. Just let the troops know they're old. I'll get you some FGM Javelins from Fort Bragg this week, but try to use everything you can out of Blue Grass Army Depot. We need to try to make use of everything we have. We don't know how long this conflict will last. The last civil war lasted four years."

Paul Randall clicked the icon that displayed his images on everyone's monitor. "Intelligence has gathered these photos of the Port of San Francisco and the Port of San Diego. If you look closely, you will see that they each have the Chinese flag flying over the California flag on all of their flag poles. We also have reports of Chinese troops in the Port of Los Angeles. The troops have on Chinese uniforms, but the insignia's are red ships where the red star would usually be. Chinese naval ships are in all three ports. We don't know what this means, but we suspect that Howe has granted the ports to China for some sort of deal. We don't know if he's getting military support from China or what, but we need to stay very aware of this situation."

Montana Governor Mark Shae sounded concerned. "That's frightening. I wonder if any deals have been struck for the ports in

Oregon or Washington."

General Jefferson answered him. "We haven't heard anything. Howe would be a fool to let them get their foot in the door that close to Seattle. His nuclear subs are stationed right outside of there. I'm sure he would give up Portland, though. If the Chinese wanted it, that is. At any rate, it is a disturbing development."

The men continued their meeting. The discussion focused on the possibilities of future attacks on the Coalition States and how best to position troops and assets to defend against such attacks.

CHAPTER 48

"Give, and it will be given to you. A good measure, pressed down, shaken together and running over, will be poured into your lap. For with the measure you use, it will be measured to you."

-Luke 6:38

Matt and Karen woke up early Monday morning. In a few minutes, Adam would be dropping off the young wife of the new militia member who would be staying with Karen for the week. As Matt finished packing for his patrol, Karen scurried around the house to make it neat and to finish preparing the spare room for the new houseguests.

"It will actually be nice to have someone else around. You're gone every other week on patrol. It gets a little lonely around here," Karen said.

"You spend most of the time over with Janice and the girls when I'm gone, don't you?" Matt asked. "Besides that, you always have the sweet Miss Mae." Matt reached down to pet the small cat rubbing against his leg.

"Miss Mae is wonderful, but she doesn't talk much." Karen

smiled. "I don't go to Janice's much because I have so much to do in the garden. By the time I am done, it's dark and I don't like to walk over there by myself at night."

"Well," Matt said, "I hope it works out. Maybe she can help you keep up with some of the chores in the garden."

They heard Adam's truck as it pulled into the drive.

Before anyone came to the door, Karen said, "Be careful on your patrol. I know DHS has troops stationed on the other side of your checkpoint. I wish you didn't have to go."

Matt pulled her close and held her tight. There was a knock and Matt opened the door. Adam came in first followed by the young couple and Wesley. The young man was short, but looked very strong. He was in full militia gear. He wore camo from head to toe and a chest rig with several magazines. The girl wasn't very tall either. She was pretty but looked a bit scared. She had on jeans and a sweatshirt and carried a backpack. The pack was the size a student might use to carry books to school. It wasn't what you would expect a person to have carrying all of their worldly belongings.

"Come in." Karen took the girls bag and asked, "Do you have any more luggage?"

"No." The girl's voice was shaky.

Karen could see that tears were starting to well up in the young girl's eyes.

"That's Okay, we have everything you could possibly need right here," Karen said.

Adam introduced the couple. "This is Justin and Rene." He then held his hand toward Matt and Karen. "And this is my city boy cousin, Matt, and his beautiful wife, Karen."

Karen said, "Come sit down and have some breakfast."

Adam replied, "We'll have a quick cup of coffee, but we gotta roll out."

Everyone had a cup of coffee and Karen wrapped up a few biscuits for Justin to eat on the road. They said their good-byes and the men headed out.

Karen showed Rene to her room. She felt sorry for her. She couldn't imagine being in her position. She knew they were doing the right thing by letting the young couple stay with them.

"I'm getting ready to wash clothes. Do you have anything to wash?" Karen knew they had been staying in a tent at Lt. Joe's for a few days and probably didn't get the chance to wash.

Rene said, "Yes. Thank you." And dug out her clothes from her backpack.

"If you'd like to take a shower, I can give you a robe when you get out and wash what you have on as well," Karen said.

"That would be nice," Rene said.

Karen got the laundry going and Rene got cleaned up. Karen fought back the tears as she thought what it was like to be a refugee. She thought of all the others that were living in camps without the comforts they were used to having.

After Rene came out of the shower, Karen fixed her a big breakfast and sat down to have a cup of coffee while Rene ate.

"So tell me all about yourself. Where did you grow up? When did you meet Justin?" Karen tried to make the girl feel welcome.

Rene lost the look of dread that had been on her face and the two women chatted for over an hour as they got to know each other.

CHAPTER 49

> "Among the natural rights of the colonists are these: First a right to life, secondly to liberty, and thirdly to property; together with the right to defend them in the best manner they can."
>
> -Samuel Adams

Adam, Wesley, Matt and Justin went out to Adam's truck. Justin jumped into the bed of the truck as the cab would be too tight to haul all four men. Matt jumped into the back with Justin to keep him company. It was early morning and the air was cool, but spring was here and it felt much better than the frigid winter air.

Matt said to Justin, "Nothing like a cold miserable winter to make you appreciate spring." It was small talk, but Matt really did have a deep gratitude for the warmer weather.

Justin nodded and smiled but didn't say anything.

"I guess you're used to the cold winters, but it's been a while since I suffered through such bad weather. Being in the militia and training out in the elements, I learned how much I don't like being cold," Matt said.

"You never get used to being cold," Justin said.

"What did you do in West Virginia?" Matt asked.

Justin responded, "You mean before the crash?"

"Yeah." Matt stuck his hands in his pockets to keep them warm. The air blowing by the moving truck made the air feel much cooler.

Justin said, "I did fence installation and repair during the spring, summer and fall. When it was slow, I helped a buddy build and repair barns. I worked at my uncle's auto repair shop in the winter."

"Who did you work for in the fence business?" Matt asked.

"That was my own business," Justin said. "I worked with a big fence company in Huntington for a couple years. I learned the business, saved up and bought my own equipment."

"You're pretty industrious." Matt looked at the ambitious young man and thought of what Justin could have made of himself if the rug had not been pulled out from under him.

The two men talked and got to know each other during the hour and a half drive toward the 421 checkpoint. Matt told Justin about his adventures in getting out of Florida at the last minute and how God had blessed them to find their little farm.

Justin told Matt about his training with the West Virginia militia and about his family, most of whom had decided to stay in the Huntington area.

Adam pulled off US 421 onto a narrow one-lane road just before the hairpin curve in the ascending mountain road. The turnoff was about a mile away from the checkpoint. Matt looked around to see what was going on. Adam continued down the road about a half mile until he came to a pond. Gary Brewer, Brian Mitchum, JC Hunter and some of the Marines who had defected from Virginia were there when they arrived.

Matt jumped out and introduced Justin to the other members of Bravo Squad. After that, he went to Adam to ask him what was up.

"Why are we stopping here?" Matt asked.

Adam replied, "I didn't want to say anything in front of Karen. I know she worries enough, but the border has been breached. Yesterday, the checkpoint at US 119 was overrun by DHS troops. The Kentucky National Guard patrol that manned the checkpoint were all killed or captured. They haven't taken any more ground, but they are setting up an outpost on the Kentucky side of the Big Sandy River. US 119 jumps back and forth from Kentucky to West Virginia in that stretch. Whoever controls that stretch of US 119 would also control that stretch of the river. Howe might want control of the Big Sandy to move coal from the area up to Huntington.

"Right across the bridge from the checkpoint is Williamson, West Virginia. DHS has set up a prison camp about five miles east of there. It's a big one, so they must be expecting to put a bunch of people in it."

"I wonder why they would put a camp there?" Matt asked.

"They'll probably use the prisoners to mine coal," Adam answered.

Two more trucks pulled up with Michael Marino, Lee Jessup and the remaining men from Bravo.

Adam called everyone to gather around himself so he could brief them on the change of plans. He repeated the latest developments to the newcomers to fill them in on the situation across the river from Williamson, ninety miles north of them. "Franklin Johnson is coordinating with the rest of the military and militia forces in Kentucky to strengthen the checkpoints. We don't know what DHS will do next, but we know this isn't the end. Johnson expects they'll try to build their presence near Williamson and look for other crossings into Kentucky. We think they took Williamson because it was one of the most lightly guarded crossings. Our checkpoint at US 421 would also be a good candidate for DHS to hit because it's relatively lightly guarded.

"Rather than build it up, Johnson wants us to maintain a low show of force at the border on 421. We're going to set up an ambush at the hairpin curve right before the checkpoint. The few guys from Alpha holding the border are going to melt into the woods if the federal forces take the bait and the checkpoint gets hit.

"One of the guys from Alpha Squad is related to the man who owns this pond, so we are going to keep our vehicles right here in the tree line. We are going to set up sniper positions up on the sides of those two hills that look down on the hairpin curve."

Adam opened a duffle bag and pulled out two sticks of dynamite. "Harlan Mining Company made this generous donation to the militia effort. We have a whole bag of dynamite. We are going to tunnel under the road at two points on the hairpin curve up on 421. The first just past the turn off to Davis Lane and the second just after the turn coming out of the hairpin. This will do two things. It will shut down US 421 from being a throughway for Federal forces, but it will allow locals to still get through on the little one lane roads. Davis merges with Garret Hollow, which is where we are now. Garret Hollow goes back up to 421 which will create a bypass for locals. The stretch of road in-between will be a kill zone for any DHS vehicles trapped in the middle of the two explosions."

Adam opened another duffle bag and pulled out two bowed, green plastic objects about the size of a book. "Anyone know what these are?"

One of the Marines that had defected and joined Bravo shouted out, "Claymore mines."

"Claymore mines," Adam echoed. "We have fifty of these, courtesy of Blue Grass Army Depot. These are old and were scheduled to be demolished, but now they'll be assisting us in our struggle for freedom. They aren't exactly fresh out of the oven, but we'll take what we can get.

"Once the vehicles are trapped in the kill zone, the objective will be to get the DHS troops out of the vehicles. If they come across the border in MRAPs like they did up near Williamson, Claymores and small-arms fire won't do much. After the initial explosions take out the road, we'll give them a while to try to maneuver out. On one side they'll have rock and on the other side they'll have that gulley. If they can get their vehicles in the gulley without rolling over, they'll be stuck when they hit the tree line. My guess is that a few of them will roll over.

"Most of these DHS agents are as green as this mountain. Several of them will panic and start pouring out of the vehicles on their own. As soon as you have a shot, take it. If you get a few of them near one of your Claymores, blow it. For the ones smart enough to stay in their truck, we'll smoke them out."

Adam pulled out a glass bottle with a rag hanging out of it. "You don't always have to be high tech. Sometimes low tech will do just fine. These Molotov cocktails are filled with gasoline that has been thickened with Styrofoam. The propellant will stick to whatever the glass breaks against. Ten or twenty of these will turn any MRAP into a convection oven. They'll either get out where we can shoot them or cook inside the vehicle until they're well-done.

"That stretch of road is short. Depending on the spacing and the number of vehicles in the convoy, they may not all get in the kill zone by the time we blow the road. Alpha Squad is going to be inside the tree line between the checkpoint and the hairpin. They have eight old shoulder-fired Stingers to light up any vehicles that try to retreat.

"That is the big picture. I'll be going over your individual assignments in detail with each one of you. Are you guys ready for this?"

Everyone yelled, "Yeah!"

CHAPTER 50

"Rebellion to tyrants is obedience to God."

-Benjamin Franklin

Justin tapped Matt on the shoulder to wake him. Matt looked around groggily, trying to remember where he was and why he was here. The anticipation of the ambush had his adrenaline running full speed the day before. His watch had ended at 2:00 a.m., but he wasn't able to fall asleep until just before dawn. When he finally fell asleep, he went into a deep slumber. He was in his sleeping bag under a shelter built beneath a huge fallen tree. The forest was too dense to see the road from their small campsite. The upside was that it could not be seen from the road. Matt climbed out and started a small fire in the Dakota fire pit they used for cooking. He brewed a small pot of coffee and made a sandwich out of a sliced boiled egg and a piece of bread.

Along with Gary Brewer, Matt and Justin were stationed on the western hillside looking down onto the road at the very end of the hairpin curve. It was a magnificently beautiful place and the serenity could easily make one forget why they were here. The subtle pinks and pure whites of the dogwood tree blooms took Matt to a place far away from war and revolution.

Gary's radio earpiece chirped and he called out to Matt and Justin. "This might be it. Alpha says multiple vehicles are approaching the checkpoint from Virginia."

Matt looked around. He didn't have on his vest or his hat. He dropped the rest of his sandwich and slugged back his coffee. He quickly put on his vest and his camo boonie hat. Justin and Gary started heading down the hill to their sniper nest. Matt grabbed his rifle and followed them.

Gary looked over at Justin who was obviously shaken up by the mission and asked, "You been in a firefight yet?"

"No," Justin said.

"Me, neither," Gary said. "We're all scared. We'll just do everything we trained to do and pray God will give us victory."

Justin nodded and found the road through his rifle scope.

To Matt, the minutes seemed like an eternity as they waited for more information or to see a DHS vehicle come around the turn. Gary's earphone chirped again. He put up a finger to signal for Matt and Justin to wait while he listened to the message.

Gary said, "Its four Cougar 6x6's and eight Humvees. The Cougars all have .50 caliber machine-gun turrets on top. There are two Cougars in the front, one in the middle and one at the end of the convoy."

"That's a pretty serious invasion," Matt said.

Gary nodded. Gary was watching through the spotter scope and Matt had the trigger to detonate the road explosion. The hairpin curve required any vehicle traveling through this stretch of road to go no faster than twenty-five miles per hour, but Matt was nervous about timing it just right.

Justin lined up his scope to the approximate area where the second machine-gunner should be after the explosion.

Gary said, "Here they come!"

Everyone's heart was racing a mile minute.

"Okay, Matt," Gary said, "get ready to blow the charge in five…four… three…two… one."

Matt hit the trigger. BOOM! Dust and smoke billowed up from underneath the lead vehicle as it popped up off the ground, on the guard rail and rolled over several times as it descended into the ravine below. The second vehicle stopped just short of the crater in the road left by the explosion.

Justin saw the machine-gunners face as he looked up into the trees, right at their sniper nest. The soldier saw them, but before he could react, Justin took the shot and the soldier slumped forward.

The men heard the second explosion which sealed in all of the remaining vehicles except the last Cougar. The vehicle sat on the east side of the crater caused by the second explosion. The machine gunners in the middle and rear Cougars began to pepper the hills with suppressive fire although they had no targets as the militia were well camouflaged and sitting silently. Moments later the machine gunners were struck dead by the militia snipers.

Adam called out on the radio. "Anyone with a Claymore near a Humvee can blow it. Everyone else, try to take head shots through the glass."

Several of the Claymores had been strapped to trees at eye level to increase their effectiveness. Rifle fire and the eruption of the Claymores rang out from all around the valley. The federal troops were unable to get a location on their assailants as the militia was all around them in the trees.

The militia began to patiently pick off the federal troops as they made themselves visible. Those who could get close enough to a vehicle to lob a Molotov cocktail did so. Soon several of the vehicles were blazing with the home-brewed napalm.

The rear guard Cougar made a five point turn on the narrow road and tried to escape. Within seconds, the sound of the Stinger missile that took out the fleeing vehicle rang through the hollow.

The Cougar in the center tried to make a run down into the gully. It was too steep and rolled over and over.

In roughly twenty minutes, all the federal troops were dead except for those who surrendered from the last two Humvees. They were quickly secured with zip tie restraints.

Adam led a team of eight men down into the gully to find the rolled over Cougar. When he was within earshot, he called out, "This is your one and only opportunity to be smart and surrender."

The vehicle was upside down. He could see one man stick a pistol out the crack in the door.

Adam yelled, "Light it up!" Most of the men in the rolled over Cougar were probably unconscious. It was tragic that this one imbecile was making the decision for all of them.

The militia began hitting the upside down vehicle with Molotov cocktails. Soon troops were coming out of the flaming death trap only to be cut down by the militia's rifles.

Adam and the rest of the militia went through the vehicles to check for survivors and to harvest any useful equipment. The dead federal troops were well outfitted with high-end ballistic chest plates and Kevlar helmets. The lethal shots from the militia snipers had hit some troops in the face or neck. Other shots struck femoral arteries causing the victims to bleed out in minutes.

They found several cases of fragmentation grenades and a few thousand rounds of ammunition. They built a makeshift bridge out of logs to get the two operational Humvees back across the crater. These would come in handy as well.

Alpha and Bravo cleaned up the mess as well as they could and Franklin Johnson sent in a different security team to watch the road for the remainder of the week. London Company deserved a few days of R and R. Besides that, Adam and his militia had proved they may be better used in a different role than standing guard duty.

CHAPTER 51

"All the believers were together and had everything in common. Selling their possessions and goods, they gave to anyone as he had need. Every day they continued to meet together in the temple courts. They broke bread in their homes and ate together with glad and sincere hearts, praising God and enjoying the favor of all the people."

-Acts 2:44-47a

On Friday night, the congregants of Liberty Chapel living at Young Field held a barn dance to get their minds off the worries of the world for a night. A few of the folks put together a Bluegrass band and had been practicing during the evenings. This would be their first live show.

Pastor Robinson stepped to the stage to introduce the band. "Folks, everyone has done such a wonderful job making the barn look so festive. The hay bales, streamers, even the refreshment table all look so nice. I want to thank everyone involved. Before I introduce tonight's talent, I want to touch on a few business items that I hope will add to your joy.

"We have completed the construction on our first residential building. This will provide a more permanent living facility for some of our residents. We're going to name it Rust Hall in honor of Albert Rust who gave everything in the battle of Minot. We'll be honoring Albert and all those who fell at the Battle of Minot and at the assault on Young Field by making the first spots in Rust Hall available to the widows and children of the men who died in the conflicts.

"The first sprouts in the corn and potato fields are coming up and with God's blessings, we should have more than double the amount of those two food items that we need for the coming year. We've committed to give 10% of all of our crops and produce to the military and militia to support those who are fighting for our freedom. We hope to barter some of the excess for livestock such as cattle and chickens.

"If we're able to meet all of our livestock goals and still have more left over, we'll try to barter for things that we'll be able to pay out to everyone in the form of a dividend. We'll strive to barter for things like silver coins and ammunition which will be compact and standardized in weight and quality. The widows of the men who died will receive a double dividend once we're able to make the payments. This year may be slim, if we have a dividend at all, but the following year should be much better.

I have nothing but praise for everyone here at Young Field. You've all been so gracious in making sure everyone has enough. That's as it should be in times of crisis. If the Church cannot pull together and look after her own, we would be hard pressed to call ourselves Christians.

"The early Church in the Book of Acts had all things in common and from what we know, that worked out fine for a while. Of course, the flesh crept in and soon enough there was squabbling. I believe that communal living has been a blessing over these past months to get us through these hard time, but I hope that as things stabilize, we will be able to each pursue our own gifts and industry. Once all the crops are planted, folks will have a little more time on their hands. I encourage each of you to find something to do for your own economic advancement. Perhaps sewing clothes, repairing shoes, cutting hair, cleaning guns or any number of things that you can use to barter with one another for goods and services. Tonight's talent is a wonderful example of folks taking the initiative to find something they are good at that will benefit the community. They are playing for the love of music tonight, but perhaps in the near future they will play at weddings or birthday parties in exchange for a shirt or a pie.

"I pray that you'll all continue to work together as diligently as you have. If the Coalition can persevere through this trial, it will be communities like you that will rekindle the American spirit. I know this sounds like a very optimistic speech in such tough times, but I truly believe that God is going to bless us. (Even when the flood stripped the earth of all the inhabitants,) God spared Noah and his family. (Even when fire fell from the sky,) God spared Lot. (Even when famine struck the land,) God provided for Israel through Joseph's position in the palace of Egypt and (even when the plagues destroyed the livestock, crops and first born of the Egyptians,) God shielded the land of Goshen where his people lived. God is able to punish the wicked and spare the righteous. He discerns between the wheat and the chaff.

"Well, that's enough business talk. That isn't why you folks are here, so without further ado, please welcome the world premiere of the hottest Bluegrass band in Idaho, Hole in the Pocket!"

The crowd cheered. Pastor John's news of hope had already lifted everyone's spirits. They were ready to celebrate being alive and the fact that they had made it through a brutal winter.

The four-piece band consisted of a banjo player, a fiddle player, a bass fiddle, and the singer who alternated between singing and playing the harmonica. The band played for three hours with only a few breaks. All the congregation members of Liberty Chapel had the time of their lives at that simple barn dance.

CHAPTER 52

"Firearms are second only to the Constitution in importance; they are the peoples' liberty's teeth."

-George Washington

Karen and Rene cleaned up the breakfast dishes while Matt and Justin headed out to start working on a larger pen for the goats. Matt traded some silver bars with Eli Miller for another nanny goat and a buck that had just been born. He also bought a young rooster from Eli in the deal. Eli sold Matt his first goat and a few hens last fall.

Justin's fencing skills were proving to be very handy on the farm. Rene and Justin were helping out a lot with all of the chores. The young couple was eager to make themselves useful. This allowed Matt to complete many more projects than with only Karen to help around the farm.

Matt and Justin tried to work quickly so they could finish before Adam picked them up for the meeting at Lt. Joe's. Franklin Johnson would be at the meeting along with most of the militia men from London Company.

They finished in time to have a quick venison sandwich before Adam was scheduled to arrive.

"We'll be back by dark," Matt said to Karen. "Y'all keep the walkie-talkie radio on and keep your eyes open. DHS has infiltrated to Pikeville. No one has reported any movement around here yet, but they aren't more than 100 miles from here."

Rene asked, "Do you know what the meeting is about?"

"We don't really know yet. Even if we did, It would probably better if we didn't discuss it," Matt said. "If you don't know anything, you won't have anything to say if you are interrogated."

Karen said, "That's fine by me. I didn't want to know as much as I knew about the last ambush."

Rene said, "If I don't have the details, I start making up stuff in my mind."

The two women had their own individual ways of dealing with the stress of having a husband in combat.

Adam and Wesley pulled in the drive. Wesley jumped out to ride in the truck bed with Justin. Matt and Justin went to the truck.

Adam called out to them, "Y'all got your rifles?"

Matt said, "We have our pistols. Do we need rifles?"

"Probably not," Adam said. "But it doesn't cost you anything extra to bring them."

Matt smiled and went back to get the rifles.

When he stepped inside, Karen asked, "Why do you need rifles? I thought it was just a meeting?"

Matt answered, "I think Adam wants us to carry them all the time. Technically, we have been invaded. We should probably start acting like it."

Matt kissed Karen on the head to comfort her and grabbed the two new Colt M-4s they had appropriated in the ambush. Matt and Justin's old AR-15s now stayed at home for the girls in case they needed them. The new Colts were well equipped full-auto rifles. They had EO Tech reflex sights and EO Tech 3X magnifier sights (that could be flipped to the side for close quarter firefights.) He put 6 magazines in his small backpack and headed back out to the truck. Matt handed Justin his M-4 and jumped in the cab of the truck.

As Adam pulled out of the drive Matt asked, "Can you give me a little heads up on what we're talking about tonight?"

Adam said, "Michael's brother-in-law from Baltimore is with the DHS team that is occupying Pikeville. He has some information about a supply convoy coming in this week. We're coming up with a plan to hit it."

Matt was doubtful. "The guy just volunteered the information?"

Adam answered, "Michael is buying him off. The guy was on welfare, living in public housing before the crash. When Howe cut the gravy train, he had to sign up with DHS to eat. He is one of the geniuses that Howe has fighting the war. They have no loyalty to anything but their stomach."

Matt said, "So these new DHS agents are bigger degenerates than the old TSA agents."

"Much more useless," Adam said with a snicker. "Same concept, though. They have no thought for liberty or virtue and they sold out their country for a loaf of bread. Once, when I was getting on a plane, I asked one of those TSA idiots how they could look in the mirror. He told me his family had to eat too."

"That sums it up," Matt said. "That's how we got into the position we're in. Rather than fight to find something productive to do or get their hands dirty doing blue collar work, these TSA bags of filth signed up to work for the tyrants. That 'feed my family' line is a poor excuse. Any self-respecting patriot who loves freedom could find something else to do to feed their family."

Adam said, "But in their defense, the TSA agents probably had no idea things would get this bad when they took the job."

Matt shot back, "Throwing Jews in ovens wasn't on the job description for being a Nazi soldier when Hitler's boys signed up either. Those who stuck around when they found out what Hitler was up to will have blood on their hands on judgment day. Same thing with DHS and TSA. There is no excuse at this point."

Matt tried to think about something else. He had just eaten a wonderful sandwich right before they left, and now he felt sick to his stomach. The power-hungry Democrats and the Neo-Con wing of the Republican Party didn't anger him so much. He thought of them as pigs wallowing in the mud. Yes, it was nasty, but they're pigs and it was their nature to wallow in filth. What made Matt sick was the American people who had no value for their freedom; those who paid no attention to politics or economics and let this great country decline to such a state. And he was sickened by those who turned on their own countrymen by accepting jobs as TSA and DHS agents.

When they arrived at Lt. Joe's, there were maps hanging on the wall. Joe's kitchen table had some small toy cars and what looked like props for planning another ambush.

Franklin Johnson and Michael were there. JC, Gary, Jeff, Bobby, Eddie Cooper, Brian Mitchum, the two new Marines that joined Bravo and several guys from Alpha were gathered at Lt. Joe's.

Johnson called the meeting to order and started speaking. "You guys did a bang up job on US 421. I wish I could've been there.

"This next operation is not going to be as easy. The convoy we have information on is coming out of West Virginia on 119. It's a much wider road than 421. It's four lanes plus a center lane and wide shoulders all the way from the border to Pikeville. The road is regularly traveled by DHS. Adam, you guys are going to have to come up with some new tricks."

Adam looked at the maps for several minutes. "What can you get us from Bluegrass Army Depot?"

Johnson said, "Anything you want except the chemicals."

"Yeah," Adam said, "I don't want anything to do with those. Can you get me vehicles?"

Johnson said, "Probably from Ashland National Guard Armory.

Write down your wish list and I'll see what I can do."

Adam asked, "Michael, what are the vehicles in the supply convoy?"

Michael replied, "Two Cougar 6x6s and six supply vehicles. Two are fuel tankers, two are provisions, one is medical supplies and the other is loaded with barter stuff to try and buy off the locals in Pikeville. They are looking to recruit as many new troops as they can."

"Do the Cougars have .50 caliber machine-gun turrets?" Adam asked. "And do you know if they will be one in the front, one in the back?"

"I didn't hear for sure, but I would guess that's the case," Michael said.

Adam pointed to a place on the map. "This isn't as tight of a choke as we would like to have, but we don't have much to choose from. Most of 119 has residential or commercial buildings along the side of it. I don't want to put those people in harm's way if I can help it. This bridge that takes 119 over Raccoon Road looks like our best shot. Approaching from the east, 119 cuts through the rock before the bridge. That puts vertical walls on both sides of the pass for about 1500 feet. The bridge is about 1000 feet across. If the vehicles are spaced the same way they were spaced on 421, all eight vehicles should be inside that 2500 foot kill zone by the time the first Cougar hits the end of the bridge. When that happens, we'll blow the end of the bridge right underneath the first Cougar. We can take out the last Cougar with a Stinger and put four vehicles loaded with charges on the east side of the pass between the rock walls. Hopefully, we can take the supply vehicles without destroying them, but if not, worst-case scenario, we'll blow them up when they try to retreat.

"The last stretch just before the bridge has an opening in the rocks that exit off the road to the west. It is a nice wide open field lined by trees that we could use to stage the ambush and the retreat.

"Well, the location isn't optimal, but we should have a lot less resistance than the last hit. This will be a nice pay off for the militia.

That food can go straight up to the camp across the river from Huntington. Those guys are the only thing keeping Howe's men from taking Interstate 64. If federal troops get across that bridge, it'll be bad news."

JC asked, "Why don't they just blow that bridge?"

"I think they're hoping they can get enough strength to cross it and take Huntington," Johnson responded.

Wesley had a question. "I though Paul Randall was dead set against an offensive war. Wouldn't invading Huntington be an offensive maneuver?"

Justin said, "We still have a lot of militia in that area of West Virginia. They stayed despite instructions to leave, but it is because they are going to launch a gorilla campaign against the federal forces in Huntington. It would be great if they could still get support from Kentucky."

Franklin could see this wasn't getting anywhere so he said, "Well, orders for blowing a bridge to a main artery like I-64 has to come from the governor, so we don't have much say in that one, boys. The bridge on US 119 can be cut around by Zebulon Highway. It will cause an inconvenience to the Federal troops trying to supply Pikeville, but locals can still get around."

Franklin also promised to get the team more Stingers and explosives. The payoff for this ambush promised to provide a much needed dividend in the form of supplies for the Kentucky Militia and National Guard. It would profit the Kentucky forces, and equally cost the federal forces.

CHAPTER 53

"Unhappy it is, though, to reflect that a brother's sword has been sheathed in a brother's breast and that the once-happy plains of America are either to be drenched with blood, or inhabited by slaves. Sad alternative! But can a virtuous man hesitate in his choice?"

-George Washington

General Jefferson and Texas Governor Larry Jacobs came by Paul Randall's ranch for a change of pace. It was Wednesday and they held their midweek pow-wow in person. The security of the internet connection was stellar, but these men preferred meeting face-to-face once in a while.

It was the first time either the governor or the general had been to Paul's home since the improvements had been made. Paul showed the two of them around and pointed out all of the special features. General Jefferson had instructed the contractors on which improvements were to be made in Randall's home, but he had not seen them in person.

"And through this steel door is my bunker." Paul opened the heavy metal door and led the way.

"Now this is nice!" Jacobs exclaimed.

"It's a smaller version of the subterranean bunker under the White House," Jefferson said.

"I can't tell you how thankful I am for all of this, General. Not for myself, but for Kimberly's sake. She's still traumatized after the raid on the cabin that killed Robert," Paul said.

"That's understandable," The general said. "It wasn't a normal event. The bunker was no trouble at all. We have to maintain continuity of leadership, Paul."

The men conducted their meeting in the boardroom located inside the bunker.

"General, I know you have some bad news, so I'll start with the good news," Randall said. "The entire northwest section of the Coalition is completely severed from the western grid. Likewise, the Southern Coalition is also independent from the eastern grid."

"And Texas is still independent from all the grids." Larry Jacobs chuckled.

"This is a big step in the Coalition becoming a separate entity from the Federal States," Randall said. "The cities in some of the Federal states are drawing much more power than they're producing. It was starting to cause brownouts and dirty power in Coalition areas. Howe just doesn't have the ability to keep it all going. Now that they aren't sucking off of the Coalition, New York is in a complete blackout, Philly is off and on, and even D.C. is having rolling brownouts to spread the pain around."

"And now, I get to be the bearer of bad news," Jefferson said. "Howe has taken most of the Gulf states except Florida. He has DHS controlling all of the major cities throughout Louisiana, Alabama, Mississippi and Georgia. There are a lot of militia down that way, but without the support of their states, they're getting slaughtered. Don't get me wrong, they're putting a dent in Howe's forces, but he is drawing from an unending pool of resources.

"As far as the Coalition States are concerned, Kentucky has been invaded and occupied on the eastern border. The local militias are biting at their ankles while the state military organizes a response. One of their small towns has been completely taken over by DHS. Tennessee is sending support up to assist in a response, but they have to be careful not to hurt any citizens of the town."

The men continued their meeting discussing the state of affairs in the Coalition and discussing their future plans.

CHAPTER 54

"You armed me with strength for battle."

-2 Samuel 22:40a

Early Thursday morning Adam, Wesley, Matt and Justin arrived at Lt. Joe's. The plan was to rendezvous with the rest of Bravo and Alpha, pick up the weapons and vehicles for the ambush and head straight to the staging area.

Gary Brewer arrived with JC and rolled out of their truck.

Adam called out to them, "Gary! You guys were supposed to pick up Michael. What happened?"

Gary said, "He has the flu."

"The flu?" Adam asked.

"Yeah, he couldn't even come to the door. His wife Susan said he's been in the bathroom all morning," Gary answered.

"Well," Adam said, "that wouldn't be good for anybody. We'll just have to get it done without him. Is everyone else feeling okay? We don't want anyone coming down with a fever in the middle of this operation."

Everyone agreed that they all felt as well as could be expected the morning before a stressful operation like this.

Adam sighed. "Okay, but if anyone starts feeling sick, tap out right away. No one is going to think any less of you. If you get a fever or start vomiting in the middle of an operation like this, you'll get yourself and your buddy killed. You're all heroes already. Don't feel like you have to prove it by doing something stupid."

Adam went inside to talk to Joe and inform him of the situation. "Joe, do you have a thermometer in your medical supplies?"

"I believe so," The older gentleman replied.

Adam asked, "Could you do me a huge favor and go around and check everyone's temperature? I can't take any chances."

"Be happy to. I'll get a bit of the recipe to sterilize it with between checking each man," Lt. Joe said.

"Which recipe might that be?" Adam's curiosity was stirred up.

"Shine. It's my granddaddy's recipe." Joe grinned. "I make up a batch now and again. For medicinal purposes you see."

Adam shook his head and tried to conceal his smile. "Thank you, Lieutenant."

Lt. Joe confirmed everyone's temperature was within a normal range before they mounted up.

Everyone was given a set of the body armor that Bair Platoon had commandeered in the raid on US 421. They could have easily disguised themselves as federal troops since they had all of the DHS insignia on their body armor, helmets and the official weapons. They had also taken the uniforms and still had the two DHS Humvees parked out in the woods behind Lt. Joe's. They decided against it as their mission was top secret and had not been announced to the other militia teams and National Guard patrolling the area. While evading the scrutiny of federal troops in Pikeville, they could attract friendly fire which could ruin the day.

Since they were obviously a coalition force, they decided to hook north past Pikeville and come back down to Raccoon Road. That would allow the militia to access the field without ever having to drive on US 119. The vehicle with the charges to blow the bridge could drive right underneath the end of the bridge. The low elevation of the bridge at the demolition point would make it much easier to repair than other points as the bridge towered nearly 200 feet in the center over Raccoon Road.

The men headed out and were set up about an hour before the convoy was scheduled to arrive.

Matt, Gary and Justin were the drivers for the vehicles that would be blocking the retreat after the bridge was blown. Adam, Brian Mitchum and Wesley were responsible for the demolition vehicle that would be going just beneath the bridge. A couple of guys from Alpha were one mile up the road and would be sending three clicks over the radio when they saw the convoy approaching. Lee and JC were at the top of the bluff overlooking the US 119 choke point from the southeast. They would be firing Stingers from their position. Jeff Nolon and Eddie Cooper would be doing the same thing from the northwestern bluff.

The rest of the guys from Alpha and Bravo were set up in firing positions to take out the drivers, machine gunners and any other personnel that did not surrender immediately.

Matt looked at his watch. He whispered, "It's still fifty more minutes before the convoy is scheduled to arrive. I feel like I've already been waiting an hour." He looked at Gary and Justin but they didn't say anything. The tension and the suspense was crippling. Matt waited what felt like another hour when he looked at his watch.

Only fifteen minutes have passed, he thought.

Five minutes later, he motioned for Justin and Gary to get into position at the wheels of their respective vehicles.

The plan was to drive their vehicles onto the road which would block the retreat as soon as they heard the bridge blow. They would then leave the vehicles there and run to the cover of the tree line to see if the supply vehicles would try to escape the kill zone. If they did, each man was in charge of blowing his vehicle as the federal supply vehicles approached. If the federal supply vehicles could be captured without destroying them, the militia's vehicles loaded with charges would be taken back to Lt. Joe's for use in another operation.

Matt looked at his watch again and there was still twenty minutes left before the scheduled time. Two minutes later, the men at the observation post one mile away broke radio silence.

The radio chirped. "We've got three helicopters coming out of the east. They have to be enemy. The choppers have a very thin frontal profile, I'd say Cobras."

Matt heard Adam's voice next. "Roger. Everybody look alive. We may have been spotted by a drone. Everyone take visual cover under trees or bushes. Matt, have your team pull those vehicles back inside the tree line. Do it quick!"

Matt depressed the talk button on his walkie and said, "Roger!" Matt, Gary and Wesley started the engines and pulled the trucks back into the tree line close to the road.

POP POP POP! Rifle fire was coming from across the open field from Matt's position.

Matt called out on the radio, "We're getting hit by rifle fire from the tree line on the northwest side of the field!"

Adam called out, "It's a trap! Everybody bug out. Engage hostiles as necessary, but get out of here as fast as possible. I am going to blow this bridge anyway. Keep that in mind when you're planning your retreats. Can anyone on top of the western ridge give Matt and his team some suppressive fire?"

One of the Marines that had crossed over from Virginia called out, "Roger!" Soon, gunfire was raining down into the tree line on the hostiles.

Matt motioned for Gary and Justin to leave the vehicles. Adam was blowing the bridge which meant they couldn't get back to the other side in the trucks. Besides, the trucks were loaded with explosives. One tracer round would light up any one of the trucks and cause a chain reaction which would incinerate them all. Matt's team started working their way back into the woods to try to get back down the mountain to Raccoon Road.

When the charges blew that took out the southern side of the bridge, the earth rumbled beneath their feet. The vibration resonated all through their bones. Matt said a short prayer under his breath that Adam, Wesley and Brian had gotten far enough away when the explosives went off.

They heard gunfire from behind. Justin said, "Should we set up a position and try to fight it out?"

Matt said, "I think we need to get out of here. Adam has ordered a retreat. I think this is a trap."

The radios chirped again. It was the voice of the observation post a mile up the road. "You guys have more choppers coming in from the north. Might be Apaches. We're working our way towards you."

Adam's voice called back, "We are outfoxed. Don't come this way. It is a trap. Everyone get out anyway you can."

Matt's team soon heard the Cobra helicopters overhead. The fire from the Cobras' 30mm chain guns rang out through the hills.

Seconds later, Matt looked up as he saw a huge explosion. The team on the bluff had taken out one of the Cobras with a Stinger. Shortly after, the northwest ridge was glowing from the Cobras' 70mm rockets that pounded the top of the hill.

The suppressive fire coming down on Matt's assailants stopped. The militia team on the northwestern ridge must have been killed. Matt's heart sank. Another Cobra exploded in the air just as the three Apache helicopters arrived. Another stinger from the southeastern ridge clipped the tail of one of the Apaches and it went spiraling down onto US 119. Matt heard the explosion then saw the smoke billow up from over the mountain ridge.

"Nice shot JC and Lee!" Matt said.

Soon, the remaining two Apaches were igniting the southeastern ridge with Hydra rockets. The resisting fire from the ridge ceased and Matt knew it meant he had just lost more of his militia brothers.

Matt, Justin and Gary reached the train tracks at the bottom of the mountain. They were in a hurry to escape their pursuers, but they still practiced precautions when crossing an open area. Gary crossed the tracks first then covered Justin as he crossed next. They covered the front and rear as Matt crossed the tracks last.

Meanwhile, Adam, Wesley and Brian were weighing their options. Their truck was down the hill on the side of Raccoon Road. Their current position was in the trees on top of the hill.

Adam said, "The path down the hill is exposed to the sight of the three remaining choppers. There are four Humvees and a Cougar driving up from the southwest on US 119. I think we should make a run for the truck below."

Halfway down the hill, they saw four more Humvees approaching from the southeast on Raccoon road. There was no way they could get to the truck and escape.

Adam called out, "Drop down in those shrubs." It was too late. Troops from the Humvees below started taking shots at them.

They laid down in prone positions. Adam said, "This is a bad situation. We've been spotted, we're cut off from our vehicle and we have bad guys closing in on two sides. We're going to have to shoot and move. Those woods back there are about a thousand feet away. We've got some bushes between here and there, but nothing that will stop a bullet. I think we are just going to have to make a run for it. That bunch of shrubs looks like it might have a small ridge behind it for cover. It's about halfway to the woods. We'll leap frog to that point, then on to the woods.

"Wes, you and Brian roll out first. I'll lay down cover fire until you get there. Then you guys lay it down until I get to you. When we hit the woods, we'll all run back into those woods as fast as we can."

Wes and Brian nodded that they understood the plan. Adam put in a fresh magazine and yelled, "Go!"

Adam started firing and Wes and Brian started running. Adam went through three magazines before he heard suppressive fire coming from behind him. He knew that was his cue to make a run for it.

As he started running, he saw the muzzle flash from one gun in the brush he was running to.

He thought as he ran "One of their rifles must have jammed. Why isn't he firing with his pistol?"

No sooner had the question crossed his mind than he got his answer. Thirty feet in front of him lay his little brother's body. A paralyzing wave of panic shot through his organs. Adam skidded in beside his brother. Wesley lay face down in the field. Adam called out, "Wesley, get up!"

He took five shots at the enemy before he rolled him over. He saw his throat covered in blood. He had been hit in the back of the neck. The bullet severed Wesley's spinal cord and blew out his windpipe. He was dead. He probably never felt a thing. Adam felt the emotion welling up inside. He had been through this in the sandbox, but this was his brother. It was different. Still, he knew what he had to do. Adam still had a wife and two little girls to get home to.

Adam whispered out loud, "I have to keep fighting and mourn later."

He switched his magazine and pulled three magazines out of Wesley's kangaroo mag pouch on the front of his plate carrier. Adam stuck them in his own empty magazine pouches and continued to the bush.

He slid in behind the bush where Brian was. Brian said, "Sorry, man."

Adam shook his head and said, "Go!" Adam laid down fire as Brian took off toward the woods. He seemed to take longer than he should have, but eventually, Adam heard the suppressive fire coming from over his shoulder. Quickly, he jumped up and ran as hard as he could.

Adam reached Brian in the tree line. He turned and laid down three shots. "Okay, let's go!" Adam said.

Brian said, "I'm all done Captain. You go, I'll hold them down."

"What are you talking about?" Adam demanded.

"I'm hit and bleeding bad." Brian looked down at his leg.

Adam looked down. Brian was bleeding heavily out of the middle of his thigh. Adam took out an Israeli Battle Dressing and applied it to the wound. He tightened the compression as tight as he could get it.

"Adam. I'm going. I can feel it. I'm getting cold and I can't focus," Brian said.

Adam didn't want to admit it, but he knew Brian was right. "You just lost a lot of blood, buddy. You'll be okay."

"I knew I should have listened to you," Brian said.

"About what?" Adam said.

"About church, about Jesus. You tried to tell me, but I knew if I committed my life to Jesus, that I would have to stop drinking and runnin' around with chicks. It seemed like too high of a price for salvation at the time. Now, I feel like I cheated myself. Now I'm scared. I'm going to hell," Brian said.

Adam laid down three more rounds. The DHS agents pursuing them did not want them bad enough to risk getting their head shot off. They were just taking potshots from a distance. The multitude of random pot shots had killed Wesley and it looked like the end for Brian as well.

Adam said, "It's not too late, Brian. Jesus was born in a barn."

Brian said, "What is that supposed to mean?"

Adam replied, "It means he always leaves the door open. You can come on in whenever you want."

Brian made a faint smile as he squeezed off a couple of rounds at a couple of federal troops who were sticking their heads up. "It's too late. I have nothing to give. I'll be dead in a few minutes."

"It's not too late as long as you have one more breath," Adam said. "In Matthew 27, we read about the two thieves who were hung on the crosses on either side of Jesus. In that account, both of them are mocking him. In Luke 23, one of the thieves continues to mock Jesus, but the other thief says to the mocker 'Don't you fear God since you are under the same sentence? We are punished justly, for we are getting what our deeds deserve. But this man has done nothing wrong.' Then the thief said, 'Jesus, remember me when you come into your kingdom.' Jesus answered him, 'I tell you the truth, today you will be with me in paradise.'

"The thief admitted that he was a sinner by saying that he was punished justly, and he acknowledged that Jesus was the Messiah by asking Jesus to remember him when he came into his Kingdom. That thief had no more to give than you do, but Jesus saved him."

Adam could see a look of hope in Brian's eyes as he lay dying. Brian closed his eyes and said, "Jesus, I admit that I am a sinner. I have been a drunk and never made time for you. Please forgive me. I know that Adam is right. I know you're the Son of God and only you can save me. Please save me."

Brian opened his eyes which were streaming with tears. He said "I feel so clean, so..."

"Forgiven?" Adam asked, the tears rolling down his own cheek.

"Yes. Forgiven," Brian said. "I wish I would've done that a long time ago."

Adam grabbed Brian's hand and said, "Better late than never."

Brian smiled and repeated, "Better late than never."

Brian's eyes closed and an expression of perfect peace came over his face. His body fell limp. The tears streamed down Adam's face, but he knew he had to get home. Adam took a shot at the soldier that was making a run towards his position. The federal soldier stopped instantly and fell backwards. The well-placed shot robbed the others of their courage. Adam took the full magazines from Brian's pouches and took off running into the woods as fast as he could.

On the other side of the bridge, Matt, Justin and Gary were crossing the creek that ran alongside Raccoon Road. They used the same method they used to cross the train tracks. This time, they had more ground to cover. They were heading to the tree line on the other side of the road. There were mobile homes and houses along that side of Raccoon Road and the hills behind were dense forest.

Matt called out, "Gary, you cross first and run to the backside of that car parked in the drive. Justin, you go next."

Gary crossed without incident, but as soon as Justin left the cover of the trees, a Humvee pulled up the road from the northwest. The vehicle stopped and the men inside began firing at Justin. Matt and Gary laid down suppressive fire until Justin could cross.

By the time Justin reached the other side, two more vehicles had approached and enemy troops were pouring out.

Matt radioed to Gary and Justin. "You guys keep moving. I can't cross here. I've got to get back in the woods. God speed."

Gary depressed the talk button on his walkie. "Roger."

Matt went back across the creek and returned to the other side of the railroad tracks. He knew if he headed back up the hill, he would wear himself out. He elected to move through the woods and follow the road from inside the tree line. Matt could hear the original pursuers from the field above. The few moments back at the road had allowed them to catch up. He started running as fast as he could.

Matt looked up ahead and said to himself, "There is an enemy team approaching from the front. I've got nowhere to go." He had to make a split second decision. "Should I go out in a blaze of glory or should I let myself be captured?"

"Freeze!" The voice came from behind.

There would be no blaze of glory. He could drop his rifle or commit suicide by turning it on the man behind him. Matt placed his hands on his head and let the rifle dangle in front of his chest by the single point sling.

CHAPTER 55

"It is when a people forget God, that tyrants forge their chains."

-Patrick Henry

Anthony Howe finished the Friday morning briefing. He was pleased with the progress the federal forces were making. They successfully locked down all of the southern states that had not committed to the Coalition or pledged their allegiance to the Federal States. In addition to that, they established a foothold in Kentucky. It was the first step in taking control of the gold held at Fort Knox and regaining Tennessee and the Carolinas.

Alec Renzi approached the President. He hesitated when he walked in, so Howe knew he was bringing bad news.

"What is it Alec?" Howe asked.

"It's former President Al Mohammad, sir," Renzi replied.

"I'll take it in my office," Howe snapped.

Howe had come to grips with the fact that he was not in absolute control. For Anthony Howe, to find out his lust for absolute power would never be fulfilled was like losing a friend. He was going through the stages of grief. He had moved past denial and was moving through the anger phase, but the lingering residue of rage would likely be with him for a long time. He had better get on with the bargaining phase, or he would lose control of what power he still possessed.

"Mustafa," Howe said as he picked up the phone.

"Hello, Anthony," the voice said. "I understand that you don't like me. I know that you would rather see me dead. However, I hope that you have come to your senses; for your own sake that is. I understand that your father had a little chat with you and that you now have a better understanding of the way things work in the world. I am willing to bury the hatchet. All I ask is that you speak to me with respect. Does that sound like something you can handle?"

"I think I can do that," Howe replied.

Mustafa said, "Good. I understand that you are considering some relatively drastic measures against the Coalition."

Howe thought, *I am surrounded by moles! Does this man have a bug in my head? I only discussed those plans with the Joint Chiefs. No one else on my staff even knows. Who could be leaking information now?*

"What measures are you referring to?" Howe asked.

"If we are going to get through this Anthony, we are going to have to be honest with each other. Part of speaking to me with respect includes not talking to me like I'm an idiot!" Al Mohammad yelled. "I'm talking about your plans for a nuclear strike against the Coalition States."

Howe was slowly beginning to realize that he needed to start playing ball. He didn't know who was pulling the strings, but they were more powerful than he gave them credit for.

"Okay." Howe kept his submissive tone.

"The only thing this country has left is its natural resources," Mustafa began. "If you start this scorched earth campaign, you are going to turn half of the country into a nuclear wasteland that will be useless for more years than you'll ever live to see."

"Respectfully, Mr. Al Mohammad, may I make a point?" Howe asked.

"Of course," Mustafa said.

Anthony said, "These rebels have brainwashed all of our best and brightest from the armed services. As you say, they have control over much of our resources. Without a definitive way of dealing with them, I'm afraid that we are not going to prevail."

"I agree completely," Mustafa said. "More importantly, so do others. There are some very good alternatives. Alternatives that have been put forth to the elite decision-makers. Alternatives that have come from your own staff. They're afraid to mention their ideas to you because of your temper. I must say, things have been tolerated from you that have ended badly for many other people in high positions. It would be very beneficial to your health to start listening to your staff. Many of them are there because they were placed there. Some at great expense."

"I'm listening," Howe said.

Mustafa said, "Rather than destroy your enemy and the spoils of war, just eliminate the enemy. Rather than nuke the Coalition, set off the nuclear warheads at a much higher altitude. This will generate an EMP that will fry all of the electrical grids, computers and every device with any sort of processor. One year later, the Coalition will be depopulated by 90% or more. At that point, you will be able to knock them over with a feather. Just imagine what it would have been like to fight 5th century barbarians with modern weapons of warfare. That's essentially what your advantage will be."

Howe felt something inside he didn't recognize. "That's a fantastic idea," He said. "I don't know why I didn't think of it."

Was that feeling inside of Howe what people called humility? He couldn't be sure. Probably not. It was most likely just a form of embarrassment.

Al Mohammad said, "We're on the same team Anthony. I'm not your enemy."

Mustafa went on to explain how warheads with specific yields could be detonated at certain altitudes to generate an electromagnetic pulse that would cripple electrical infrastructure inside the Coalition. Precise strategies could uniquely target selected geographical sectors. While the Coalition had control of the ICBMs, the Federal States still had nuclear subs armed with Trident missiles and B-2 bombers capable of launching AGM 158 JASSM, a smaller stealth version of the cruise missile, armed with nuclear warheads. Extended range versions of the AGM 158 JASSM could be launched from B-2s in Federal airspace to any detonation point within the Coalition.

Howe was conflicted between his absolute hatred for Mustafa Al Mohammad and his admiration for his connections with the Masters, and of course, this ingenious plan.

CHAPTER 56

"We are hard pressed on every side, but not crushed; perplexed, but not in despair; persecuted, but not abandoned; struck down, but not destroyed."

-II Corinthians 4:8-9

Karen and Rene ate a light breakfast. They didn't know exactly what the mission was that Justin, Matt and the others had gone to do, but they knew they should have been home before dawn.

Karen dropped her fork to the table. She couldn't eat. "I don't have any appetite." She fought back the tears. "I am going to walk over to Adam's and see what Janice knows. Would you like to come with me?"

Rene nodded. Her young eyes were filled with dread.

Both of the girls took pistols for the short walk through the woods. Karen did not want to start speculating, but she knew something wasn't right. They didn't say anything on the walk over. Karen knew it wouldn't do any good to speak her fears out loud.

Janice opened the door when they arrived. Her eyes had dark circles. She obviously hadn't been to sleep.

"Come in," she said.

Karissa grabbed Karen's waist to hug her when she came in the door. "Where's Uncle Matt? Where's my daddy?" She asked.

Karen looked over at Shelly and Mandy sitting on the couch. They looked at her with hopeful eyes, but she didn't have any news for them.

Karen held Karissa close and said, "I don't know, sweetheart, I don't know."

The morning light woke Adam from his light sleep. Every time he had closed his eyes, he saw the body of his brother lying on the ground. Adam wondered if the Federal troops took Wesley's body or if it was left to the birds. Neither option was good. He said to himself, "It's best not to think about it right now. No sense in getting bogged down with something I can't do anything about."

Adam wasn't sure of his exact location. He had kept moving last night well after dark to put as much space between himself and the federal troops as possible. He found shelter in the loft of an unused barn that was approximately ten miles southeast from the area of the operation that had gone so terribly wrong.

To get focused, Adam said out loud, "This morning, the mission is to find water, hopefully something to eat and start walking toward a militia checkpoint that could get me back home. The first order of business is to get out of everything that will mark me as militia."

He ditched his body armor, his rifle and his Kevlar helmet. He took off his sidearm holster and tucked the pistol in the small of his back. He took out everything that could be of use and stuffed it into his pockets. His camo pants would not necessarily mark him as militia. Out here, camos were as common as jeans.

He stepped out of the barn, looked at the sun to orient himself and started walking.

There was no chance of Gary and Justin bumping into Adam. Their path of escape and evasion had taken them eight miles northwest of the reverse ambush. The night before, they constructed a small shelter of brush and leaves near a creek. The two men had a water source, but otherwise their mission was the same as Adam's, get home.

Miles away from everyone else, Matt had not slept a wink. He had been restrained with zip ties, blindfolded and transported somewhere about thirty minutes from the place he was captured. Now, he did not know where he was. It was dark and there was only a little light coming through the cracks of the door. His zip ties were cut off and the blindfold was removed. From what he could tell, it was the inside of a metal shipping container that was sectioned off with chain-link fence. The makeshift cell was small. He could see two buckets. One was filled with fresh water and the other was empty. He said to himself, "I suppose these are my facilities."

Matt wondered how everyone else was. Had Adam or Wesley been captured? Did Gary and Justin survive?

His thoughts raced. *What's going to happen next? I'll probably be interrogated. They say everyone has their breaking point. How long can I hold out? Everything I say will put Karen and the rest of the family in danger. Perhaps I should have just raised my weapon and let them shoot me. It's too late to second guess the decision now.*

Matt lay down on the floor of the cell. The other cells were empty. There were no other prisoners to ask where he was. The silence was haunting. Matt had to shift his mind away from the terror of the situation. He began to recite Bible verses that reminded him that God was still there. Matt started with Psalm 23.

"The LORD is my shepherd, I shall not be in want. He makes me lie down in green pastures, he leads me beside quiet waters, he restores my soul. He guides me in paths of righteousness for his name's sake. Even though I walk through the valley of the shadow of death, I will fear no evil, for you are with me; your rod and your staff, they comfort me. You prepare a table before me in the presence of my enemies. You anoint my head with oil; my cup overflows. Surely goodness and love will follow me all the days of my life, and I will dwell in the house of the LORD forever."

Thank you for reading
American Meltdown,
Book Two of The Economic Collapse Chronicles.

Amazon reviews are the most important method of getting The Economic Collapse Chronicles noticed. If you enjoyed the book, please take a moment to leave a 5 star review on Amazon.com. If you don't feel the book quite measured up to 5 stars, drop me an e-mail at prepperrecon@gmail.com and let me know how I can make the next book better.

Keep watch for
American Reset,
Book Three of The Economic Collapse Chronicles.

Stay tuned to PrepperRecon.com for the latest news about American Reset and preparedness related subjects. While on the website, you can link to our Facebook page and YouTube channel to stay up-to-date with the most recent posts.

Listen to the Prepper Recon Podcast to get great interviews from preppers around the world. It will help you to be better prepared for everything from a hurricane to the end of the world as we know it. You can download or listen to the podcasts at PrepperRecon.com or subscribe to the show on Stitcher, iTunes or YouTube.

Made in the USA
Middletown, DE
02 August 2015